A Lover's Betrayal

A Lover's Betrayal

Nikki K. Hail

www.urbanbooks.net

Urban Books, LLC
300 Farmingdale Road, N.Y.-Route 109
Farmingdale, NY 11735

ISBN 13: 978-1-64556-755-4
EBOOK ISBN: 978-1-64556-756-1

First Trade Paperback Printing January 2026
Printed in the United States of America

10 9 8 7 6 5 4 3 2 1

Distributed by Kensington Publishing Corp.
Submit Orders to:
Customer Service
400 Hahn Road
Westminster, MD 21157-4627
Phone: 1-800-733-3000
Fax: 1-800-659-2436

The authorized representative in the EU for product safety and compliance
Is eucomply OU, Parnu mnt 139b-14, Apt 123
Tallinn, Berlin 11317, hello@eucompliancepartner.com

A Lover's Betrayal

Nikki K. Hail

CHAPTER ONE

Hiding hatred makes you a liar, and slandering others makes you a fool.

—Proverbs 10:18

As she sat behind the cherry-wood table, Ridah's heart beat rapidly. This courtroom wasn't just her trial. It was her reality check. Her stomach churned at the thought of her fate resting in the hands of mostly white jurors. When she glanced their way, two of them looked half asleep. She inhaled sharply and let the breath out slowly. Inhaling deeply, she then sighed, glancing at the DA, and finally, her eyes landed on her court-appointed attorney. Were they in on something? Maybe she was just paranoid, but why the hell were they wearing matching colors?

Each minute that passed made her more irritated.

Ms. O'Kelly, seated beside her, scribbled notes. She was pleased that Ridah followed her advice: dress soft, innocent, young. Let the jury see a young girl, not a criminal. The goal was to appear innocuous to her peers.

Ridah kept that in mind as she dressed in a two-piece sky blue Chanel suit. Her face was graced with a pair of Chanel frames. Ridah's looks fit the description Ms. O'Kelly needed the jurors to see.

The district attorney, on the other hand, was dead set on making her look like another ruthless adolescent to society. But outside this courtroom, in public view, thanks to Ms. O'Kelly, Ridah didn't look destructive. She didn't look ruthless.

When someone Ridah didn't know stepped on the stand, she bounced her leg more out of anger than a nervous habit. It was a challenge to sit quietly and listen to people labeled "character witnesses" stigmatize her. Some of these people Ridah had never seen a day in her life.

Getting clout for snitching was obviously the thing to do. That was how it was looking. People wanted to feel like they were helping society get rid of "another problem." Ridah had done a lot of crazy and wild things in her youthful life, but on this day, her peers were so far from the truth.

Then came the next witness. Capone.

He strutted into the courtroom like he owned it, head high, arrogance dripping off him like cologne. A snake wrapped in a tailored suit, like betrayal was fashionable. Ridah leaned forward, rubbing her forehead with a hand full of stress. Capone looked too comfortable walking to the stand like it was his throne.

The DA gave Capone a stern look as she asked if the person who pulled the trigger was in the courtroom. Capone looked Ridah in the eye and ratted like he was going to be rewarded with a block of government cheese the State offered. He replied and proceeded by pointing her out in the courtroom. No one knew he was the cause of most of their shortcomings. Instead of being a man and taking responsibility for his own mistakes when he got jammed up, Capone chose to go out the cowardly way.

With each answer Capone gave freely, it was like a nail deepening into the palm of Ridah's hand. He nailed her to the cross personally, making sure she could not get off. It was hard for her to hide the hurt now displayed on her face. Even though she had seen with her own eyes Capone's griminess slip out to others who were one and the same with them, the thought of him betraying her had never crossed her mind.

Pushing her glasses closer to her eyes, Ridah watched how the odds stacked up against her like Legos. It did not matter how bad it looked. She wouldn't break. She would never reveal the identity of the person who actually pulled the trigger that fateful night. Ridah took loyalty seriously, even if it was not reciprocated on the other end. And still, somewhere in her spinning thoughts, she thought about Jesus. Judas. Betrayal. But at least Judas couldn't hide his heart from God. Capone? He raised his hand up to the public and lied like his heart was pure. He did a good job hiding his deceitfulness.

Ridah was called to the stand. She stood on the situation, not revealing who was present the night of what really happened. She admitted to being present at the party but denied seeing K.J. there. Ridah kept her answers as simple as possible. Yes, she was sure she never saw K.J. or Capone. No, she did not pull the trigger. No, she didn't see who pulled the trigger. Ms. Johnson was not convinced at all.

The district attorney had it out for Ridah. It took every ounce of breath in Ridah not to give in to the rage that was now roaring within. Closing her eyes briefly, she exhaled, trying to get her emotions under control. Ms. Johnson continued to cross-examine her. It did not matter how she worded her questions. Ridah's answers were still the same.

Photos were displayed of Ridah with other gang members to persuade the jurors not to be fooled by her attire and that she was dangerous to their society. To assassinate Ridah's character further, Ms. Johnson turned the jurors' attention to her supporters, who she believed to be gang affiliated. At least that was the perception Ms. Johnson wanted the jurors to be aware of.

Ridah's mother, Tina, was overlooked. Her eyes were puffy from the lack of sleep and all the tears she had shed thanks to the streets. Ridah had no idea how deep her mother's fear ran at the mere thought of the white man taking her daughter away while she sat there, helpless. Ridah turned to glance over her shoulder at her mother's teary eyes, and regret filled Ridah's heart for a moment. She hated to be the source of any pain her mother was enduring. Ridah knew this was the bed she had made. Now, the time had come for her to lie in it without any complaints.

Anyone who said it was sweet being born in a gang was a liar, and the truth wasn't in them. Ridah was born, raised, and trapped in! She had been down since day one until she was old enough to get sworn in.

Ridah's truth was that it was hard living up to the expectations that were blessed and yet cursed upon her. Though not fully understanding what she was fighting for, Ridah searched to define who she truly was within.

Ridah's pops, Blu Foxx, was from the Bronx, New York. He banged with the best of them until he was put in a body bag and set on fire by some Vice Lords. Her mother, Tina, was his queen. She feared for their lives after Blu Foxx was murdered. Tina packed them up in the middle of the night and moved her family to Georgia. Macon, Georgia, to be exact. To be honest, gangs there weren't any better, but that was where Ridah found her purpose, or so she thought. Ridah embraced her newfound family proudly. While Tina attempted to keep her past a secret, Ridah was out with hers, causing hell in her pops's name, banging!

The day Ridah's pops was murdered would forever be a strain on her memory.

Ridah was sitting between her mother's legs as she ran the hot comb through Ridah's thick hair. Suddenly the side door opened, and Blu Foxx came rushing in, putting Ridah on alert. He never came through there. When Blu Foxx came through the opening, a short, stocky man chased behind him.

With the hot comb in midair, Tina asked, "What in the hell is going on?" She sat still with a bewildered look.

"Run! Run!" Blu Foxx shouted, running toward his family to protect them.

Ridah didn't hesitate. She shot up to her feet and took off running toward the room she shared with her sibling. When she heard gunshots and shouting, she ran faster. Throwing the bedroom door open, she saw Prissy already sitting up in her twin bunk bed.

"Come on, we gotta go!" Ridah said, breathing hard still from running. She rushed to the window, quickly unlocking it, then turned back to her sister. "Come on, Prissy, dang!" She wanted to get them as far away from there as possible.

After they climbed out, Ridah grabbed Prissy's hand, and they ran until they reached their destination: Blu Foxx's other baby mother's house. At the top of the corner, Ridah stopped running, which caused Prissy to stop as well.

"Why we stop? We almost there," Prissy whined.

"Listen, you go ahead. I need to go back and check on momma and them." Ridah couldn't see herself just leaving and not going back.

"But—" Prissy started.

"You think they wouldn't come back for us?" Ridah questioned.

"I know they would, but what if they're dead or you get hurt too?" Prissy panicked at the thought.

Ridah couldn't stand the thought of their parents being dead. She had to hurry back, especially for her pops. Looking Prissy in the eye, she said, "Go. I'ma come back."

"You better, or you gonna get in trouble," Prissy said as she started walking down the road. When she looked back, Ridah was running back up the road they'd just come down.

When Ridah made it back to their apartment, it was destroyed. Furniture was turned over, and lamps were broken. Ridah couldn't stop the tears from forming in her eyes. She quietly stepped into the side door, which was cracked open. The first thing Ridah saw was her pops's mangled body on the floor in a pool of blood. She began sobbing loudly as she walked up to his body. Slowly kneeling down, she touched his ashen face.

"Daddy!" Ridah cried out. "Daddy, please get up!" She cried harder because she knew that he was never getting up again and her life would never be the same.

Ridah was so disturbed by her pops that she didn't notice her mother's body until she saw movement out of the corner of her eye.

Tina reached for her daughter weakly. Ridah got up and ran to where her mother lay.

"Momma, you all right?" Ridah asked, searching around to make sure the man was gone.

"Blu Foxx is dead. We're no longer safe here. We have to go," Tina said through her tears of pain.

Tina held her wounded shoulder as she got up off the kitchen floor. She told Ridah to pack up a few things. After they grabbed what their arms could carry, they left, shutting the door on the past.

It was Blu Foxx's first baby mother who helped Tina move. She knew that if she didn't take them far away from New York, Blu Foxx's killer would come back to finish what he started.

They left in the middle of the night, not sure of what the future held for them.

During Ridah's toughest late-night warfare when she couldn't sleep, death consumed her thoughts. Not knowing how she would leave this world tormented Ridah's soul. Would she end up getting murdered like her pops? The question burned her mind like setting a match to paper.

The man Ridah worshipped banged to his death. He made her feel like she had something to prove. So, closing the door on who she was had never been optional, not for Ridah. Her pops was the blueprint. He was the guide for many. With that being said, Ridah followed in his footsteps. He got it out of the mud, so she jumped in the mud, swinging. Ridah just wanted to make her pops proud, even in his death. When it was Ridah's time to rise in those streets, she ran full speed into its arms. She became street bound. It was everything Ridah dreamed of becoming. Her reality nightmare.

Only the real would be able to relate, then. There would be some people who would never understand this way of living. This once was Ridah's life, every day, all day.

Ridah's extended family gave her the name Ridah. It spoke for itself. When it was time to ride, she rode from the depths of her soul. See, because she was so rare and loyal, Ridah ended up catching seventy-five years for something she didn't do! Most of them "real" dudes (they hollered) and a few females stood with the DA like they cared about them. Right hand up, lying on the stand, speaking on things they knew nothing about.

No matter how many football numbers they threw at Ridah, she barely blinked as she told them to do their job. What did she look like helping them do a job they got paid to do? This wasn't about being cool. This was about street facts that Ridah's pops instilled in her. He and Tina raised them to be this way.

Ridah's sister was her twin. They were like night and day. It wasn't hard to tell that Ridah was the night. You couldn't pay Ridah's twin to put on a pair of Tims and get down and gritty in the streets. Sometimes, Ridah wondered why she was so thugged out. Why couldn't she have been more like Prissy? Though Ridah knew the answer, it didn't stop her from wondering. Her pops's genes ran deeper in her veins than Prissy's. He lived on through Ridah, and she vowed to die trying to keep his legacy tall and honored.

Ridah stood at five foot five. Her skin was smooth and chocolate, and she had big, round eyes. She was slightly bowlegged with an impeccable shape. In her eyes, Ridah was the sexiest goonette you'd ever stumble upon. Her homies were amazed at how Ridah aimed her blue flag–wrapped .380 snub nose with her head cocked to the left. Aim game, and be steady, ready, and deadly. She went hard in the streets without trying.

At 19 years old, Ridah couldn't help but repeatedly ask herself, how did she end up on trial, facing over twenty years in prison? Ridah's truth was about to be revealed. No fabricating!

CHAPTER TWO

Ridah was in the eighth grade when a chick named Kenyatta Patterson tried her on a disrespectful level. Kenyatta was a GD. She was normally quiet, but since she had a crew around her, Kenyatta was suddenly loud and bold. Ridah allowed Kenyatta to continue talking loudly and putting on for the people. Everyone in the cafeteria got quiet as they waited to see what was about to happen.

A lot of people did not know Ridah, let alone what she represented, and honestly, she preferred to keep it that way. It meant fewer problems unless she was tried. Now that Ridah was disrespected, she was forced to expose who she was. Ridah held her composure for as long as she could. Smiling up at Kenyatta, Ridah challenged her to repeat what she said. Like a fool, she did, and without warning, Ridah leaped across the table at her like she was a black panther. Kenyatta did not have time to react. Ridah beat her so bad that Scott begged her to stop.

From that day forward, everyone knew facts. They knew Ridah was a Gangsta Crip. So many Crips and Cripettes were coming up to her, showing love. It made Ridah feel good to receive so much love. There was nothing like that loc love. Feeling the power and movement caused Ridah to fall deep in love. Ridah found her new family. Soon after that, Lanka stepped in, and Ridah began collecting more jewels, along with a few others.

*A wise man is strong. Yes, a man of
knowledge increases strength.*

—Proverbs 24:5

Lanka was giving Ridah knowledge that her pops never went in depth about pertaining to her set. Lanka took her under her wing, and they began to build a bond as they got deep in different lessons. One day, Lanka asked Ridah a question that she'd never forget. The question was, if Queen Sheba, her mom, and the Bible were drowning, which one would Ridah save?

Without a second thought, Ridah said to her, "Momma."

Lanka was quiet as she stared at Ridah for a split second, as if she was giving Ridah a chance to change her answer. Instead, Ridah stood by her decision. Whether it was a test or not, Ridah was saving anyone she held dear to her.

Lanka smiled. "And remember, God's words are supposed to be engraved in your heart," she said as she pointed to Ridah's chest.

Not only did Lanka teach Ridah how to walk the path that was before her, but she also shined a light on some things Ridah never knew, like Crips before they had a color. Therefore, it was never about the color to them. The color came about to honor and represent Tookie's best friend after he was murdered. His friend always wore blue and a blue bandana. They were taught togetherness and to protect and serve their neighborhoods and the homeless.

Now, all that was amazing, but Ridah needed to find her own place in all of this. She was on the road to becoming a young legend, and Ridah was not stopping until she conquered and mastered it. She knew the life she lived could end any second and any day. Yet, it did not stop her from banging day in and day out. Ridah lived her life by the double-edged sword, so if she died by it, she could not blame anyone but herself. Until that time came, she would be Ridah, riding with everything in her. Ridah was content with dying, knowing her homies were going to hold a grudge until the final score was settled.

CHAPTER THREE

Welcome 2 My World

Gloccz Out

Yo Gotti's voice filled the flag-wrapped club with "Bang Bang." On one side of the room, a hyper crowd of Crips cheered a few of their "locs" on as they did the infamous dance of "The Ikey Loc," repping their set proudly without a single hint of fear, while the Bloods continued to mug, waiting to get shit popping. Neither set was on their own territory. The slightest disrespect could make bullets rain from the opposite direction.

I see blue flags (what else)
I see red flags (what else)
I see niggas that ain't reppin with they scared ass

D.J. Ruthless rapped on the mic along with Yo Gotti. He knew exactly what he was doing, and he was not showing any mercy for either rival. In a sober mind, maybe D.J. Ruthless would not have been hyping the rivals up if he thought about the brutal outcome and effect upon others. But maybe he just did not care. After all, they called him Ruthless for a reason.

Ridah's face turned stone cold when her eyes fell upon Erika with her tagalong scary friend, Dreka. The three of them went to Ballard Hudson Middle School several years back. Ridah considered Erika cool at one point, until she saw how she really got down, which caused Ridah to despise Erika for that reason alone. What irked her the most about Erika was that when she was in the presence of Crips, she did anything to prove how down she was for the blue team, then switched up in the presence of the opposite side. One day, Ridah was riding through Pleasant Hill, and lo and behold, there was Erika, dressed in a red jumpsuit with a scarf tied around her neck, kicking it with some Bloods. From that day forward, Ridah called her "All-star" Erika.

The very next day, Erika had the audacity to come around in a blue flag. Ridah had never been the type to show out in front of anyone, but when she felt disrespected, she would spazz out in front of whoever. Erika felt tried, so she stole off on Ridah. Class was now in session. Ridah was teaching Erika a valuable lesson. Dreka stood back as Ridah beat her best friend until she was pulled off Erika. From that day forward, the two had been at odds.

Ridah could smell the beef coating the air. Closing her eyes, she inhaled the aroma and began craving her favorite meat. As tempting and inviting as it was, Ridah prayed she would not give in to her hunger for violence. All she wanted to do was chill without wilding and capping. But Ridah could almost bet her life that Erika was not going to make it easy.

Smiling wickedly, Erika glared at Ridah, confirming what she already assumed. Ridah shook her head as Erika showed off the rubies in her mouth, then threw up her set "of the week." Ridah clenched down on her teeth as anger slowly filled her. It seemed like no matter how hard she tried, she could not escape the drama. If Erika tried her, Ridah did not care how many people she was up against. She wasn't going to back down, period. Ridah was the type who would bring a knife to a gun fight.

Erika smirked in satisfaction. Now that she had Ridah's full attention, she planned to finally settle the score, especially with her crew being present tonight. Erika eyed Ridah with daring eyes as she approached her. Ridah bypassed Erika's sidekick, bumping her so hard that Dreka stumbled but did not utter a single word. She was not crazy enough to do so, so she stood there as if nothing happened.

Now in touching distance of Erika, she and Ridah were in a standoff.

"What the fuck is so funny though?" Ridah was fully in beast mode. And beasts loved to eat.

With her red flag wrapped around her right wrist, Erika replied, "You!" Though Erika's heart felt like it was about to blast out of her chest, she still stood there, ready for whatever.

Erika brought her right hand down on Ridah's shoulder. Ridah flinched as if the fabric burned her. In flashing speed, Ridah had her flag wrapped around her left hand. "Shid, what's going?" Ridah shouted, going in attack mode, hooking her fist deep into Erika's pretty brown face. It was like a chain reaction. All hell broke loose. Rivals began swinging at any- and everyone who was not one of them.

Meanwhile, D.J. Ruthless, who was now out of the booth, looked down from the top tier at the mess he created. He bit down on his bottom lip, nodding his head at his own stupidity while he played the song again, remixing it with Young Jeezy's "Bottom of the Map." D.J. Ruthless must have forgotten bullets flew. How quickly he remembered when a bullet struck him right in the eye, causing him to fall headfirst over the balcony into the frenzied crowd.

Hearing the first gunshot, a crowd of screaming, panicking people rushed toward the entrance, praying to make an exit with their lives intact. Some were knocked to the floor as others tried to escape death. No one wanted to get caught in the wrath of the rivals, let alone be kissed by a stray bullet. Ridah pushed her way through the thick, frightened crowd to make a quick exit. Tripping over someone on the floor caused her to fall and get stepped on and over. Ridah pushed herself back up with her arms, but her body crumpled back down forcefully. Jerking her head in the direction the attack came from, she stared into the eyes of Erika.

"Leaving so soon, cuz?" Erika mocked Ridah, running her tongue across her rubies.

"Bitch!" Ridah roared, quickly jerking her small frame up off the floor.

Erika jumped back so Ridah couldn't get another one up on her. Ridah's arm went up in the air. She brought it down with force. Erika fell back to prevent herself from catching the vicious blow. Unfortunately, a young female happened to be standing next to Erika and caught Ridah's wrath. The innocent bystander's hand shot up to her ripped face, and she withdrew it in horror as she screamed at the sight of her bloody hand. Ridah silently uttered profanity right before turning toward the front door to make her exit. She quickly glanced over her shoulder for any sign of Erika, causing her to run smack into a muscular chest. Ridah tried to go around him, but he blocked her. Giving him a death look, she attempted to get past him again.

The man shoved Ridah hard, but she recovered quicker than he expected. She charged him like a bull. After all, he did have on red.

"Cute!" He smiled amusedly, shaking his dreaded head. "Such a shame dat shit goin' to waste!" He wrapped a thick, rough hand around Ridah's neck, causing her eyes to bulge. "Let's see how hard you are then," he uttered, reaching behind his back.

Clawing at his hand, Ridah fought hard to breathe. "Nigga, get off me!" She tried to jerk out of his strong grip.

Ridah's rival continued to laugh. He was so focused on taunting her that he never saw her homie, Smirky, sneak up on him. Ridah braced herself while preparing for the fire that Smirky was about to set on their rival. Before she could hold her breath, Smirky cleared the dude's thoughts clean out of his head. Ridah could not keep her body from jumping as the blood of their rival sprayed her.

As the night breeze hit them, Ridah thanked God as she attempted to calm herself down. She rubbed at her face as her eyes roamed the almost empty parking lot. Gunshots echoed in the air from an unknown direction. The sirens were getting closer. They were not trying to be around when the police got there.

Smirky passed Ridah a gun as he told her to follow him. Ridah despised the fact that she did not have the upper hand in the situation that was taking place around her. Smirky's voice broke through her roaming thoughts. Ridah turned around to a bullet separating flesh from the lower side.

"Aaahh!" Ridah grunted as she jumped back into the shadow of the building.

"Come on, Ridah." His .45 was aimed, ready to kill anything that moved near them. There was no way Ridah could make it without possibly being fully exposed. Looking at Smirky, she shook her head. "Shit," he yelled, then took off running around the other side of the building where his car was parked.

Ridah knew the longer she stayed out there, the greater the chance she could end up dead or in the back of a police car. She wasn't planning on seeing either of those thoughts prosper, even if the weapon had already formed. Taking a deep breath, Ridah prepared herself mentally. Saying, "Fuck it," she ran out in front of a gray Regal, which slammed on the brakes. Ridah's breath got caught in her throat for a split second. Surely getting hit by a car wasn't how her life would end, and if so, Ridah would be highly offended.

Seeing Smirky throw the door of the passenger side open, Ridah scrambled to hurry inside in fear of a bullet catching her. As she was closing the door, she heard a familiar call. Anwar jerked the door open and pushed the wounded J-loc in, all while busting his gun. Ridah quickly jumped in the back and opened the back door for Anwar. Smirk pulled off as he was getting in. Ridah exhaled with brief relief. After catching her bearings, she observed the red Chevy Monte Carlo speeding in the opposite direction, apparently spooked by the impending danger that came with sirens getting near. The beef was far from being over, yet Ridah felt some relief, though it was only for a moment. Then, there was the increasing pain in her side.

"Damn, I got hit in the same fuckin' leg, cuz," J-loc said with irritation in his voice.

"Nigga, stop whining up there." Anwar chuckled loudly.

"Fuck you, nigga. Easy for ya punk ass to say. Have you ever been shot?" He didn't give Anwar time to reply. "Hell nawl." J-loc exhaled loudly.

"Consider me blessed, nigga," Anwar boasted.

"Whatever, nigga." J-loc tore his T-shirt to wrap around his bleeding leg and applied pressure to his wound.

Everyone fell into their private thoughts. As Smirky drove, he constantly watched the rearview mirror. Pulling out his phone, he dialed his cousin, K.J. When he didn't answer, Smirky gave up. "Fuck," he swore, more out of frustration than anger. "Aye, y'all didn't see K.J.?" he asked in concern.

"He left wit' Trina before shit popped off," Anwar replied, then cut his eyes Ridah's way. He knew Ridah had a thing for K.J., but with K.J.'s baby mother being her mentor, she never acted on it.

"What?" Ridah snapped defensively, but only Anwar saw the malice in her eyes.

"I ain't said shit," he replied, playing dumb.

"Y'all better not start that bullshit," Smirk said.

Ridah and Anwar stayed at each other's throats. If he didn't know any better, he'd think the two of them had a thing for each other. Smirky smirked at the mere thought.

Sucking her teeth, Ridah replied, "Nigga, shut up and drive. I'm bleeding bad." Ridah's voice cracked as she spoke.

Smirky was not aware that she had been hit. He almost swerved into the next lane trying to look behind him. Anwar looked down at Ridah's shirt, noticing the blood-stained shirt for the first time.

"Aye, see how bad dat shit is," Smirky said to Anwar, pressing his foot down on the pedal, causing the car to speed up noticeably.

Anwar could not get his hand up good enough before Ridah slapped his hand away. The razor she kept hidden in her mouth was out within the blink of an eye, making it loud and clear what would happen if he touched her.

Holding up his hands, Anwar eased back into the seat.

"Damn, you gonna cut ya loc now?" Anwar asked, causing J-loc to laugh maniacally.

"Dat's some cold shit right there, cuz," J-loc said, still filled with laughter.

"Whatever." Ridah's only reply was filled with disgust. She wasn't in the mood to play. Grabbing one of the shirts Smirky kept in his car, she attempted to wipe her face clean from the earlier events.

"I'm glad y—" The back window exploding cut Ridah's words short. She froze for a split second as realization set in. Reaching for the pump Smirky kept under the driver's seat, Ridah looked at Anwar and nodded. They were on some Mr. and Mrs. Smith–type shit, letting their bullets rip into the night, hoping they would find their target.

When a bullet breezed by Anwar's head, he roared, "Fuck," as he refocused on shooting at whoever was pursuing them. "Aye, Ridah, try to hit the tires," he yelled over the wind and gunshots.

"Fuck. J-loc hit, cuz. He hit." Smirky noticed J-loc fumbling for his tool.

"I'm good, loc. I'm good. Get me to the medical center." J-loc was leaking blood between his ear and neck. He unsuccessfully tried to staunch the bleeding. Another bullet exploded into the passenger seat. The impact slammed J-loc forward into the dashboard. Gripping his tool, he had to reach deep within for strength to lift it. He was not planning to go out without a good fight.

Ridah could hardly contain her fear of the unknown. Maybe it was a good thing. Blocking out everything that surrounded her forced her mind to focus on Monte Carlo.

Anwar knocked the remaining glass out of his and Ridah's way, then put the sawed-off on the back seat. By the time his finger wrapped around the trigger, the driver flicked the bright lights to blind them. As they ducked down in the seat, a grim look of uncertainty was plastered across Ridah's stained face.

Anwar smiled to assure her that they were going to be all right. He silently counted with his fingers. Ridah nodded with the countdown until they were both up, busting at their enemies.

Smirky focused on keeping J-loc talking and getting them to their destination. "We almost there, cuzzo." Smirky ran the traffic light as he glanced in the rearview in time to see the Monte Carlo slam into a parked car. He swore he heard all of them let out a collective sigh of relief.

Ten minutes later, Smirky was pulling up to the emergency ramp doors. Anwar hopped out before the car came to a complete stop. He wasn't prepared for the sight his eyes took in. J-loc was not only covered in blood, but he also had a nickel-sized hole in his chest.

The staff rushed out with a gurney, quickly putting J-loc's body on it, then rushing him inside. Smirky started texting his cousin and a few more homies to let them know what had transpired.

When Smirky looked up at Ridah, who seemed to be in shock, his heart went out to her.

"He gonna pull through."

Judging by his facial expression, Ridah knew he didn't believe J-loc was going to pull through.

"Let 'em folks see about dat shit." He nodded his head toward the blood on her shirt.

"I'm good." Pulling at her pink tank top, which stuck to her skin, Ridah allowed Smirky to see the wound.

He bent down, leaning in to examine it more closely. "It's nasty, but you only got grazed by it. Be thankful it's not worse," he said, standing back to his full height.

"Shit don't feel like a graze." She looked down at it and then sighed. "I'ma let them clean it up. I wanna make sure J-loc is all right first."

An hour after they'd walked into the emergency room, the waiting area was filled with Gangsta Crips. Their appearance told who they were as their facial expressions showed the crew was so overwhelmed. Intimidation filled the area, causing others to flee as if the devil himself were chasing after them.

Smirk paced back and forth, mumbling to himself, while Anwar tapped his foot, biting his bottom lip as he occasionally checked his phone. Tanya, J-loc's babies' mother, sat off to the side in a corner by herself, praying as she cried silently.

A chubby woman came through the double doors in blood-stained scrubs. She held her head high as she exhaled. Approaching the already angry crowd caused her to shiver.

"Is Mr. Hill's family present?" she exclaimed nervously.

Tanya stood. "Yes." She wrapped her arms around herself, trying her best to embrace herself for what would come next.

"We're his family, lady. Tell us what's up with cuzzo," Anwar demanded.

"I . . . I am sorry. We lost him," she replied, clasping her trembling hands in front of her. "I am very sorry," she offered again as she turned to leave.

Anwar stepped in her path, blocking her. "Hold up. Ya mean to tell me y'all gave up on him that easy?"

Anyone could sense the despair in the waiting room as Smirky shook his head, then added, "I bet if he was white, y'all ass would still be in there workin' on him."

Everyone nodded in silent agreement. The doctor shook her head fervently. She thought of explaining, but after taking a look at the people she was surrounded by, she knew the angry and emotional crowd would not hear anything she said. With that in mind, she all but ran back behind the double doors to safety.

Tanya dropped to her knees. The screams that ripped from her soul were like daggers hitting the bull's-eye on everyone's heart. Anwar lifted Tanya off the cold waxed floor while others watched through blurry vision. Kicking at the air wildly, Tanya repeatedly screamed, "Why?" in a wounded voice. J-loc was her first love. In the blink of an eye, he was snatched from this earth, leaving her to raise two sons on her own.

This scene caused every member to accept whatever outcome fate had for each of them tonight. Some would be blessed to see another sunrise, while others may end up on a slab like their homie, trapped in total darkness forever.

Ridah pushed away from the nurse who was tending to her wounded side. She silently braced herself for the repercussions of J-loc's absence. No one was off-limits. Anyone could get it. Ridah inhaled deeply. Death was thick in the air, and it wasn't a pleasant smell.

As the members pulled themselves together, Ridah stood as if coming out of a thick fog.

K.J. stepped up beside his cousin, Smirky. Grabbing his shoulder, he said, "Check the move." Nodding his head in another direction, he continued, "Kia needs to get active. She say she ready to earn some strikes."

Smirky cut his eyes in Kia's direction, nodding his head in approval. "What are we ridin'?"

K.J. could not hold the chuckle that escaped his lips. "Damn sho can't ride ya Regal. Y'all ridin' with me."

"Ridah wit' me, too." Smirky gave Kia one final glance before turning his focus back on his cousin.

"Oh, yeah?" K.J. said with a mischievous grin. He had been waiting for an opportunity to kick it with Ridah. He hated it had to be under these terms though. Clearing the wicked thoughts from his head, he got back focused. "These niggas about to get penetrated since they actin' like some bitches," K.J. growled vehemently.

K.J. was a longtime member of the Gangsta Crips with the status of an OG. He was the ghetto tale you never got tired of hearing about. Every young dude in the hood strove to be a living legend and survive in the streets like K.J. in his hell-raiser days. To say he could be coldhearted would be an understatement. The streets were to blame for that. It came naturally to respect a true gangsta of his caliber. K.J. was not only street smart, but he retained a lot of knowledge on any and every level.

Outside in the now dark lot, K.J., Smirky, Ridah, and Kia piled up in the midnight blue Tahoe while the others went their separate ways to handle other matters. Ridah sat in the back, watching everyone pulling off to their destination. She fought to keep her emotions in check. The last thing she needed right now was her emotions clouding her mind while retaliating on behalf of her homie. If Ridah had a penny for every homie who had been taken away by the streets, she would be hood rich. No lie. The streets had claimed so many souls while the street avenues and signs stood tall, silently watching. Instead of taking heed of the street tales, Ridah continued to stand stuck as she sank deeper into the streets like quicksand.

K.J. thought back to the Monte Carlo Ridah described earlier when a chick he used to kick it with in Pleasant Hill popped in his already troubled mind. Old girl's dude drove the exact same car model. If this was the same person, K.J. was thinking he and his crew were really about to wreak havoc on their territory. Gotti's voice filled the truck with "Bulletproof," giving them all the motivation they needed in the most gangsta way. They were war ready.

Smirk rolled up a fat blunt of some good Kush. Flicking the lighter, he put the blunt under the fire to dry it. When the blunt was to his satisfaction, he lit it and put it in rotation. K.J. passed the blunt behind him to Ridah. Retrieving it happily, Ridah inhaled the thick smoke. She passed the blunt to Kia, who declined but still took it and passed it to Smirky.

She shook her head. "I can't smoke that shit. I gotta keep my mind clear," Kia explained as she went back into her thoughts.

Ridah cut her eyes at the girl and slightly frowned. "So, what?" She shrugged her shoulders. "My mind ain't clear because I'm smoking?" She tightened her lips to keep herself in check. At the end of the day, they were riding for the same side.

Kia raised her hand in an attempt to dispel any negative thoughts of what she meant. By reflex, Ridah caught Kia by her wrist.

"Girl, a hand movement can get ya ass killed," Ridah warned before Kia snatched her hand out of Ridah's grip.

Kia's eyes widened. She looked Ridah dead in the eye. "Just because we on the same team don't give you the right to disrespect me. Cuz or not, shit won't end good. Now, all I'm saying is this my first time doing some shit like this. I don't wanna fuck up," Kia snapped at her. She did not care how long Ridah had been down. No one was going to disrespect her gangsta. She was an up-and-coming jewel who had something to prove.

Ridah couldn't do anything but laugh as she thought, *this rookie bitch.* She had to respect Kia's gangsta though. Ridah remembered feeling like she had to prove herself when she first came to Georgia. Without saying anything, Ridah nodded her head in agreement.

Turning her attention back to the front, Ridah raised her arched eyebrow. "What y'all snickering like some bitches about?" Licking her dry lips, she frowned, eyeing K.J. and Smirky.

"K.J. bet me Kia wasn't gonna back down from ya mean ass," Smirk revealed as he continued to chuckle.

Ridah shook her head. "I swear sometimes y'all can act like bitches!" She rolled her eyes. Although she wasn't used to being around K.J., she could tell he'd become a problem.

"Bitch," K.J. and Smirky said in unison. They were offended, yet laughter filled the air.

"Let's see who the real bitches is when it's time to put in this work," K.J. said, looking in his rearview mirror.

"I ain't the one who got shit to prove. I been ridin', nigga." She turned to Smirky. "Smirk, let this nigga know how I earned my name." Then she turned her attention back to K.J. "Don't sleep on me, nigga."

"All right, Ridah, damn!" K.J. replied, giving up. He admired her hood ethics, but he did not need her acting but showing she was about this gangsta shit they were on. He knew niggas who would hesitate when it was time to put in work.

"Shhh," Smirky suddenly said below a whisper. "Hit the light." His voice filled with excitement. Squinting his eyes in disbelief, he pointed where the totaled car was parked. "Dat's the car right there, ain't it?"

"These niggas got a lot of nerve," K.J. said bitterly. He turned the music down as they watched their prey intently.

The coldness of K.J.'s voice caused the hair on both Ridah's and Kia's necks to stand. Kia rubbed her sweaty hands on her black skinny jeans as she peeked at Ridah, who appeared calm. Quando Rondo's "No Smoke" invaded Kia's mind as she rapped along with the rapper.

Ridah tapped her finger against her leg as she listened to one of her newest favorite rappers. It was like he knew what was about to happen, and these niggas were not even aware that their asses were about to get smoked the fuck out.

Caressing the .38, Ridah took a glance at Kia, then at Smirk, while K.J.'s attention was glued to their prey, who was leaning on a burgundy old-school Chevy, flirting with some chicks. The guys were too intoxicated by drugs to realize death was hovering over them like a spider weaving a web.

K.J. looked toward the dark skies. To Ridah, it appeared he was saying a prayer. Ridah decided to speak her piece as well. Exiting the truck, Capone passed by them only to park down the road from them. To their advantage, a lot of trees and bushes in the area told them to give their rivals the element of surprise.

Before K.J. could pop off the sneak attack, Capone appeared out of thin air and got it popping. K.J. and his team had no choice but to follow suit. It was hailing bullets. Someone had to pay for the loss of J-loc. Since he was taken from them, retaliation was a must. They weren't going to rest until the situation was stood on, and they were planning to stand tall.

Ridah held the .38 as steady as she could while it spit disrespectfully through the air. Her adrenaline kept her from being drowsy due to the pain medication the nurse had given her earlier. Bullets pinged off parked cars.

The air held a pungent smell of gunpowder and the sharp smell of blood. This was Ridah's second shootout. She held it down like she had been doing it all her life. She got down on one knee as if she were about to propose to someone, but in reality she was only vowing to bring death.

Ridah was so caught up in the moment that she could not hear Capone frantically yelling her name over the gunfire. Ridah felt thuggish fill her spirit. She was so locked in on the action in front of her that she did not notice the dark figure creeping up on her from the side. He tackled her with desperation that only a frightened person could possess. The impact knocked Ridah to her wounded side. He immediately went to work trying to disengage the gun from Ridah's death grip.

Being a fighter at heart, Ridah overlooked the pain in her side and fought for her life as a desperate struggle ensued. Ridah was beyond caught off guard when the big man pulled the chrome MAC-11 from his teal-green jacket. Staring death in the eyes, Ridah briefly stopped struggling as she contemplated her options. When a gunshot rang out, it distracted Ridah's rival.

Taking the opportunity, Ridah slid the hidden razor from between her teeth, kissing the inside of the man's wrist, causing him to loosen his grip. Ridah quickly transferred the razor from her mouth to her hand.

With one explosive leap, Ridah lunged for his exposed throat. The gun clattered from his hand, dropping from his hand as if it had burned him. Her fingers locked around his neck, nails digging in deep. His eyes went wide, pure disbelief flickering in them just as a wet, strangled gasp escaped his lips. Ridah twisted hard and ripped free, leaving him staggering, clutching at the wound as dark blood sprayed between his trembling fingers. He dropped to his knees, choking on the bubbling crimson.

The night continued to fill with chaos. Neighbors stayed far away from their windows. When the police did show up asking questions, they had enough sense not to get involved in anything that would put them or their families in a deadly situation.

Someone grabbed Ridah's arm, startling her. Ready to attack further, she was relieved to see it was only K.J. She didn't waste any time taking the gun he held out for her, shooting at their rivals who seemed to keep appearing out of nowhere. Ridah followed K.J.'s lead as he formed a tight circle with her and Smirky's backs against each other. The three of them prepared themselves to make a run to the truck.

Kia was already sitting behind the wheel. As soon as they hopped in, she pulled off, leaving tire marks. Ridah thanked God and could only hope Anwar and the others made it out of the gun smoke. She did not know where they were heading. She did not care as long as Kia was putting miles between them and what was now a crime scene. Thoughts of how close she came to death tonight flooded her mind. Ridah could almost hear her mother asking, *"Did it bring back your friend?"* or *"Keep on. Ya ass gonna end up just like ya daddy."* Ridah's head started to pound at the thought alone.

Because of her pledge and loyalty, everything Ridah's mother said went in one ear and came out the other one. She was going to ride for those she pledged to be loyal to, and if it came down to it, she would die for the cause. She did not see it any other way. Ridah was not built to back down from her pops's legacy. This was her way of life, and she could not help who she was, or so she thought. Yes, there were moments when Ridah sought change, yet the streets had her in their grip. It'd only be because of her death. Ridah wondered what Tina would do if she ever got the call to come out of retirement. Would she go back to her old gangsta ways, or would she continue to run and hide like she had always done?

"Kia, ya ass was giving them hell, girl," Smirky praised her. Nothing turned him on more than a Cripette.

Kia tried hard to contain her smile but failed. "I try," she replied modestly.

"Still a rookie." Ridah rolled her eyes and leaned against the window. K.J. smirked at Ridah's little slick attitude.

Adjusting the rearview mirror, Kia looked back at Ridah. "Have you been a vet all ya life?" Kia questioned.

"I'ma product of a vet, so I'ma let you answer dat," Ridah snapped. She felt some type of way toward Kia. True, she had not done anything to her. Ridah had been the only girl in Smirky's circle for years, and now that Kia was part of their clique, Ridah felt threatened. Ridah was not feeling it at all.

"Aye, chill, Ridah. Y'all cut all that childish-ass shit out. It ain't a good look on you." K.J. spoke with irritation.

"Stop tryin'a tell me what to do." Ridah turned her attention to K.J.

"Product of a jealous-ass bitch," Kia mumbled, cocking her head to the side with amusement in her eyes.

"Bitch." Ridah leaped forward to attack Kia. K.J. snatched her back just as Kia swerved into another lane.

"Man, y'all gonna kill our ass," Smirky shouted as he tried his best not to laugh.

"Calm down, Ridah. It ain't dat serious," K.J. whispered to her.

"I'ma hit the clock with dat ho." Ridah pounded her fist into her hand and fell back into the seat.

"Ain't no problem," Kia responded, exhaling the smoke. The only way Ridah was going to respect Kia was if they fought it out. Kia stayed ready for whatever and whoever. She did not care who they were.

"Got damn. Man, y'all chill the fuck out," Smirky said, this time as he rubbed his hand across his fade.

"Dat's Ridah actin' like I done took her nigga or some shit." Kia smirked.

Ridah sat up. "Bitch, say my name again!" Ridah dared Kia.

Kia turned her attention to the rearview mirror with an open challenge. "Ridah," Kia said with a small smirk.

Ridah delivered a series of quick blows to the top of Kia's head. Kia let go of the steering wheel and was almost in the back seat throwing wild punches just as hard as Ridah was.

Kia had been fighting most of her life because girls always tried her up, and when she got started, it was hard to get her to stop. Many had witnessed this firsthand themselves.

"Got damn!" Smirky yelled, reaching over to grab the wheel. "Cuz, get this wild-ass girl," Smirky shouted as he gained control of the swerving truck.

Ridah was halfway down on the seat when she grabbed Kia's hair and kicked her in the face as hard as she could.

"Bitch," Ridah uttered, breathing hard.

Kia went crashing back into the dashboard. Her face was suddenly stinging, yet she was determined to get back at Ridah. As Kia lunged forward, she squeezed her eyes tight, seeing Ridah draw her arm up with a razor in her hand. Kia braced herself for the impact that was coming.

K.J. caught Ridah's arm as she was bringing it down. "What the fuck, Ridah? Y'all on the same team. Save that shit for our enemies." K.J. snatched the razor from her. He hated being around females because of this very reason. They always had some drama going on. "I don't wanna hear shit else outta y'all ass."

Kia sat in the passenger seat, sniffing. She couldn't believe Ridah was going to cut her like she was an enemy. Kia did not sign up to fight against her kind. She joined the gang to have something she had yet lacked: a real family. Kia wanted to belong to and be a part of something. Her pride was hurt.

Ridah wanted to take Kia's head off. She must have thought Ridah was sweet. Ridah couldn't have her thinking that. Ms. Ridah was the last chick Kia wanted to play with. She wouldn't think twice about putting some fire behind Kia! Ridah could not help but roll her eyes as a thousand ways of how to kill Kia ran through her head like a *Law & Order* marathon. That was one of the many reasons why Ridah did not hang with females. Either they were jealous or trying to sleep with your man. Ridah was ready to get out of the truck from around Kia before she exploded.

Ridah's heart damn near leaped out of her chest when she saw flashing lights. Smirky speeding off did not make it any better. Ridah didn't know about them, but she was not trying to make a top story of the morning news. Ridah had things to do, and getting her mother to post her bond definitely wasn't one of them. When Smirky thought he was out of their view, a patrol car ducked off on the side of the road and pulled back on the road. Ridah shook her head.

"Man," K.J. shouted as he clenched his teeth.

The police pulled up behind them, flashing their lights again, giving them a final warning to pull over before things got real.

Smirky summed the situation up quickly. He bobbed his head and said, "Okay," with a devilish grin, then looked at Kia. "Aye, don't you specialize in driving?"

Kia grinned a stupid grin that Ridah had grown to hate within minutes.

"Thought you'd never ask." Kia grabbed the wheel while Smirky slid into the passenger seat. Kia then climbed over him, getting in the driver's seat. Kia adjusted the seat, all while popping her neck, then pulling out her tool.

Ridah started biting her nails, more out of nervousness than habit, as she thought, *this rookie-ass bitch 'bouta get our Black asses killed.* Ridah had no other choice but to be content going out in a blaze with Kia if it came down to it.

"Might as well go out with a bang." Kia shrugged her shoulders as she slowed down, hitting the signal as if she were about to pull over.

Smirky pulled his tool, and K.J. laid his tool on his leg, ready to blow. There was not an actual plan. The officer pulled behind the truck. As soon as his foot hit the concrete, Kia sent a spray of bullets his way, causing him to stumble back for cover as he reached for his gun. Kia hit the gas, laughing, leaving nothing but gun smoke lingering and tire marks.

"Bitch, you wildin'," Ridah couldn't help but say. She had no choice but to give Kia her respect. She earned it. Looking at Ridah through the rearview mirror, Kia nodded her head with a grin.

Ridah couldn't help but think about how Cleo from the movie *Set It Off* went out in a blaze. Ridah was a rida, but she was not stupid at all. She wasn't trying to go out like that. Not Ms. Ridah. Glancing over her shoulder, Ridah exhaled and silently thanked God no one was behind them. Living this kind of lifestyle would give someone a heart attack. You didn't have to worry about anyone killing you. You'd end up killing yourself.

Kia took a few sharp turns, cutting down back roads. Although K.J. was not with ditching his truck, he knew that he could not risk them being in his truck since the police would be looking for a truck that would fit its description. In the alley, they hopped out of the truck after Kia threw it in park.

Smirky jumped a fence only to land in a nearby creek. Ridah did not know how to swim, but she was going to take her chances before she let the law take her or, worse, toe-tag her. Ridah refused to be captured.

The trio made it over into the cold, murky water and waded toward the middle. The water started to get deeper. Ridah started to panic as she kicked her legs wildly, causing her body to go straight to the bottom of the filthy water.

K.J. grabbed Ridah's arm to pull her back up. She quickly hopped on his back and held on to his thick neck for dear life. Seeing a few water moccasins snaking through the dirty water caused her to watch them to make sure they did not come near her.

Smirky screaming caused Ridah and Kia to scream too. Ridah jumped off K.J.'s back and flailed her arms and scissored her legs until she reached the muddy ground.

They ended up by a swamp-like embankment with an assortment of thick, nasty algae. There was only one way to get to the other side, which was to walk across the log that floated in the slimy murk. "Ridah, you and Kia go ahead," Smirky urged, scanning the sketchy swamp.

Ridah stepped up on the log with Kia following closely behind her. "Bitch, you better not make me fall," Ridah warned before turning her focus on the task of walking on the log without falling.

Kia was so busy flirting with Smirky that she accidentally bumped into Ridah, causing her to lose her balance. Ridah did not plan on going down by herself. She grabbed Kia's arm and brought her along with her.

K.J. and Smirky bent over, choking with laughter. Ridah looked at Kia, who was smirking while she apologized. Ridah rolled her eyes so hard, then shot K.J. and Smirky a look filled with animosity. The way Ridah was feeling, she could have put a bullet in all three of them.

Thank God the water wasn't as deep as it looked. They were able to wade to the other side after much difficulty disengaging their feet from the muddy bottom. Once they made it, K.J. and Smirky joined them.

"Damnnn," Smirky said, imitating Smokey from the movie *Friday,* then chuckling.

Kia thought it was so funny. Ridah did not find anything funny. "Fuck y'all." With a scowl on her face, Ridah gave them her middle finger.

"Come on, Ridah. Don't be like dat." Kia leaned in to hug Ridah, which caused Ridah's body to tense up. Ridah cut her eyes at K.J., who looked as if he was pleading for Ridah to play nice.

Ridah threw her arm around her new cuzzo and grinned. "I know your ass pushed me for get-back." Both of them laughed. Ridah saw K.J.'s facial expression relax.

As they walked toward the barbed-wire fence, they realized they were not left with any other choice but to take their chances on getting cut up, then bitten by those nasty snakes.

K.J. told them to give him their T-shirts. Ridah was hesitant due to the padded bra she wore under her ruined tank top. K.J. held out his hand, waiting for Ridah to give him her tank top. Ridah cussed silently while pulling it over her head and throwing it into his waiting hand.

After climbing over the fence, Ridah thanked God for the millionth time today. This time though, Ridah thanked Him for being back on dry ground. Ridah quietly assessed the bandages on her side. As filthy as they were, Ridah wouldn't doubt if she had a growing infection from the bullet graze.

Walking into the unknown had Ridah thinking the craziest things and a bunch of what-ifs. One thing Ridah knew though was they weren't wanted. Hell, the police didn't know who they were, and K.J.'s truck was well hidden. At least until things cooled down.

Ridah felt uncomfortable without her shirt on, especially in K.J.'s presence.

Ridah stole a glance at K.J. out of the corner of her eye. He still looked appealing to her, even with the grime on him. Ridah licked her dry lips, then bit down on her bottom lip as wicked thoughts invaded her trifling mind. Ridah found it very frustrating fantasizing about someone she could not have. Knowing that only deepened her desire for him.

"What's on ya mind?" K.J. asked.

Ridah attempted to keep her facial expression from revealing what she hid in her mind. When Ridah turned to face him, she silently prayed that there was not a trace of her lustful thoughts lingering. Ridah was taken aback by the look K.J. was giving her. Ridah's mind could have been playing tricks on her. It had been a long, exhausting night, and besides, she looked a hot mess. So, she knew it was not possible for him to be looking at her in an attractive way.

"Nothing really." Ridah shifted uncomfortably.

K.J. nodded his head. "I'm glad you put dat petty shit with Kia behind ya. She really good people. And she's gonna need someone like you around. For real for real, y'all are alike in a lotta ways."

"Dat bitch bumped me on purpose." Ridah could not help but giggle. If it had been the other way around, she would have done the same thing.

"Maybe, but you took her ass down wit' cha," he said, laughing as well.

Smirky and Kia walked up. He looked from Ridah to K.J. "Yeah, we good if y'all wanna know." He mugged them as they continued to laugh. "Let me find out," Smirky mumbled more to himself, but Ridah heard him.

To lighten the mood, K.J. started talking about how Kia rode on the folks to being chased. Ridah laughed so hard she almost peed on herself. All of a sudden, she felt blood squirt into the bandage. Out of nowhere, Ridah felt lightheaded.

"You good, cuz?" Smirky's facial expression filled with concern. He bent down beside Ridah and noticed the soiled bandage soaked in fresh blood.

Ridah nodded her head as a wave of nausea hit her like a freight train. She took a few deep breaths, then stood back up. "I'm all right. Just need a minute to rest," Ridah replied, not wanting to appear weak in front of them, especially Kia and K.J.

Ridah was about to say something when K.J. suddenly halted. Looking up, Ridah saw why he put his index finger to his lips, signaling them to be quiet. Smirky flashed a dangerous grin, and Kia cocked her head to the side as if she were really considering her thoughts. Ridah could see pieces of herself in Kia, and it was scary.

They stood back in the woods, only to watch a man struggle with what appeared to be a body. Ridah's heart raced, not knowing how much more it could take in one night. She was liable to have a whole heart attack.

Ridah and Kia stepped out of the shadows at the same time. When Kia told Ridah to get out of her head, Ridah smirked as she gave her a look that said, "You wish." Ridah knew Kia was trying to prove herself to her now. Instead of Ridah embarrassing her, she decided to let Kia take the lead and have her back.

As luck would have it, the man was Blood affiliated. The light in the car allowed them to see his flag, which hung loosely around his rearview mirror.

"What's crackin'?" Kia said boldly.

The man nearly jumped out of his skin at the sound of someone's voice. Kia let out a giggle, seeing the expression on his face.

"Where the fuck y'all hoes come from?" he asked while scanning the area before letting the feet of the body drop to the ground. As if an afterthought, he fixed his mouth to say, "And do I look like a hardback to you?" he said defensively.

As if she did not hear him correctly, Kia slightly turned her head to make sure she understood what he said. Ridah, on the other hand, took a closer step forward. She was not going for anything strange, especially when it came to someone disrespecting her set.

"What was that?" Kia asked, now challenging him.

Before the man could utter another word, Kia held her pointer finger up. "I want you to think 'bout what come out your mouth next before you speak."

Frowning as he looked around for the final time to make sure no one else was with them, he said, "Y'all hoes doin' a lotta cappin' to be in the middle of nowhere."

Smirky stepped out of the woods with K.J. closely behind him. "My Cripettes ain't never alone, nigga." Smirky smirked at the man, then added, "But you, on the other hand . . ." He extended his hand in a cocky way. "Can you say the same?"

Smirky spoke with so much venom that his words caused goosebumps on Ridah's bare skin. A smirk spread across Smirky's sweaty face. Ridah was over the night's events. All she wanted to do was go home and clean the filth from her abused body.

Ridah made her way to the rival and pointed her finger toward the already open trunk. The vein in the middle of his forehead seemed to strain against his skin. He sensed tonight would be the last time he'd feel the cool air and see the sunrise.

Getting in a better stance, he prepared himself for a battle. He charged at K.J. Ridah could not help but stand back and admire the fact that he was not going down without a fight. K.J. sent a mean, nasty right, catching him square in his jaw, dropping the man like a bad habit.

Smirky got in on the action. As their rival was getting up, Smirky put him in a headlock, causing him to claw at Smirky's arm as the fight slowly left from his body.

"Stop scratching on my loc, nigga," Kia warned, then started swinging on him. Ridah did not expect her to jump in on the action, but she surprised her. "Didn't I say stop scratching my muthafuckin' loc?" Kia shouted with each punch she sent to their rival.

Ridah had to pull Kia off him. She was swinging so wildly that she was hitting K.J. Kia's adrenaline was now racing through her. She paced back and forth while Ridah stood out of breath. Smirky picked the man's gun up off the ground and fired a single shot, which echoed into the darkness. Their rival already knew what time it was. He stood up, dusted the dirt off his pants, and put himself in the trunk. Smirky slammed the trunk with a deep frown.

"Damn, Kia, ya wild ass punched me in the eye," K.J. said as he got into the driver's seat.

"My bad, cuz," she said, still out of breath.

K.J. took the red flag off the rearview mirror. Ridah jumped in, riding shotgun, while Smirky and Kia got in the back. Ridah started going through their rival's glove compartment, which contained cocaine and a .45. Ridah could not contain her smile. Smirky leaned forward to look over Ridah's shoulder and hungrily grabbed the powder out of her hand, acting like a geek monster. Smirky had once told Ridah that snorting powder was a hobby, but it seemed to Ridah that Smirky had an addiction. When Kia reached for the gun, Ridah moved it out of her reach.

"Nawl." Ridah shook her head at Kia.

Smacking her lips, Kia folded her arms. "Come on, Ridah. It'll be my first toy."

"See, that's the problem right there." Ridah held the gun up. "This ain't no toy. You pull the trigger, this muthafucka take lives." Ridah thought back to the day she caught her first body.

Ridah could see the hesitation in Kia's eyes before she lowered them. Seconds passed before Kia reached for the gun. "If it comes down to it, then hell yeah."

Ridah glanced at K.J. for his approval. He slightly nodded his head. Ridah could not contain her smile as she handed Kia the gun and said, "Welcome to the family."

Kia took the gun, admiring it as soon as it touched her hand. Ridah then turned around in her seat. Smirky was already busting down a small baggie of cocaine. Ridah reached her hand toward the bag, only to put her pinky in the white snow. As she was getting close to her nose, she noticed K.J. watching her.

"Damn, can I have my face back?" Ridah sassed and felt embarrassed.

Instead of K.J. responding, Smirky said, "Aye, Ridah, don't be thinkin' ya ass Superwoman and shit," Smirky laughed.

Ridah rolled her eyes. Smirky always had something to say. "I swear, sometimes you talk too fuckin' much," Ridah snapped, then flared her nostrils. K.J. turned back to the wheel and continued driving.

Sitting back, Ridah let the narcotics take their effect. Although she did not partake in drugs on the regular, Smirky was right about one thing. Ridah felt like she could take on the whole world when she snorted powder. She was Superwoman!

CHAPTER FOUR

Block Bound

Street law: Keep ya eyez open at all times!

The sun was rising by the time K.J. pulled up on Poppy Avenue. There, the trappers were known for their hustling skills, and the fiends used what they had to get whatever it was that they wanted when their money was short. Today wasn't any different from the rest. Crips were posted on the block. A few were leaning on a gold Honda that sat on four old, crumbled bricks.

Ridah yawned as she exited the car to follow K.J., who made his way to the porch of the beige and white house. When Capone stepped out of the house, K.J. told him and Kia to get rid of the car they'd just exited. Capone rushed to hop in the idling car. K.J. strolled in one of his trap houses, as some people referred to them.

They entered the house, which was filled with intoxicated people scattered throughout the living room. A few of them were passed out on a money green sofa, obviously unaware of anything going on around them. The air reeked of stale behinds and cigarettes. Empty beer bottles, overfilled ashtrays, and old food littered the wooden coffee table. Ridah scrunched her nose in disgust as she continued to follow closely behind K.J.

In the hallway, some dudes were shooting dice. One acknowledged K.J. as he was coming from a room adjacent to another room. "Damn, cuz. What the fuck happened?" he asked, taking in their appearance.

Ridah slightly moved behind K.J. "Jumped in a creek." Ridah squinted her eyes as she bumped K.J. in his lower back.

"Damn," was all the man said as he went on about his business.

Giving Ridah a shirt, K.J. said, "I'm abouta jump in the shower right quick. I'ma take you home when I finish." K.J. started making his way to the bathroom. Ridah followed but stopped short at the frame of the door.

Watching him pull the soiled shirt over his head, Ridah looked down at her appearance. "I need one too."

"Come on then." K.J. continued to strip down shame-lessly.

Seeing his muscular arms and ripped chest had Ridah in her feelings. She was raping him in her thoughts as she attempted to pull herself out of her head. She failed tremendously. Biting down on her bottom lip, she fought the lustful thoughts of what she would do if the opportunity ever presented itself. Lost in her salacious thoughts, she jumped when K.J. waved a hand in front of her face. Embarrassed by her fantasy, Ridah held her head down, shame written all over her face.

Suddenly, she felt disloyal to her mentor, Lanka, who just so happened to be K.J.'s baby mother. Lanka taught Ridah most of everything she knew pertaining to her set, as well as other things. Ridah looked up to Lanka like everyone else did. What girl did not want the kind of respect Lanka got from around the way? Not only that, but what girl didn't want a nigga like K.J.? That was most of the young girls' hood dream, to be like them. The hood equivalent of Jay-Z and Beyoncé.

"Aye, man, you good?" K.J. asked.

Snapping out of her thoughts, Ridah stuttered, "I was thinking about taking a shower. Look at me." She extended her arms to show him as if her disarrayed appearance weren't apparent.

"Come on then. I won't bite." K.J. exposed a mischievous grin.

"I might though," she said nervously while silently thinking that she should not have made that statement.

"I like to be bitten." He turned the water on while still staring at her with daring eyes.

"I bet you do. I'ma wait 'til you finish," Ridah willed herself to say, then sat on the toilet seat.

K.J. frowned as if he was confused. "Hold up. Let me make sure I got this right. Ain't no problem with you being in here and I'm butt-ass naked. But it is if you get in with me?" K.J. raised his thick eyebrow in question.

Ridah let out a nervous giggle. "Exactly."

"Oh, okay, be like that then." He splashed water her way. "With your stinky ass." They both laughed.

It was awkward for a minute. Ridah and K.J. had never been alone or shared a full conversation without everyone else around. Now here they were, getting acquainted with each other in the bathroom. To clear the uncomfortable silence, K.J. began telling Ridah a little about himself.

Ridah could not help but see how Lanka fell for someone like him. K.J. had a side of him that most people hardly ever got a glimpse at. So, Ridah valued the moment he allowed her a peek at his inner self. K.J. peeped quizzically from behind the curtain at Ridah, who was leaning forward with her elbows on her knees.

"I know Lanka took you under her wing when you came to Georgia. So, y'all pretty tight?" he asked, breaking the uncomfortable silence between them.

"We're close," Ridah admitted, yet she hated her, and Lanka was so close in this moment. It made her face reality. She couldn't have K.J. Ridah filled him in on how Smirky and her childhood friend, Bagz, introduced her and Lanka after discovering Ridah was a Cripette yet needed molding and sharpening. What Ridah's pops did not teach her, Lanka filled in.

"Damn," K.J. commented with a thoughtful expression on his face. He couldn't care less how cool and tight Lanka and Ridah were. He was going to smash Ridah. K.J. wanted Lanka to experience what it felt like to be betrayed by someone close to her heart. Lanka slept with K.J.'s childhood friend, Fetticain. "So, the real reason you declined gettin' in the shower with a nigga was because of Lanka?"

Ridah thought for a few seconds as he stared at her intently, waiting for an answer. "No," she revealed.

"Prove it and get your sexy ass in here then," K.J. said in a lustful tone. He knew he had Ridah then.

"Nigga," she said in a girlish tone.

Hesitation filled her, but one look at his muscular body chased away any doubts she had. Ridah pulled off the muddy skinny jeans, followed by her filthy bra and panties. She was so relieved to free her body of the soiled clothes. Kicking them in the corner, she exhaled as she stepped in the steamy water.

"I ain't never had to convince a woman to get in the shower with me," K.J. confessed as Ridah's body was immersed in water.

Ridah laughed. "Well, now you have."

K.J. turned to face her. Ridah's eyes widened as they traveled down to his enlarged penis. She was in awe. *Sorry, Lanka, I gotta get some of this beef stick,* Ridah thought with lustful eyes. As she shifted to stand directly in front of him, she brought her hand up to touch his face. A loud banging came on the door, interrupting their betrayal act. K.J. stared at the door with annoyance at the intrusion.

"What?" he shouted, clearly irritated for being disrupted.

"Nigga, I gotta shit," responded a desperate voice on the other side of the door.

"Man," K.J. said regretfully. He had been wanting Ridah for a while. Now, the opportunity presented itself, but he still couldn't smash, at least not in this moment.

"Come on, cuz. Don't do a nigga like dat, man. Hurry up," the male voice shouted even more desperate than before.

"Give me a minute," K.J. replied as he turned the water off.

Ridah eyed him with an attitude etched all over her face. "Nigga, I know you ain't abouta let him in here while I'm naked," she stated while cocking her head to the side.

K.J. paused, pretending to contemplate it, then smiled. "Nawl, I'ma grab you somethin' to throw on," he said, stepping out of the shower, then glancing back. "Don't go nowhere," he joked.

Ridah leaned her head forward, shooting him an evil glare. "This shit ain't funny." She pointed her finger at him.

When Ridah heard the bathroom door open, she assumed K.J. had returned until she heard a series of farts and grunts. She automatically frowned when the caustic smell burned her nostrils. *What the fuck?* Peeking out of the curtain, Ridah snarled as her eyes fell on a guy sitting on the toilet. He sat with his legs apart and head back. A look of euphoria covered his greasy, stubby face. Ridah was beyond disgusted. She silently cursed the man to hell, hoping he'd be finished soon.

"Damn," the dude moaned after a loud plopping noise escaped from the toilet and brought Ridah a new wave of disgust.

"Nasty ass," was all Ridah could mumble as she shook her head. It took everything in her not to interrupt him. Ridah did not have the nerve to interrupt him anyway. She would have been more embarrassed than he would. Ridah stood there, shivering, regretting letting K.J. turn the water off.

K.J. opened the bathroom door. He immediately halted, like someone physically stopped him.

"Nigga, you gonna kill dat girl," he voiced, referring to Ridah. "I'ma leave the clothes on the sink, Ridah," K.J. said as he quickly closed the door.

Looking dumbfounded as he reached for the tissue, then proceeded to wipe his soiled buttocks, he said, "Damn, my bad, cuz. Why you ain't say shit?" he asked shamelessly while continuing to clean his butt.

"You didn't give me a chance to. Pass me that towel," she said from behind the curtain.

Ridah couldn't wrap the towel around her body fast enough. She grabbed the sweatpants and shirt on her way out of the bathroom.

In the living room, Smirky sat on the edge of the sofa with a blunt in his mouth, telling his version of what went down last night. Smirky, being a natural comedian, couldn't help but make them laugh at his antics. He was so animated. Smirky stood up and reenacted from the patrol car pulling them over to taking their rival's car, all while continuously puffing the blunt. K.J. smiled as he listened, occasionally cutting his eyes open to where Ridah stood. Smirky was having too much fun. K.J. decided to join in, and he revealed how loud Smirky was screaming when he saw those snakes in the water, causing everyone to double over in tears.

"Nigga, I wasn't screaming." Smirky licked his lip as he chuckled, trying to hide his embarrassment.

A woman with a matted hair weave said, "Oh, not Papa Smirky." She giggled as she and another woman high-fived each other and erupted with boisterous laughter.

"Shut up, bitch." Smirky jumped up off the edge of the sofa with Ridah close beside him.

Anwar jumped in to diffuse the situation. Everyone knew Ridah would ride on anyone who disrespected Smirky in the slightest way. The living room became deathly quiet as Ridah stepped in front of Smirky, now in a standoff with the two women. Smirky smirked as he inhaled the blunt and knew the tension had deepened.

K.J. clapped his hands together to get everyone's attention. "All right, enough of the dumb shit. I need this place to be tightened up."

Although the women had attitudes and smacked their lips, they were glad K.J. saved them from getting rolled on by Ridah. The women began picking up the empty bottles and various trash that engulfed the living area. Once the living area was cleaned, they left. Ridah busied herself with examining the small cuts on her arms and hand.

Last night, Ridah really didn't think she would make it through. But somehow, she did. They all did, and she was so thankful. Being that close to death made her question a lot of things, like why would her pops mold her for the streets, or why would he want this for his daughter? Ridah really needed to find her own identity instead of living in the shadow, chasing her deceased father.

CHAPTER FIVE

The streets ain't for everybody. That's why they made the curb!

—Moneybagg Yo

K.J. jumped off the porch at the age of 11. He was tired of being without. Like most, there was not a father figure in K.J.'s household. You were lucky if there was a father around. It seemed as if they did not have those in the hood. All they had were drug dealers, jack boys, OGs, and a bunch of jaded people to look up to. K.J. had to step up and be a man for his mother and younger sister. Even as a youngster, K.J. wanted a better life and knew there was only so much the drug game could offer. He was among the other youngsters who had hood dreams of being a rapper, trapper, and the hardest that would intimidate the devil himself if he ran up on him.

K.J. considered himself one of the smartest OGs on the west side of Macon. He mastered school and the streets at the same time. K.J. always wanted more out of life than the one he was living. Although it was a challenge to get rid of all the grime that the streets seeped into one's pores, he never stopped striving for better. K.J. could not help but think of Tookie, the cofounder of the Crips. He knew where Tookie came from and that he reached the level of elevation that he had reached. If he could change, anybody could. Most chose to find an excuse to stay on the lower level where they felt comfortable at. Not K.J. though. He sought to reach his height in life.

K.J. vowed to himself that he was not going to be one of the ones who got cast out. He always felt like he was smarter than the streets, so they were going to get him. Most people had this logic that people joined gangs due to abandonment issues. That could be the case for most, but it was not the case for K.J. His mother showed them love. They may not have had whatever their heart desired, but she made sure he and his sister had what they needed. K.J. got down because he already had the heart of a lion. If he was thrown in a forest with wolves, or any other animal, K.J. would come out leading the pack every time. Not only did K.J. have the heart, but he also had the respect to match. No one knew the fear he could instill, and K.J. felt like people needed to acknowledge that.

A lot of things came with the image a person built for themselves. If you went hard in the streets and it was time to step up, the streets were watching and waiting. The pressure could cause one to be explosive due to the image they sent out. In a heated moment, one would draw the tool and threaten to kill. But the difference was, would they pull the trigger without a conscience? There were very few who could actually pull the trigger and take someone's life.

At an early age, the hood taught K.J. to smash or be smashed. Most stood down without thinking about the pride of the other one, vowing that if he escaped his death, he was coming back with a vengeance, and it shall be his if you allowed him to live.

Every time K.J. looked at Ridah, he could not help but admire her realness and respect, how loyal and down she was. In a lot of ways, she reminded him of Lanka back in her younger street days. If K.J. did not love anything else, he loved a thugged-out female. There were not many females who made K.J. want to invest his time in them besides Lanka, who was his middle-school sweetheart.

No one could have ever told him that Lanka would have crossed the line of betrayal. K.J. would have bet his life on that, and apparently, he would have lost and died. Now, he lived his life with the statement of "trust nobody." He did not care who it was. K.J. only trusted in two things in life: God and his gun. He trusted that God would keep him covered while his gun made bullets hail on the streets.

CHAPTER SIX

*Hell and destruction are never full, so the eyes of man
are never satisfied.*

—Proverbs 27:20

K.J. navigated his black-on-black box Chevy through
the traffic. Tupac's poetic ghetto words trapped Ridah
in her own thoughts. Lately, she had been boxing round
for round with her demons. Sometimes, Ridah didn't
think living a normal life was possible for her. Nothing
in her life had ever been normal, even as a little girl. She
had been banging so long that Ridah couldn't see her life
without doing so. Just thinking about her life caused her
to sink deeper into the leather seat.

K.J. yielded at the red light. When a black Charger
pulled up beside them, a beam flashed across the outside
mirror.

Not having time to indulge in what was happening,
Ridah quickly grabbed K.J.'s arm, forcing his upper body
to take cover. She hit the gas pedal with her hand as
the driver's window exploded. "Drive," Ridah shouted
hysterically, looking back in time to see the Charger
turning off the main road. Ridah's heart beat so loud in
her eardrums. K.J. regained his composure as his eyes
jerked around cautiously. He couldn't believe he almost
got caught slipping. If it weren't for Ridah's impeccable
reflexes, he probably would have made top news.

Without a doubt, K.J. knew if he didn't get off the main street, there was a chance whoever had it out for him would come back to finish the job. He had an idea of who would boldly come for him. K.J. was kicking it with a south-side chick named Meka. She failed to mention that she was married to her Blood, Big Slim. That alone complicated things on Meka's behalf. She attempted to be as discreet as possible, though K.J. wasn't. He boldly came through, flag banging loudly, with the blue Dickies and Chuck Taylors. His cripping was not a secret. K.J. made sure people in their neighborhood knew he was coming to see her.

On a Thursday night, while it was raining, K.J. was laid up in Meka's spot when Big Slim walked in on him and Meka. K.J. stayed ten toes down whenever he was on a different territory. He already knew Big Slim would not let him slide if he ever caught him up in his spot. With that in mind, K.J. released a single bullet, kissing his neck, only giving him half a chance to react. Big Slim pulled his tool out, two hitting Meka in the chest, before crashing to the floor.

K.J. knew it was only a matter of time before they came his way to retaliate on the death of their fallen one. K.J. knew someone tipped Big Slim's people off. He was the last person seen at Meka's house about two weeks ago. As much as K.J. hated to admit it, his ego was a little crushed.

Entering Terrance Park apartment complex, K.J. turned his head in Ridah's direction. He found her eyeing him. "Damn, I know a nigga look good and all but close your mouth," he stated in a joking manner.

Sucking her teeth, Ridah rolled her eyes. "Don't flatter yourself, nigga." She giggled then asked, "What you about to do though?" Ridah barely had company and could use some about now.

"Shid, chill with ya for a minute." K.J. had plans on picking up where they left off in the shower. He had known that Ridah had a thing for him. K.J. chose to ignore it due to his baby momma, Lanka, and her relationship. But all that went out of the window when Lanka pulled her flawed move a few years ago. K.J. felt it was time to return the favor.

Ridah glanced at him with curiosity in her eyes. In this moment, she felt her weakest. She attempted to find an excuse to have K.J. and not feel guilty. She knew if they crossed that line, it could never be undone. Ridah knew how Lanka felt about K.J., but that didn't stop the urge between her legs for him. Ridah decided right then and there that she would deal with whatever consequences for her acts when the time came because Ridah was crossing that line tonight.

K.J. turned the car off. For a brief moment, he questioned whether he should go inside. Throwing the thought out of his mind, K.J. threw the driver's side door open to exit the car.

There was a small crowd in front of the building, hanging out. One of them approached Ridah. With K.J. already being edgy, he reached for his gun. Ridah peeped his sudden movement out of the corner of her eye. She put her hand on his arm, letting him know there was no threat.

"What's up, Ridah?" he said cheerfully, never noticing the move K.J. almost made.

"Scott, what you doing out this early?" Ridah's eyes swept the scene before she fully had her focus on him.

"Kicking shit with friends." He pointed back with his thumb to the few guys still sitting on the porch, drinking. "Man, some crazy sh—" Scott started to get hyper until Ridah cut him off.

"What I told you about calling these niggas your friends? They ain't ya friends, Scott," Ridah scolded him.

"You my friend though?" Scott questioned.

"Ya one and only." Ridah's heart smiled. She really cared about Scott and considered him a friend. Scott stuck his hand out to do their lame handshake he had made for them. Ridah secretly loved it, but she would never tell anyone.

Scott gave her that silly grin she loved so much, then turned his attention to K.J. Poking out his chest, Scott said, "What's up, big homie?" He slapped hands with K.J., then closed it into a fist.

"Shit, you got it, little homie," K.J. replied with a sly smile. He could see the innocence in Scott. As sad as it was, K.J. couldn't remember the last time he had been around a teen with that kind of innocence about him.

"Scott, I'ma get at you later," Ridah said as she and K.J. headed into the building of her apartment.

K.J. took in Ridah's apartment as he entered it. He admired her style. Ridah's living room was decked out in a chocolate color with sky blue and gold trim. Two crystal lamps sat on the glass edge tables against the wall. K.J. nodded his head in approval. He loved a woman with class yet who was still hood. Ridah was definitely about her business in her home and on the streets. K.J. admired that.

Ridah told K.J. to make himself comfortable, then went to the back room to strip out of the clothes he had given her. Sinking down in the water, Ridah sighed. Tears stung her eyes with thoughts of J-loc's death. She could not help but think, *why does life have to be so hard to live?*

Most people admired the fact that Ridah was born in a gang. The only thing she had to do was step up, and boy, did she take off like a rocket. The streets were taking their toll on Ridah while holding her tightly in their deadly grips. There had been plenty of nights when, deep in her troubled thoughts, she wished she could be more like her sister than the person she had become. Ridah hated how obligated she felt to her deceased father.

Now, dressed in an orange tank top and yellow boy shorts, Ridah entered the kitchen, finding K.J. She peeked around him as he put the final touches on two sub sandwiches. "Let me find out." Ridah put her hand over her mouth as a giggle escaped.

"This all a nigga had to work with. I can't believe you got all this junk and no real food. If I'm gonna be comin' over here, you better hit the grocery store," K.J. said as he continued to focus on the subs.

"Nigga, eat before you come over or go buy food yourself if you don't wanna eat what's here. It's that simple." Ridah raised her eyebrow as she sassed.

K.J. shook his head. All the time he had been around Ridah, he never noticed how fly her mouth was. "Maybe I will if I decide to stay around," he stated.

"Decide?" Ridah repeated with a tight lip. "Humph, yeah, okay."

She knew K.J.'s type. He was used to females giving in to him. He was in for a rude awakening though. Ridah was known for making the hardest gangsta weak for her without trying. This was going to be very interesting. Ridah couldn't wait to see where their journey led them. She smirked at the thought.

Ridah kept trying to convince herself that she was not going to mess with K.J., but lust always ended up being most people's downfall. Last night, they formed a bond after facing death together. Taking a shower with him was something she would have never expected to happen. No matter how much Ridah denied it, the reality was that the line had already been crossed. So, why not go ahead and have fun? At least, that was what was going through her mind when she got the tingling feeling between her legs.

K.J. passed Ridah a paper plate with sub bread, turkey, lettuce, tomato, cheese, and mayo. To top it off, he added her favorite, plain chips. They went into the living room to eat.

When K.J. sat down, Ridah all but yelled, "Nigga, you ain't eating on my damn couch. I know your momma taught you better."

The look on K.J.'s face was priceless. Ridah set the plate down on the glass table to go retrieve a blanket from the hall closet. Once she spread it, K.J. gave her a quick glance.

"Mother, may I?" he smarted off.

"Yes, you may." Ridah giggled as she sat Indian style. K.J. grabbed the remote and pressed play. "What we watching?" Ridah asked while putting a chip in her mouth.

"*Straight Outta Compton.*" K.J. leaned his back against the couch.

"One of my favorites," she stated. As they watched the movie, Ridah suddenly asked, "Do you and Lanka still kick it?" She licked her lips as she cut her eyes at K.J.

K.J. stared at Ridah as if he was challenging her question. "What cha mean do we still kick it?" Setting his now empty plate on the glass table, he said, "I think the real question is, are we fucking?" K.J. didn't wait for an answer. He already knew. Every female he kicked it with had always been more concerned with Lanka instead of themselves.

Ridah swallowed the food that was in her mouth. Cutting her eyes, Ridah looked K.J. directly in his eyes.

"It's simply a yes or no." Ridah wasn't in the mood to play mind games. Although there was no such thing as in-between loyalty, Ridah felt she'd rather not rock with K.J. if they were still messing around. Then again, she felt as if she was contradicting herself. Deep inside, Ridah knew she was going to sleep with K.J. She was hoping she could do it without feeling an ounce of guilt.

"Those days been over."

It was really none of Ridah's business what he and Lanka had going on. K.J. would never reveal that he was still in love with Lanka, especially after her ultimate betrayal.

As Ridah relaxed against K.J.'s chest, he adjusted to her position.

"I hear you," she said, half believing what came out of his mouth. She decided to change the subject. "When do you plan on slowing down out there?" She nodded her head toward the front door.

When she felt him stiffen, Ridah knew her question caught K.J. off guard. Other than Lanka, no one had ever seemed to care enough about his well-being to ask such a question.

"I wanna go to college for journalism or something. Maybe even become a public speaker for troubled teens to help detour them off the road of self-destruction."

This was a side Ridah never allowed people to see, her more sensitive side. Her pops always taught her that if you showed a hint of weakness, then you would appear weak to others. He told them that people preyed on the weak, and no daughter of his was going to appear weak if he could help it. Ridah remembered Blu Foxx pushing her and her sister to fight each other, and if one cried, he would beat them himself. His goal was to beat the softness out of his innocent daughters. And if Tina ever tried to get in between Blu Foxx's lessons, she would get punished as well. Thinking back though, Ridah could not help but wonder if her pops was doing it all to protect them or prepare them for a certain type of life.

"I been on the block since a li'l nigga. When you see as much shit as me, a lotta shit becomes normal. I've written two books as of this moment. A lot of authors do make-believe about the streets because they've never been there. The shit they write is too farfetched and fucks up the streets. But if you from the streets"—K.J. pointed at himself and then Ridah—"everybody don't make it out alive."

"Yeah, that's true." Ridah nodded her head in agreement as her mind began to fill with things she could pen.

K.J. was right about one thing. A person from the streets, or who had been through something, could pen a successful book because they lived it. Ridah did not know a damn thing about selling drugs, but her lifestyle was a story within itself. If she did pen a few novels, it would be the beginning of a beautiful and promising career.

"Put me on your team," Ridah said, trying to hold in her excitement. She would try to write her book, *Diary of a Cripette*. Just that little part had her hooked.

"Can ya ass sit still enough to pen a book?" He didn't try to hide the doubt in his voice. K.J. had met so many people who capped about writing a book. But when they realized it took a lot of self-discipline and required a lot of one's time, they weren't as hype as they were going into it.

"I can," Ridah said with determination, overlooking the hesitation displayed in K.J.'s eyes.

"Only time will tell." K.J. had wasted his breath so many times on this particular topic that it wasn't funny. Though the scenes had always stayed the same, it was the people who changed. There had been many who thought their desire was to write a book, only to discover it was a nice idea that formed yet they were not passionate enough to follow through. Even if Ridah did write a few chapters, he doubted she would complete it, so why lecture her? She would have to show him.

"I'ma show you." Despite K.J. doubting that Ridah could pen a book, he went along with throwing out ideas, book titles, and even discussed what her book covers would be like.

K.J. had gotten comfortable, so he began to open up more about himself. They jumped from one topic to the next, and K.J. was pleased at how he enjoyed conversing with Ridah. He remembered a time when he and Lanka used to stay up all night, talking about everything under the sun. K.J. missed those times. He missed them as a couple, even as best friends, because at the end of the day, they were one hell of a team. Staying under the same roof, they had become more like strangers and were at odds most of the time.

Ridah woke up to the smell of bacon heavy in the air. The smell willed her out of the bed, stretching her limbs. She dreaded going to school today. Dragging herself to the bathroom, Ridah got herself together. She did not remember getting into bed last night. The only thing that she remembered was lying with K.J. on the floor. Making sure her boy shorts weren't in her butt, Ridah exited the bathroom and headed to the kitchen.

"Oh, let me go get my phone." Ridah turned to skip out of the kitchen. She was about to capture this scene.

"Oh, fuck nawl!" K.J. shouted and took off after Ridah. Lanka would kill him, them, if she got wind of a picture of him floating around. K.J. wasn't going for that at all.

Ridah dove on the bed, landing on her back with her legs and arms out, trying to keep K.J. at arm's length. He landed on top of her and grunted as her foot crashed into his chin. Her finger laced the back of his neck. Gently, she pulled him closer. K.J. leaned in, fighting temptation. Ridah held back with no punches. She wrapped her legs around his waist. The moment their lips touched, Ridah's body had a mind of its own. She started grinding her hips against him with urgency. She needed him inside of her. Ridah was ready for whatever came her way from sleeping with K.J.

"Ridah," he grunted as he battled against his other head that was ready to get wet. K.J. had cheated numerous times. However, he had never cheated with anyone as close to Lanka as Ridah. K.J. was still hurt by Lanka's actions, and he wanted her to feel his pain. K.J. never thought there would be a time when he'd become as disloyal to her as she was to him.

Ridah sensed his struggle. "I know. We can't." Ridah wanted K.J. so bad it almost brought tears to her eyes. She couldn't help but question why he had to belong to Lanka.

K.J. pushed himself up off Ridah, who sat up and went into the kitchen. K.J. punched into the air in frustration. He wanted Ridah badly, but it was a challenge for him to walk the line of betrayal. To make it worse, he was actually fond of Ridah, which would eventually complicate things more within his home with Lanka. K.J. wanted his cake and to eat it, too. He could not see himself letting Ridah go nor was he going to let Lanka go. If he played it right, he could have it all.

After filling their bellies up, K.J. took Ridah to school. There was so much to be said, but neither of them uttered a word. When he pulled up to the West Side High School ramp to let Ridah out, she put her hand on the door handle. Looking over at him, Ridah searched for a sign of regret. All she saw was a man struggling against what he knew wasn't right. This made Ridah more determined. She now had her sights set on one thing, and that was getting K.J. Ridah wanted him, and at this point, she couldn't care less about who got hurt in the process.

Ridah leaned in to kiss K.J. on his cheek. "See you later."

"Most definitely." A smile spread across his handsome face.

"All right, see ya," Ridah said, exiting the car. K.J. watched her enter the building before pulling off.

Ridah made her way to the gym with everyone else until the first bell rang. All eyes seemed to be on her. The attention did not go unnoticed to Ridah. When she went to sit by Chase, he slid over as if she had something he'd catch if she got too close.

Ridah took in his sudden action with confusion. "What's up? Something wrong?" Ridah quizzed.

"Toni talking reckless, insinuating me and you fucking around. Remember the night you let me crash at ya spot?" Chase explained.

"What?" Ridah was not expecting to hear that. There had been so many times when Chase crashed at her spot. He even brought Toni over to chill. That was what really blew Ridah away the most. That was another reason why she did not kick it with many females. It was always something. "Toni knows better than that shit."

"Toni ain't trying to hear shit! She don't want me talking to you," Chase said in a frustrated voice. He considered Ridah his friend who had always been there in his time of need. But to keep down confusion, he wanted Ridah as far away from him as possible.

Chase was like a brother to Ridah. Truth was, Toni had a problem with anyone Chase hung around. She was jealous and rude to anyone Chase gave his attention to. So many people tried to warn him of how Toni was, but he didn't take heed. Chase always believed Toni over his close friends. Ridah was one of the last friends he had left until now. Toni had pitched another deceitful ball in the air.

Toni strutted toward Ridah and Chase's direction with a deep frown on her face. A few students whispered among each other as others watched with anticipation. Ridah stood with her hand on her hip, ready to defend Chase. Toni strolled right up to Ridah and boldly slapped her. Ridah was so startled by Toni's sudden boldness that it took her a second to react to the disrespect.

Ridah pushed Toni, causing her to trip over her own feet and land on the gym's waxed floor. Ridah straddled her and brought a series of vicious punches straight to Toni's face. No one attempted to break up the fight. A lot of them wanted to see Toni get beat unmercifully. It was Chase who jumped up and punched Ridah in the head hard enough to daze her. Ridah jumped up blindly as she attacked Chase. Although she was no match for him, she still fought him. Within seconds, a few Cripettes jumped in, too. Ridah felt herself being lifted in the air. She continued to swing hard and kick wildly.

"Get her outta here. That toy cop coming," Scott said as he put Ridah down but didn't release her until Smirky restrained her.

Students began to take off running in different directions, knowing they could get expelled for the rest of the school year if they were caught. Others pretended to have been breaking up the fight but really stuck around to see what was going to happen.

The Humpty Dumpty toy cop walked up to Ridah and Smirky, smiling hard like he had just caught a killer. "Ms. Girl, you just can't stay outta shit, can you?" He shook his head, showing disapproval.

"What are you talking about?" Ridah forced out while trying to catch her breath. Ridah acted as if she were confused about what he was talking about.

"Is that blood on your shirt, ma'am?" The toy cop grinned, focusing his attention on the bloodstain on her lower shirt.

Ridah glanced down at the stain. Before she could come up with a logical answer, Scott appeared. "Man, leave her alone."

The toy cop turned his attention to Scott and then Smirky.

"Y'all think y'all thugs, huh?" He nodded his head like he was answering his own question. "Bring that thug shit to my hood. I swear them niggas will get shit popping," the toy cop said, sizing them up.

"I might just take you up on your offer," Smirky replied with challenging eyes.

Smirky turned away, and Ridah followed suit, leaving him where he stood. "Aye, Scott, stay around and keep me in the loop of what's being said," Smirky said.

"I got cha, big homie," Scott replied as he glanced at Ridah before walking off into the now thinned-out crowd.

Pushing open the double door, exiting the school, Ridah saw Chase and Toni making their way to his car. Rage filled her. Without thinking, Ridah took off running in their direction. Toni happened to look up in time and noticed Ridah heading her way. Toni quickly hopped into Chase's car for safety and locked the door. That did not stop Ridah from leaping through the half-open window and attacking Toni. Screams could be heard in the school lot. Smirky stood back, laughing, until Chase started up his Honda. Ridah did not realize the car was moving until she felt herself being dragged. Once she gained her footing, Ridah pulled her upper body out of the small opening as the car started to pick up speed.

Ridah stood back, breathing hard as Chase sped off. She felt so dumb being that none of her homies cared for Chase. Ridah used to defend him every time one of her homies used to talk down on him. She had fallen out with a few people and still didn't speak to a few people because of Chase until this day. What happened today would forever be remembered as her weakest hour.

Smirky stood by his old-school baby blue Chevy, laughing. "Got damn, cuz," was all he could say.

Walking over to his car, she got in. "Shut up." She was still trying to catch her breath.

"Aye, I got something for ya." Smirky held a blunt up. She happily accepted, wasting no time lighting it up. Hitting it twice, Ridah leaned back into the blue and white leather seat, allowing the substance to take her higher. Ridah's problems began to rip away and blow in the wind like pages.

CHAPTER SEVEN

Moment of Truth

Ridah was 14 when Smirky gave her her first taste of white snow. Ridah's mother had kicked her out on a Friday night. She strutted out of the house happy. Leaving her mother's house meant one thing to Ridah. "Party and bullshit!" She could stay out as long as she wanted. Ridah ended up in the bottom court in Unionville where all her homies were rooted. They were deep like any other night, playing craps, clowning, drinking, and getting high in the wee hours!

Ridah and Smirky had always been cool. He showed Ridah love off the rip. That night, Ridah did not know what came over her when she asked to hit Smirky's sack. Smirky did not hesitate. He warned Ridah about the effect it'd have on her. Since that day, Ridah had been on it. Being around Smirky was like having the brother Ridah never had. Ridah and Smirky were so close that most people thought they had something going on.

Smirky gave her the name Ridah. He started calling Ridah that when she was 13 years old and caught her first body. Although she was not proud of it, it was what it was. Ridah had gained a lot of knowledge through many of her homies, but Smirky and Lanka were the only ones who kept it raw with no cut, as well as Bagz. Although Ridah had not seen Bagz in a few years, he was a part of her growing into the person she was today.

Back in the day, Ridah used to sit around Smirky and Bagz, sharing war stories about being shot at. In Ridah's young mind, getting shot at was cool. Ridah wanted to get shot at so she could have a story to tell. Ridah used to go where Bloods hung out, with her flag around her neck and dressed down in blue, gray, and black. A few rivals jumped her, and Ridah left some damage, but never had she been shot at.

One day, it was pouring down raining, and a blue bonnet covered Ridah's head. She was dressed in a blue khaki St. John jumpsuit. She was not paying attention when, out of nowhere, she heard gunshots. Ridah froze. Her mind screamed, *run,* but her feet felt like they were stuck to the concrete. When the dark green Ford Taurus's back light showed white, Ridah knew the driver had put the car in reverse. Ridah took off running as the gunshots filled the air. At the time, she did not know she had gotten shot in her right leg. But from that day forward, Ridah knew firsthand that there wasn't anything cool about getting shot at, and it sure was not funny when you were running for your life, not knowing whether a bullet was going to catch you. Being shot was only the beginning of Ridah's troubles. She became a target for any rival who was not one of them.

Smirky pulled up to Young's convenience store. The owner was protected by the Crips in the area. Across the street was the fish dock, which was Mafia territory. As strange as it sounded, Crips and Mafia beefed at times, but nothing separated the territories but two lanes. What was really crazy was some of those Mafia cats used to be Crips until something popped off that forced them to choose sides. If you were from the area, then you knew what took place and made history, and if you weren't, then it didn't matter to you. Loyalty was tested and left friendships torn. There wasn't any real beef between the rivals. The Crips stayed on their side of the road and so did the Mafia.

Bringing Ridah out of her thoughts, Smirky said, "Aye, ya feel like goin' to pay for the gas and grabbin' some blunts?" Smirky got out of the Chevy.

"If I don't, you gonna make me do it anyway!" Ridah replied as she held her hand out.

Smirky could not help but chuckle. "I swear ya ass acting like Ma Dukes!" Smirky shook his head. His mother always gave him hell when it came time to go to the store.

"Whatever, and I ain't using my money to fill this boat up!" When the $20 bill hit Ridah's hand, she retorted, "I can't even keep the change with ya cheap ass."

"Y'all hoes all the same," he yelled after her, then chuckled. Smirky loved Ridah before all the gang activities they were involved in. He was amazed at how Ridah transformed into the person she was today.

Smirky considered Ridah in his top six of the most real females he knew. With that being said, Ridah was not just another female to him. He cared about her and would hate to see her get caught up in K.J.'s web of deceitfulness. What bothered Smirky the most about the situation with his cousin and Ridah was, at the end of the day, it did not matter what Lanka had done in the past or how many females K.J. smashed. He was always going to choose Lanka. No one could change that. Smirky had seen the couple go through this so many times. This time, Ridah, someone he loved, had fallen victim. Although he wanted to warn her to be careful with K.J., he decided to stay in his lane. Besides, Ridah was a grown woman. She could handle herself.

Ridah entered the store, and her eyes landed on Lanka and K.J. She didn't even notice K.J.'s or Lanka's car outside. If she had, she definitely would not have come into the store. Ridah could tell the two of them were engaging in a heated conversation. It was her guilt that caused her to push back against the door to exit. Smirky pushed the door in to come in, drawing unwanted attention to Ridah as she tripped over her feet, sending her falling. Ridah pulled herself up off the floor so quickly that you would have thought she never hit the floor. It took everything in Smirky to keep a straight face.

Ridah felt like she was busted when K.J. strolled in their direction. Lanka followed him but stopped short. Ridah couldn't help but wonder if Lanka could sense the attraction she and K.J. shared. Lanka's eyes roamed over Ridah, which caused her to shift uncomfortably as she stood as normally as possible. Ridah knew Lanka was reading her body language.

Ridah's guilty conscience kept her from doing her norm whenever she saw Lanka. Of course, Lanka picked up on it. She could always feel the slightest shift in people, and something was off with Ridah. She had known Ridah since Smirky and Bagz introduced them. Lanka silently fumed on the inside as she thought back to her own betrayal. It broke Lanka's heart. Ridah was like a little sister to her.

She knew this was possible and that K.J. was more than capable of pulling something this grimy. What she did not understand was, why continue to be in a relationship and say you forgave the person if you were going to be on some revenge shit? That was exactly what K.J. was doing with the one person Lanka would have never thought would betray her. Lanka molded Ridah into who she wanted her to be. No matter what Lanka thought, the reality was that she and Ridah were alike in a lot of ways. They both crossed the line of betrayal.

"Since when we did it like that?" Lanka questioned, burning a hole into Ridah's eyes.

Ridah was caught off guard with Lanka's sudden question. She did not know what she was even referring to. "Huh?"

Lanka smacked her teeth. "Girl, don't play with me. You heard what the fuck I said." Lanka had a full attitude now. She felt like Ridah was playing on her intelligence.

Smirky stepped up to defend Ridah. "Let up off her. The girl just got jumped at school." Ridah stood still as she was frozen, not uttering a single word.

Snaking her head around Smirky to look at Ridah, Lanka said, "Since when you can't speak up for yourself, Shanna?" Lanka knew calling her by the nickname her family called her would get a reaction out of her.

"What you wanna know, huh? Oh, you think I'm fuckin ya nigga. Is that what this is about?" The minute the statement left her mouth, Ridah cut her eyes at K.J., wishing she never uttered a word.

After baiting Ridah, Lanka smirked bitterly. A part of her wanted to believe Ridah would never commit such an act, yet there Lanka stood, in front of another snake who always claimed to be so real. Lanka was beyond disappointed. This situation stung her. Lanka lowered her head as she turned to exit the store before she did the unthinkable. K.J. was right on her heels, ready to defend himself. Ridah heard him telling Lanka he would never sleep with Ridah and how it was her own guilt that was making her think that way.

Smirky shook his head as he made his way to the counter to get some cigars and the gas that Ridah was supposed to get. This was the drama he did not want Ridah to be caught up in. At the end of the day, Ridah was going to do what she wanted. As her friend, all he could do was be there for her when she needed him.

Ridah walked out of the store with apple juice in her hand and a pack of Black & Milds. The only time Ridah smoked was when she was stressed. What took place minutes ago put her on edge. This was a much-needed smoke. Lanka was insinuating that she and K.J. were messing around. The line had been crossed. Ridah could not undo the damage that had been done.

K.J. and Smirky were deep in their conversation as Lanka stood off to the side. Making her way to Smirky's car, Ridah rolled her eyes at the sight of Lanka. Ridah was in her feelings. K.J. did not glance in her direction one time in Lanka's presence. She felt played. Ridah had to really get a grip on herself. She and K.J. had not even slept together, and she was already tripping. Ridah had to get her mind right. As Smirky made his way to the car, Ridah sat up, grabbing her phone to appear busy.

Smirky dropped down into the seat and started the car up. He pulled off onto the road without a single word. Ridah sighed as she dropped the phone in her lap.

"Fix your crown. Never let nobody see you stumble," Smirky stated without looking at Ridah.

Ridah smiled. Smirky's statement was one of the many reasons Ridah loved him as much as she did. He had never judged her. He had always had her back, no matter what she had going on.

For the rest of the ride, Moneybagg Yo's voice filled the car. Pulling up to Ridah's apartment, Smirky cut the car off and exited before Ridah could. "Nigga, you actin' like you stay here," Ridah said while giggling.

Smirky shook his head. "I got a key to this bitch, don't I?" Smirky said.

"Open the door then, nigga," Ridah playfully snapped.

"Yes, Master Loccette," Smirky said in a joking manner, causing Ridah to punch him in his side. "Damn, man!" Ridah walked into her apartment after Smirky.

Smirky went straight to the kitchen while Ridah went to the back. She needed to change her bandages. "Aye, can I bring Kia over tonight?" Smirky asked, now sitting on the couch with the remote in his hand.

Entering the living room, Ridah joined him on the couch. "Y'all smashin'?" Ridah questioned.

"I could ask you the same about you and K.J.," Smirky stated with his infamous smirk.

Ridah snarled at him. "Boy, you don't know what you talking about. Don't be tryin'a dodge my question!"

"Why do it matter, Ridah?" He was now inches away from her face. "You miss this dick, huh?" he whispered, like the question was forbidden to speak out loud.

Ridah held her breath as she stared back into Smirky's hazel but grayish eyes. She hated it when he did this to her. She knew he got a kick out of it every single time. Smirky was Ridah's first when they were both living in a foster home. Over the years, the young teens secretly sexed each other on the low, without being exposed. A lot of their homies assumed Smirky and Ridah were messing around. Of course, they denied it. But they had not slept with each other for almost two years now.

Instead of answering him, her arms found their way around his neck. Pulling him closer, Ridah attacked his full lips while moaning softly. Smirky lowered his upper body on her as he gripped her thighs tightly. Over the last two years, Smirky had daydreamed of these private moments. He had not met another female who could compete with Ridah. Smirky led her to believe that the name he gave her was given due to how well she handled herself in the streets. That was partly true, but it was her riding-dick skills that formed the name Ridah.

Coming up for air, Smirky eyed Ridah. "Is this what you want?"

"Nigga, don't kill the mood!" She aggressively squeezed his hard penis through his Polo jeans. While gripping it tightly, she moaned. "Damn, how the fuck I make it two years without this good-ass dick?" she wondered out loud.

Smirky smirked as he picked Ridah up and carried her to the bedroom. Throwing her on the queen-sized bed caused her to giggle. Smirky hungrily eyed her as he stripped out of his clothes. After Ridah came out of her clothes, she spread her legs apart, then plopped up on her elbows.

Ridah knew Smirky was about to bring pleasure and pain to her body. One thing she loved was his aggressiveness. When the two of them had sex in the past, it was always like they were rivals going to war with each other. He was the only one who could bring out the savage in her. Smirky gripped her legs roughly, snatching her closer to the edge of the bed. Biting the inside of her thigh, Smirky kissed it before slamming his thick mushroom penis in her slippery, wet tunnel. He ground a little before pulling it back out slowly. Kissing her shoulder, he rammed it back in even harder. Ridah moaned loudly as her back deepened into a perfect arch.

"Miss this dick, don't cha?" Smirky grunted, putting his hand on top of her head. Still inside of her, he kissed her open mouth as she moaned. When she didn't answer his question, Smirky bit down on her nipple before sucking it hard, then slammed his penis hard and deep inside of her again before going stiff.

"Ahhhh. Yes. Yes. I miss this big-ass dick. I miss it. Please give it to me." Ridah was on the verge of tears. She loved how Smirky worked her body.

"Nawl." Smirky shook his head, thinking differently. "You ain't fuckin' me like ya miss this dick." Smirky slammed his large penis into Ridah hard again as if he were trying to break something.

"Aaahh." Ridah ground on his penis as she dug her nails in his back.

"Yeah. Now you starting to act like you miss it a little," Smirky said. "I'm abouta show you just how much I miss this pussy though." Smirky took Ridah's leg and placed it across his shoulder. Putting both hands on the top of her head, he began to pump her with nothing but his hard dick as his balls slapped her butt.

Ridah could not control the loud moans as tears rolled down the corner of her eyes. Smirky hurt her body good. The room filled with moans, making her wetter than before. Ridah dug deeper into his skin as she matched his speed. Her body started shaking as she screamed K.J.'s name. Smirky stopped mid-stroke as he looked down at the shocked Ridah.

"Oh, so dat's who you throwing this pussy for like dat?" Smirky flipped Ridah over and slid his penis back in. "Well, let me show you how I'ma give this good dick to Kia's sexy ass."

Ridah glanced over her shoulder at Smirky with a devilish look. "Nigga, you know damn well Kia will never fuck you like this." She threw her behind in a circle. Before Smirky knew it, she had him on his back. "Yeah, nigga, what was that?" Ridah taunted him as she rode him backward while looking back at him, talking trash.

Smirky did his trademark smirk. This was what he missed with Ridah. With them, one always tried to outdo the other one.

"You better put on for ya city before Kia outdo you," was all he said as he slapped her ass hard.

Smirky allowed Ridah to have her frame while she performed on top of him before he took control again. Gripping her hips, he lifted Ridah up and then slammed into her. Smirky did it repeatedly until she came all over his beef stick. Smirky attempted to lift Ridah but failed as she moaned loudly, grinding into his penis. He gave up and came deep inside her as he clenched his teeth.

Ridah giggled as she got her sweaty body off Smirky. "Get ya shit and go, nigga," she said, out of breath, then headed to the bathroom.

Smirky laughed. "Damn, ya ass still cold." Now sitting up, he gathered his clothes to put them on. Pulling out a $10 bill, he chuckled as he placed it on the nightstand. Smirky knew Ridah was going to cuss him out, but it would be well worth it. Making his way to the kitchen, he opened the fridge and grabbed the container of apple juice and a bag of plain chips off the counter. Just like old times, snickering like a little kid, he left.

CHAPTER EIGHT

*Let's take it back to when we were breaking down dope
in the trap, baby, you were my rider.*

—Moneybagg Yo, "Pride"

Beads of sweat formed on K.J.'s forehead as he flipped
the smoked ribs over on the grill. He and Lanka were
on good terms for the moment, so he could not find one
thing to complain about. When li'l K.J. came over and
patted K.J. on his lower leg, he reached down to pull him
up on his shoulder.

Although a secret was hovering over their household
like a dark cloud, K.J. did a great job pretending it didn't
faze him. Truth was, every time he looked li'l K.J. in his
innocent eyes, he could not help but think of Lanka's
betrayal.

No woman had ever humiliated him the way Lanka
had, but K.J. stayed by her side, more so to save face than
from any love he had for her. If he did not love her the
way he did, K.J. would have ended her existence.

Lanka came up behind him, wrapping her arms tightly
around him. "How's my favorite men?" she asked as she
rubbed li'l K.J.'s legs gently.

K.J. gave her a quick glance before passing li'l K.J. off to her. He really wanted to feel her forehead but quickly decided against it. He knew her like the back of his hand. Lanka had to be up to something. She was being a little too nice.

"What's up with you?" he asked, eyeing her with suspicion.

Lanka eyed him as she tried to hold in the laughter that escaped her glossy lips. "Damn, am I dat bad?" She cupped his chin, forcing him to look down at her. "I just miss us. I know it's hard to deal with the past when you have to stare—"

"I don't wanna talk about that." K.J. grabbed her wrist, only to remove her hand from his face.

"Fuck it then." Lanka stormed off with her son in tow.

Minutes later, Smirky was pulling up in the driveway. K.J. slightly frowned while watching Smirky, Ridah, and Kia exit the car. Ridah's eyes burned a hole into K.J.'s, and he was forced to look away. Smirky closed the distance between himself and his cousin with a brotherly handshake, then embraced. Ridah folded her arms as she continually shot daggers at K.J. with her eyes. Kia smiled as she leaned in to hug him in a brotherly manner.

"What y'all doing out this way?" K.J. asked curiously as he avoided Ridah's heated stare. Smirky had never popped up at his house without letting him know he was coming over.

Smirky frowned, a bit confused. "Lanka invited us. Said y'all having a cookout. You know a nigga ain't turning that shit down. Told me to make sure I brought Ridah," Smirky said while making his way to the grill to see what all was on it.

When Lanka came back out the front door with a deep mug, Smirky already knew coming over there was a setup. Closing the distance, Lanka threw something at Ridah before she swung on her. Ridah instantly defended herself.

Kia sealed her loyalty and started throwing punches at Lanka too. It took K.J. a full minute to react due to the shock of what was unfolding before his eyes. There was so much pressure between the women that K.J. decided this was something that needed to happen. With that in mind, he walked off, frustrated. When he heard Lanka screaming at him, he turned in time to dodge the lighter liquid she attempted to douse him with while holding a lighter in the other hand.

"What the fuck?" K.J. shouted in shock. He knew from experience that Lanka could be fatal if pushed, but he would have never imagined her going to these measures.

"I found dat bitch charm bracelet in ya car, nigga." Lanka pointed to the shiny object she threw at Ridah.

"That's what this shit about?" He shook his head at Lanka. "I ain't got shit to hide. She been in my car, Lanka. You thinking foul shit because that's how your ass get down," K.J. said to shut her up with false allegations.

"And, Ridah, I taught you better," Lanka said, breathing heavily. She then turned to Kia, who stood in a fighting stance. "And you, bitch." Lanka squirted the fluid on her without hesitation, struck a match, and lit Kia up. Standing back, Lanka watched Kia scream as she quickly pulled the shirt over her head.

Ridah stood, frozen, while Smirky helped Kia stomp the ruined shirt out. After Kia's shirt was out, she went to attack Lanka. Wrestling the fluid out of Lanka's hand, she emptied the contents in her face. Li'l K.J.'s cries brought everyone out of their trance. Kia looked over at the crying child trying to pull her off his mother. She hit Lanka in the face one final time before getting off her.

Now pacing back and forth, Kia mumbled things no one could understand. Suddenly, she stopped. "We didn't get invited for no cookout. This bitch tricked us here." Kia shook her head, making her way to Smirky's car.

Looking back to face her once mentor, Ridah said, "This ain't over! I'ma catch dat ass in the streets." Ridah nodded her head at her own threat. "Matter of fact, I just might fuck ya nigga now." As if in deep thought, she said, "Yeah, dat's what I'ma do." Ridah followed Kia to the car. Kia laughed, then high-fived Ridah.

"If you think the dick worth dying over, try ya luck," was all Lanka replied before picking up her son and going back in the house.

K.J. shook his head. "I gotta hear this shit all fuckin' night." He rubbed his head, already stressed. "Man, get these bitches outta here before she comes back out here busting and shit!" he said to Smirky.

Smirky replied, shaking his head, knowing they had just declared war. "All right, I'ma holla at cha later. But nigga, I better get some of them ribs, too."

"Nigga," K.J. said, not believing his cousin was thinking about food at a time like that.

K.J. took the meat off the grill as he prepared himself mentally for any eruption Lanka was going to release. He knew a peaceful day without him and Lanka bickering at each other was too good to be true. Sometimes, he felt like Lanka made it her business to piss him off and see how far she could push him. That was the main reason why he did the things that he did. He did not understand what they were holding on to each other for.

Entering the quiet house, K.J. went into the kitchen and put the foil pan on the countertop. His eyes roamed the living room area for a sign of Lanka. To his surprise, she was nowhere in sight. Although the couple had lived together for a little over seven years, their house had not felt like a home in years.

When his former friend revealed li'l K.J. could possibly be his, K.J. could not believe Lanka would be grimy and lead him to believe li'l K.J. was his son. After that situation, he kind of lost a lot of respect for Lanka. She was the one female who was supposed to always keep it one hundred with him. Not only did she betray him with his childhood friend, but Lanka also had a child by him.

Heading to their bedroom, K.J. threw the door open, causing Lanka to jump and drop the ice pack she had on her cheek. For the life of her, she could not bring herself to look into K.J.'s eyes. Lanka knew her betrayal put a wedge between them. Instead of letting the relationship go, the couple stayed grasping at something that was no longer there.

"Nawl, don't look all innocent now! I don't feel sorry for your disloyal ass." He could no longer contain his anger.

Cocking her head, she said, "If I'm so disloyal, why the fuck you still here?" When he didn't reply, she said, "Just like I thought." Lanka rolled her eyes as she got off the bed. Making her way to the bathroom, she slammed the door behind her.

K.J. sat on the edge of the bed. He remembered lying side by side with Lanka, confessing their young love for each other and planning a bright future. She was his Bonnie, his one and only, always down to ride. But Lanka slipped along the way while riding with him. No one could have told him she would have been disloyal to him.

The pact they had made, K.J. had taken very seriously. No matter what came between the two of them, they vowed to never leave each other's side.

Although K.J. cheated every chance he got, he never allowed that to interfere with his family. One thing about the streets, they were always watching, so he could not afford any mishaps. There was a time when K.J. would have never considered sleeping with Ridah or anyone Lanka was close to for that matter.

Standing up, K.J. made his way to the bathroom. Opening the door, he began stripping out of his clothes. Lanka peeped out the shower curtain, making eye contact with him. K.J. stared intently at the one woman who got to live and tell a story of breaking the heart of a gangsta such as him. Lowering his head, K.J. glanced back up, making stronger eye contact with her. She pulled the shower curtain back with an eyebrow raised, as if daring him to join her. K.J. shook his head with a tight-lipped smirk.

Stepping into the shower, he grabbed Lanka's hips, spinning her around. Grabbing the back of her neck, he bent her over. Lanka gasped as she rose on her tiptoes, mouth set in a perfect "O." K.J. lowered his head as the water hit him, then kissed down Lanka's back until he reached her perfect, round ass. He bit on her ass softly but roughly. Suddenly, he stood, and without warning, he slammed his penis deep into Lanka's slippery wet folds, causing her to become vocal as her hands pressed into the wall.

"I miss you," K.J. grunted, caught up in his emotions. Before slipping out of her slowly, K.J. teased her opening.

Lanka's moans echoed in the shower, and she bit her bottom lip so hard she drew blood.

"Oooh, my God," she moaned as she backed K.J. against the wall, spreading her legs invitingly as she bent over and grabbed her ankles.

K.J. loved it when Lanka got into this position. Looking back at him, she gave him a half smile. That smile. The one he fell in love with. For a split second, he could see them putting the past behind them and moving forward, but within a blink of an eye, that second was gone. Masking his pain, he entered Lanka from behind again.

In that moment, K.J. decided that he no longer cared about hurting Lanka by sleeping with Ridah. Ridah reminded him of who Lanka once was in so many ways. Ridah had not produced any deceitfulness since he'd been dealing with her for the last couple of months.

"I'll always love you, Lanka. Never forget that." Minutes later, K.J. was emptying his seeds deep in her roots.

It had been a week since the incident that took place at Lanka and K.J.'s house. Kia was so set on getting revenge on Lanka that she could barely sleep at night. She was glad the day had finally arrived where she could finally rest well at night, knowing she got to Lanka unexpectedly.

"I can't believe that bitch tried to set me on fire," Kia vented, thinking she had to get revenge for what Lanka pulled. She pulled the black hoodie up over her head, ready for whatever, whoever, and whenever. Kia felt just that bold tonight.

"Bitch, she didn't try. She set ya ass on fire," Ridah said, making it no better. She was in her own feelings, so she hyped Kia up more. She and K.J. had not even slept together, and all this drama was kicking off. "Listen, after tonight, we ain't speaking on this shit. Not even to Smirky, Kia," Ridah warned her.

"Say less," was all Kia said while standing back, looking at herself in the full-length mirror. Anytime she was in all black, she felt anxious. Knowing that it only meant one thing, she was about to get hyped.

Pulling up in a black stolen Pontiac, Kia texted the woman she had paid earlier who would play a part in her scheme against Lanka. Ridah got out of the car. She was ready to get it cracking. She could not wait to see the look on Lanka's face when the sneak attack happened. The thought caused her to burst out laughing.

Ridah and Kia got in position just as Lanka ran out of the building into the hallway. After Lanka rushed past Ridah, who was hidden on the staircase, she quickly went into action, wrapping the pillowcase around Lanka's neck. Her hands automatically went up to her neck as her eyes widened from the sudden attack. A wicked smile found Kia's face as she gripped the iron bat. Kia swung as hard as she could, like she was aiming for a home run. The bat made contact with Lanka's stomach, causing her to fold over and clench her midsection. Ridah snatched the pillowcase tighter around Lanka's neck when she started bucking on her.

"Let that bitch go," Kia demanded, ready for her get-back. She planned to make Lanka pay in full tonight.

Ridah released Lanka, giving her a chance to redeem herself.

"Yeah." Kia nodded her head. "What's up now?" Kia was fully hyped. She had been daydreaming of that moment for a week now.

"Bitch!" Lanka weakly reached to grab Kia, but she hit the ground instead.

Kia pulled a small bottle out of her hooded sweater. Taking the top off, she threw the contents in Lanka's direction, causing her to release a wrenching scream.

Ridah stood motionless, shock covering her face. The minute the acid hit Lanka, she knew their beef had gone to a whole other level. Ridah knew right then and there that Lanka should not live after this, but she did not have enough heart to end her once friend's life.

Instead of going with her instinct, Ridah shouted to Kia, "Let's go." The two of them fled into the darkness, leaving Lanka wallowing in pain as her screams pierced the air.

CHAPTER NINE

Started from the ground, building to the sky now
Watch it fall down, but how you gon' survive now?

—Yo Gotti feat. J. Cole, "Cold Blood"

The streets of Macon were sizzling with beef from around every way and every corner. The mayor admitted that the events that were taking place were unlike anything he'd seen in his years living in Macon, Georgia.

He also stated that the gang problems continued to escalate to new levels of violence. "If all these drug-dealing gang members want to shoot each other, that's fine with me. I'm just tired of the taxpayers having to foot the bill. Let them bleed to death on the street." The truth was that he was right in so many ways, yet his statement wasn't enough to make the violence stop.

It had been almost a month since the incident with Ridah, Kia, and Lanka took place. Ridah and Kia were not hiding. They were out and about, looking over their shoulders every other moment. Ridah wasn't willing to risk Lanka rolling up on them and slipping out into the streets. If no one else knew, Ridah knew how Lanka moved and the force that came along with her movement. She may not have the army that Lanka had, but Ridah had enough heart to go up against them and not care about the outcome.

Ridah admired herself in the full-length mirror one final time before grabbing her .380. She kissed it before tucking it safely behind her back. "Can't leave without my li'l ridah!" she stated to no one in particular. Laughing, she made an exit out the front door.

"Where you going all thugged out?" Scott asked admiringly. He always tried to do something that would impress Ridah. He even fought a few times just to score points. Even if he wasn't hard, he would fake it 'til he made it.

"To a ceremony," Ridah replied, continuing to make her way to the white Charger.

Grabbing Ridah's hand as if he were a child, he said, "I wanna go! Please, Ridah, let me go with you!" His whiny voice reminded her of Prissy.

Ridah pulled her hand away and looked into his gray eyes. "Scott, ain't shit inviting or fun about watching the innocent getting blessed in this shit." When his face filled with disappointment, she couldn't help but add, "I tell you what though. How about I take you to the cookout this weekend?" Scott's face lit up, causing Ridah's heart to smile. "Now pull them damn pants up. You ain't no thug, Scott."

Pulling his pants up, he said, "Bet that up." Scott only wanted to fit in, and if fitting in meant acting like something he was not, Scott was willing to do just that.

Leaning her head out the truck window, Ridah gave Scott a caring look.

"What I told you about tryin'a be gangsta? It ain't cool. Besides, I like you better when you yourself." With that said, she put the Charger in reverse before backing out of the parking space, heading to her destination.

Despite the gray clouds, which were heavy in the sky, the Unionville gym was still packed with Gangsta Crips. Blue, gray, and black colors filled the gym. The marvelous sight was tainted only because a child was about to be blessed into the gang. It was a natural process that took place when both parents were a part of the gang.

Everyone stood when Pacman and Peaches entered the room with their son tightly in Peaches' arms. Members bowed their heads as the couple walked down the aisle to the final stop, signing their son's blood over to the streets. Ridah stood back, taking in the whole scene. Her mind began to roam, wondering if this was the same way she was blessed in. Shaking the thoughts away, Ridah focused her attention on Script, who stepped up and placed a blue flag around the child's neck. The baby looked at Script and gave him a toothless grin, as if he knew what was going on around him.

Script motioned for everyone to quiet down before he spoke. When the gym settled, he cleared his throat then began speaking with much authority. "We cuzzos are gathered here today to welcome another one of our youngest members to the family, our family. May he be loyal to the fullest like his pops and receive much knowledge as he finds his place in the world." Looking at Pacman, Script motioned for him to come lead them in prayer.

Pacman stood before his innocent son as he prayed. When he finished, he leaned in, kissed his son's forehead, and whispered, "Welcome to the family." His son began to cry as if he felt the burden being placed upon his weak shoulders.

Members started coming up to greet their newest member. Peaches' soul quivered as thoughts invaded her mind of what her son's life would now become when he reached that certain age. The thought alone made her want to protect him from the world. Little did she know the world needed to be protected from him.

K.J.'s dilemma had him deep in thought. Pacman walked up, interrupting his thoughts. "What's going on, cuz?" he greeted K.J.

"Shid, you got it, cuz." Doing their signature handshake, then locking C's, K.J. leaned in to embrace Pacman.

"Aye, buzz, the ceremony turned out pretty good, huh?" In Pacman's heart, this was not the path he wanted to accept for his son. He wanted him to have a better life than the one he had.

"I wouldn't have it no other way, cuz. It's just the beginning." He signed.

K.J. could tell something was troubling Pacman by the stress lines on his face. Not one to overstep anyone's privacy, he decided to give Pacman his space. "All right, cuz, I'ma see ya around," K.J. said as he got lost in the crowded gym.

After Ridah finished speaking to a few of her homies, she walked toward the restroom area where Smirky and Capone were shooting dice with a group of tiny locs.

"What it do, Ms. Ridah?"

"What's up, young nigga?" Ridah responded, thinking of how young kids were getting down.

"Ridah, tell ya homies stop now. I'm abouta take all this nigga here money, honey," another younger boy spoke.

"Li'l nigga, you ain't abouta take shit." Smirky liked the li'l nigga's cockiness. Shaking the blue dice in his hand, he let them go, watching them bounce off the wall. Smirky snapped his fingers. "Fuck."

Capone shook his head and laughed out loud. "Cuz, luck ran dry."

"Fuck you, nigga." Smirky snapped, licking his lips. "Y'all bad-luck ass breathing all ova the dices and shit."

"Whatever makes you feel good, nigga." Capone continued to laugh.

"Let me get dat, nigga," young boy Trey yelled out as his little homie capped him up, and then he scooped the money up. "Here you go, Ms. Ridah. Buy you something nice," Trey said with his chest poked out as he held two hundreds out to her.

"Keep ya change, li'l nigga. Shit won't keep my Charger full two days." Ridah laughed, causing a few others to crack up.

"Ridah, that's cold," Smirky said, watching Trey's eyes go from hurt to a cold glare. Smirky knew that look. It was a look any nigga had when it came down to his pride. It would make a muthafucka do the unthinkable.

"Fuck you then, ugly-ass bitch," Trey shouted, walking up on Ridah with his hand on the handle of his tool. He was ready to air Ridah out right where she stood.

Ridah saw the rage in his eyes. He wanted her to pay for dissing him. Trey had something to prove in front of his little homies who stood behind him, ready for whatever. As Kia cut the corner, she walked up to Ridah, feeling the tension when she asked what was up. Instead of replying, Smirky and Capone took their place beside Ridah. Kia followed suit and stood in front of Ridah without knowing what was going on.

"Aye, cuz, villains stick together. Ain't no need to catch feelings behind some bullshit." Capone attempted to clear the air.

Ridah held in the smirk that was slowly creeping up on her face while staring deeply into Trey's cold eyes. The streets had already captured his mind and soul. And young Trey was ready to prove just how gangsta he was.

"I respect ya gangsta and homies backing ya. But this shit ain't no game over here, li'l homie."

The younger homies awaited their uncertain fate, knowing the situation could turn real stale for them. The young wolves were not scared to go to war at all.

Trey swallowed hard. The look in Trey's eyes filled with straight hatred. He wanted to smash Ridah's face in. "It ain't no game over this way either." Looking over his shoulder, he said, "Let's ride, y'all." Turning back to Ridah, he nodded his head. "You got dat," Trey forced himself to say as he continued to hold Ridah's cold stare. With a wicked smirk on his face, he added, "See ya 'round, Ms. Ridah." He posed a threat.

"I'll keep that in mind." Ridah flashed a smile and then winked. Watching the youngsters leave, thoughts filled her mind of their pride clouding their common sense, causing them to act violently. It could force them into an early grave. The thought made Ridah's stomach flip.

If Ridah thought there was going to be trouble, she would have taken the money. Now, she had to worry about some hot-headed young nigga trying to take her life to soothe his ego. Ridah was not built to back down. But she was beyond tired of having to shoot her way out of problems. The thought caused tension in her body. When she got like this, blowing some good Kush was the only thing that could bring reassurance to her soul.

"Think it's gonna be a problem?" Capone asked, bringing them all back to the present.

"Ridah, what cha ass done did?" Kia cut her eyes over at her.

Before she could reply, Smirky spoke. "Done hurt that li'l nigga pride in front of his homies. I won't put shit past a nigga when it comes to they pride." Smirky kept his eyes on the corner the youngsters turned off on.

"Damn, cuz!" Kia shook her head and giggled.

"Look at this sight!" Ridah said, taking in her surroundings.

Everyone seemed to be enjoying themselves. That was the highlight of it all, chilling and just having a gangsta ball. It was a privilege to be a part of something Tookie started. It was times like this that made Ridah feel so blessed. If only her twin had stepped out with her, she would have been whole. But Prissy refused to be a part of something their mother claimed was a curse from hell.

Ridah was speaking to some of the homies when K.J. came into her line of vision. She ended her conversation and made her way toward him. She stopped short when she saw Lanka standing beside him. K.J. was too caught up in conversing with her to even notice Ridah was in touching distance. She felt a sense of jealousy as she watched intently how the two of them interacted.

Despite what Lanka had done to K.J. in the past, anyone with eyes could see the passion oozing out of him for Lanka. It made Ridah's stomach clench. K.J. showed her that Lanka is, was, and would always be top priority. Why did it feel like an unexpected blow to the gut when Ridah already knew that? Blinded by lust, Ridah went against everything she believed in. She felt so out of character. She was secretly beginning to hate her once friend.

Lanka was aware of Ridah's presence, especially after the stunt she and Kia pulled. Lanka was on guard. They wouldn't get another up on her. Fortunately for her, the acid Kia had thrown on Lanka did not cause much damage. However, specks of it hit her neck, shoulder, side, and the inside of her hands when she tried to cover her face. As bad as Lanka wanted to go into attack mode, she knew this was not the time or place to smoke their asses out. There was no way in hell Lanka would allow Ridah and Kia a pass for what went down.

Lanka was deep in thought while watching Ridah storm out of the gym. Shaking her head, she could not believe K.J. would stoop this low to settle a score. Ridah wasn't just a random female to Lanka. She was like a sister. Now that the line had been crossed, there was no turning back. The two women were now rivals. Not even death could make her forgive Ridah's deceitfulness. Lanka was the type who killed all competition, literally!

Cutting her eyes at K.J., Lanka asked, "Why you dragged her in this shit?" Sucking her teeth, she stormed off. She had to get away from him before she exploded.

Lanka knew K.J. would eventually get his revenge for what she had done a few years ago. That was one of the many reasons they were not together now. K.J. had always cheated on Lanka. There had never been a time where she had to check any of K.J.'s hoes. They knew what would happen if one were to swerve in Lanka's lane. No one had to tell her K.J. and Ridah had something going on. Ridah reeked of disloyalty, but so did she.

Lanka continued to party as if nothing happened. She already knew that before the day was out, she and K.J. would have a blowout. There was too much frustration built between the two. K.J.'s eyes were glued to Lanka until he lost her in the thick crowd. Walking off in the other direction, he was heated, and the last thing he wanted was for their business to be aired out in public. He could not wait to deal with Lanka in the privacy of their home.

Opening the double doors, Lanka exited the gym to clear her mind and smoke a cigarette. Inhaling the smoke deeply, she looked up into the sky as she thought of how many days there were before the month was out. Out of nowhere, Kia sucker punched her so hard that it blinded Lanka. The sneak attack caused Lanka to stumble and drop her cigarette on the ground.

Kia nodded her head, licking her lips. She had been waiting for this moment. A smug look covered her face while she stood back, waiting for Lanka to recover before she went in for the kill. Lanka made her way to where her car was parked, which just so happened to be a few feet away.

"Punk-ass bitch wanna leave now!" Kia shouted after Lanka, who nodded her head as if she was agreeing with Kia.

Highly disappointed, Kia began to walk off. She had heard all these stories about how Lanka was about that life and how quick she was to get it cracking. When Kia heard Lanka call her name, she turned around with a cocky grin, which caused her to miss what Lanka was concealing in her hand. Her tool game was so swift that Kia never saw it coming. Suddenly, she felt a sting in her upper chest, and Kia touched the dime-sized hole. Withdrawing her hand, she glanced down, confounded, then looked back up at Lanka in shock. Kia could not grasp what happened until another bullet pierced her flesh.

"Still think I'm a punk, bitch?" Lanka stated, watching Kia crumble to the ground. Turning away, Lanka exhaled deeply before she fled the scene before someone saw her.

Ridah jumped at the sound of the gunshots. Thoughts of Trey and his crew coming back to retaliate invaded her mind. Squeezing her eyes tight, Ridah deeply regretted what went down. Now, bullets were sparking on a day where unity and peace should be the main focus. Grabbing her .38 from under her seat, Ridah hopped down out of the truck. When she turned the corner, she halted briefly upon seeing Kia scaled out on the ground.

A few people ran out of the gym, gripping their tools tightly, ready for some action without knowing what was going on. Ridah dropped down to the concrete next to Kia. She became so choked up that a minute passed before she began feeding her lies, telling her she was going to pull through. From the look in Kia's young eyes, she knew that this was a battle she was not going to win. Kia had already experienced pain, though this pain was different from all the other pains she had felt in her eighteen years. All she ever wanted was to belong to a family. She wanted to experience love, the kind she did not receive within her household.

"I'm sleepy. If I close my eyes, I'ma die in my sleep," Kia whispered. She was tired of fighting to keep her eyes open.

"Rest, Kia. You gonna be okay." Tears burned Ridah's eyes. She did not care if her tears fell. She was once again losing someone she had become close with. The funny thing was that Ridah did not realize it until this moment.

"Lanka, she caught me," Kia fought to say as blood began to fill her mouth and spill down the corner of her mouth.

Anger quickly replenished Ridah's veins. She took Kia's hand and kissed it. "I got you!" She leaned in to kiss Kia's forehead. Trapped in their own world filled with stillness, their eyes spoke loudly as they stared into one another.

Ridah sat dazed while Kia bled out in her arms. Although Kia was terrified of dying, not one tear spilled. Her life had always been hard, so if she was going to die, death had to be easy. But most of all, Kia would be able to rest peacefully and not feel the pain of life beating down on her.

Smirky burst through the crowd aggressively. He was not ready for the sight that was in front of him. Smirky's eyes fell on Kia's body. Although he hated that it was she lying on the ground, he was relieved it was not Ridah. Balling up his fists, Smirky brought them to his head as he closed his eyes, then opened them again as if the scene would somehow change, but the gruesome sight remained the same.

"Fuck!" he shouted, thinking about the little problem that had taken place earlier. Smirky could not believe he underestimated those youngsters, and because he had, Kia ended up being the victim, or so he thought.

Kia squeezed Ridah's hand tightly as she fought the grim reaper over her soul. Though she knew it was a fight she would not win, Kia still fought like hell because she wanted to stay. She wanted to live.

"G . . . get the . . . dat bitch. Get her for me, cuz." A single tear spilled down the side of Kia's face. Her hand fell to the filthy ground as her eyes became lifeless, staring off in the sky.

Smirky squatted down, closed Kia's eyes, then placed a kiss on her forehead. Ridah moved from under Kia's body as Smirky slid under her. Smirky's cousin approached them. It really saddened K.J. to see Smirky in this state of mind. He had never seen him like this with any female.

"Come on, cuz. You gotta let her go." K.J. reached out his hand to help Smirky up.

"I got him," Ridah said emotionally, still on the ground next to Kia's body. No, this may not have been the time for her to be in her feelings about K.J., but him not offering to help her up hit her in her chest.

How did something that started out so beautiful turn out to be a big disaster? Only God ever knew. It began to rain lightly. Smirky attempted to shield Kia's face from the rain, overlooking her blood seeping into the cement. Repeatedly kissing her forehead, Smirky started talking to Kia as if she could hear him.

While everyone else veered off, Smirky and Ridah waited until the ambulance came to get her body.

CHAPTER TEN

Ridah's Life Lessons:
Tears of a Gangsta

Tears of a gangsta unseen but felt like the wind, deep within the soul. Leaving the pain cutting like a sharp knife, penetrating the most tender spot of your body. Most people had a choice whether to become involved in daily activities. It was fun when you didn't really understand what was going on around you. Members of different gangs fighting over street signs, repping avenues that didn't belong to any of them. Deadly deceived. Watching the ones you loved dearly being carried off in a black hearse. Not understanding why or how this could happen to them. Those were the questions that were wondered out loud. Fighting, we were all fighting, but no one knew what we were fighting for. Some saw people they grew up with or used to kick it with die over petty beef, bruised egos, and a drunken state of mind. And they expected you to believe there was a ribbon in the sky. Life was so deceitful, and you thought this wasn't enough to bring a gangsta to tears.

It had been almost a week since Kia was killed. The streets had been so quiet that it was critical. The storm was brewing, and a lot of people were praying lightning didn't hit their way. Some nights, Ridah jumped up, drenched in cold sweats, dreaming of her death. The life she chose was filled with teardrops and closed caskets.

Ridah's pops passed on such a heavy burden that it could never be reversed if she wanted to. Besides, Ridah would never turn her back on her set, even though it called for a deadly violation. Ridah would die before she stained her pops's legacy. She was not going out like that, but if Ridah continued to live her life on the edge, she'd eventually fall. These thoughts were suddenly terrifying.

Staring in the mirror, Ridah could not help but get trapped in the eyes that stared back at her so cruelly. Ridah was blindly searching for something without a clue what it was. Could it be a glimpse of hope for what truly lay ahead in her life? At her moment of truth, Ridah realized that she did not want to die. Ridah tried to reshuffle her hand as if her life were a card game. As it would have it, her decisions were the ones who cut the cards, messing up her whole hand. Death had breezed past Ridah so many times and taken people in touching distance from her. Life, as well as death, was bold. Both would come after you.

Before Ridah started banging, it never crossed her mind that there would be so much death around her. She did not know every Crip who died, but because they were one and the same, it was a loss to them all. Because they were family, and Ridah took an oath to ride to the very end, turning away was not an option. She took those vows, and she was not taking them back. No matter how cruel the streets were, she signed her name in blue blood.

Ridah had not heard from Smirky since Kia was murdered. She had witnessed how tight Smirky and Kia had gotten, so Ridah knew he was taking her death hard.

Lanka sneaking Kia the way she did still blew Ridah away, and at the same time, Kia's death ate at Ridah like acid. She knew Kia died from being loyal to her. Ridah would have never entertained thoughts that Lanka, the mentor who taught her everything she knew, would pull something as grimy as she did.

Although Ridah and Kia did Lanka dirty, she still did not have to snake Kia in Unionville where it was a unity event. Now, Ridah had to make Lanka feel her statement. Kia's death tore her up deep inside because she knew Kia died for being loyal to her. Ridah and Kia may have started out on the wrong foot, but Kia was becoming friends outside of the gang stuff. When Ridah's pops was murdered, that was her first harsh reality of life's lesson. It did not matter how hard or real a person was, life or death did not care about those things. It would still come for you in any shape or form.

Ridah grabbed her .38 snub nose with a slight sigh. She opened the front door to some dudes sitting on the staircase, drinking and blazing the hallway down. Ridah held her head up to the sky, noticing the gray clouds promising rain. She took it as a sign of Kia crying. Sweet tears of a gangsta.

"Hey, Ridah." Scott suspiciously looked at her. Sometimes, he did not know what to think of his friend.

She mumbled, "Hey."

Ridah's heart was so damn heavy right now. When she first came to Georgia, Smirky introduced her to Lanka, who walked with Ridah and fed her the politics she needed to know and knowledge. Ridah studied Lanka and became her shadow. She never strove to be like her but better. Now, the two were at a crossroads. Ridah was not getting over the fact that Lanka touched her cuz. The loyalty Ridah had for Kia would not allow her to pass on that. It was a must that Ridah handle it accordingly. Ridah vowed to make Lanka wish she had kept their beef about K.J. between them and quiet.

Ridah pulled up at Little Rock Baptist Church, hating every second of the gloomy morning. Out of all the funerals she had attended over the last few months, this was the one that hit her the hardest. She wasn't ready

to see her hitta laid up in a casket. Ridah hated that
meeting Kia's mother for the first time would be under
these terms. Honestly, she and Kia were starting to get
to know each other on a personal level. Ridah remembered her always talking about her brother, but other
than that, they never really talked about their personal
life like that, something Ridah wished they would have
taken more time out to do.

As soon as Ridah entered the church full of mourners,
tears instantly blurred her sight. As she walked down
the aisle, her eyes were glued to the cherry-wood casket
with gold trim. Ridah's heart filled with sorrow and rage.
How could Lanka take her life? was the only thought
repeated in her troubled head. When Ridah saw Smirky,
her throat became tight. There was so much she wanted
to say. Ridah needed to empty her heavy soul. She had to
quickly pull herself together. The last thing she wanted
was people witnessing her falling apart.

"God, why you let them take my baby?" Kia was a
mirror image of the rail-thin woman who cried out. She
had to be Kia's mother.

Ridah bowed her head, closing her eyes. There was
nothing worse than hearing a mother mourn her child's
death. Hearing her weep had others weeping for her
loss. When the woman laid her head on the lower part
of the casket, sobbing uncontrollably, Ridah stood up
and made her way to comfort the woman, but Smirky
interfered instead. He pulled Ridah back.

"She's gone, Ma Dukes," a younger version of Kia said.

Looking at him as if it were her first time seeing him,
she said, "She can't be, Kell. I wanted to take her out to
celebrate. Now, she can't see me clean!" Kia's mother
cried into her son's chest while he consoled her.

Ridah stood back, high on emotions with a new cross
to carry. If she had not brought Kia into her drama, she

would still be alive. Ridah's knees suddenly became weak. There was so much she wanted to say to Kia but would never get the chance to say. Smirky held Ridah tight as she cried silently. It wasn't just Kia's death that broke her down. It was also the guilt of her being disloyal to her former friend. There were so many things that stained her soul.

"Girl, I heard Kia got killed because Ridah got into it with li'l Trey and his crew," a female spoke above a whisper.

"Yeah, I was there when that shit went down. But listen, bitch, you know her, and Lanka got some shit going on too. I wouldn't be surprised if Lanka didn't have nothing to do with Kia's murder. I heard they caught Lanka slipping and jumped her a couple of weeks ago."

"What?" one of them said with wide eyes at the new information.

"Oh, you didn't know?" The girl rolled her eyes toward the sky in a dramatic way.

"Yeah, they jumped Lanka out in Bloomfield. Kia had paid some chick to go to Lanka, saying something was wrong with her son or some shit. Them hoes slick and grimy as fuck!" The female shook her head, cutting her eyes in Ridah's direction. "I ain't never like that sneaky-ass bitch!"

"Oh, did y'all know K.J. and Lanka had an altercation about that bitch, Ridah, and him? Yeah, bitch! That ho was fucking with him," another one said as she lustfully watched K.J.

When the choir began to sing "After While" by Deitrick Haddon, there was not a dry eye in the church. Ridah thought about her life. A part of her did not want to be labeled as another gang member who lost her life on the streets. Ridah had seen this same movie so many times that she watched emotionlessly, while other times like this were unbearable.

Although she knew what came with this type of lifestyle, it was still hard to accept some of the things that came along with it. Ridah had made such a mess out of her life that she did not have the first clue where to start cleaning it up. Ridah wanted to do something positive with her life before it was too late. There were times when Ridah just felt trapped.

The choir finished singing. There was a moment of silence as "One Sweet Day" by Mariah Carey and Boyz II Men filled the church. Ridah closed her eyes as she listened to the words of the song. Boy, she could not wait to see all the homies who'd passed. She definitely could not wait to see her pops, Blu Foxx. That would be one sweet day.

Ridah and Smirky approached Kia's casket. It appeared as if she were only sleeping. Kia's pecan brown face was done up nicely with makeup while her hair was pulled up in a bun on the top of her head with a tiara, which Smirky blessed her with. Her dress was white and gold sheer. She looked like a sleeping princess, Hood Princess.

Ridah found it hard to grasp the concept of Kia's misfortune. Maybe it was the image and the representation of Kia being the kind of female she built herself up to be over the last seven months. It was hard for Ridah to accept that Kia was gone. Staring down at Kia's angelic face made her wish she had gotten to know her on a different level. The only bond they had was that they were both tied to the streets. It was like when they began spending more time together, the streets snatched her. Ridah could not help but reminisce on the times they shared.

As Ridah was turning to leave the casket, K.J. came up to hug her. She leaned into K.J.'s muscular arms. In his arms, she found comfort, but she also felt guilty. She held her breath while tears filled her eyes. Placing her hand on his shoulder, Ridah pulled out of his arms with her head down. Her emotions were all over the place, and she hated not being able to control what she was feeling, even for him.

"I need a minute." Before excusing herself, she placed a single black rose on Kia's mother's lap and then exited the church. Ridah felt that if she did not get out of there, she would have died from suffocation.

Halfway out of the church doors, Smirky called Ridah's name. Turning back in his direction, she waited for him to catch up with her.

"Kia's momma wants you to come by the house."

"All right, text me the address." Ridah licked her lips as she tried to keep herself from rolling her eyes at the women who were walking past them.

"I'm right here. I ain't letting you deal with this shit alone." Smirky wrapped his arms around her shoulders. "What you thinking in dat big-ass head of yours?"

Ridah stopped short, fighting the urge to hit him, and then stared into Smirky's eyes. She fought the urge to tell him who killed Kia but knew she could never betray Kia's trust by exposing the truth.

"Death," she decided to say instead. In reality, death was on her mind, Lanka's death, but he didn't have to know that.

"Dat's a part of life. It comes for the best of us. Shid, I'm tryin'a take that muthafucka out if it comes for me. Feel me?" Ridah nodded her head before shaking it. Only Smirky would say something dumb like that.

Smirky fell in love with street life at the young and tender age of 12 years old. He was buried so deep in the streets that he couldn't see anything past it. Street life was the only life he knew. Until he figured out another way of life, Smirky would forever be thugging.

"I know." Ridah took a moment of silence, then added, "But let me get my mind right before this repast. I'ma holla at you later, cuz."

"Fix your crown," Smirky said while hugging her again before making his way to his Chevy as a group of women passed by him. His mind was so far away that he did not hear what one of them said as he walked past them.

"Girl," one of them said, smacking her big, glossy lips, "now the ho all hugged up with Smirky." She nudged the one next to her to get her attention.

Ridah, on the other hand, saw drama coming her way. She heard the women stigmatizing her but held her tongue on the church grounds out of respect. One of them bumped into Ridah as the group of women passed by her. Ridah started laughing like she had just heard the funniest joke. Suddenly, on impulse, she grabbed the stunned woman up by the top of her dress. Irritation filled Ridah's face as she fought against the temptation to buck back.

"Stop playing with me!" Ridah exclaimed, shoving the now frightened woman into one of her friends. Ridah hopped up in her truck and hit the steering wheel repeatedly out of frustration. Pointing a finger in their direction, she added, "Today is ya lucky day."

Ridah watched the woman scramble to get out of her path. Thoughts of what Lanka once told her penetrated her mind suddenly. *"If a person can't control their emotions, it shows people you're not in control of yourself. People begin to come at you sideways, and then you start slipping, and once you start slipping, you make mistakes."* And Ridah could not afford for that to happen. Closing her eyes, Ridah exhaled silently. In that moment, she was grateful for the jewel.

CHAPTER ELEVEN

Crime is the entertainment of the fool. So is wisdom for the man of sense.

—Proverbs 10:23

"I'ma forever be a Gangsta Cripette. With the action to stand on my loyalty and the street code, even when I know the streets ain't gonna always be loyal to me, I still remain the same."

After Ridah made a quick stop to change out of her clothes, she was in Bloomfield in no time. Crips were deep on Deeb Drive, throwing up gang symbols. Ridah was not feeling any of it, but out of respect, she acknowledged them. There were different kinds of Crips. Although they all repped the same set, Ridah learned firsthand that every loc was not her loc. There was griminess in every group. It didn't matter what color a person was repping. The ones who got envious in their hearts were the worst kind. So, it was hard to trust the ones in their crew. In the game they were in, everyone had to be watched.

Kia's mother's house sat right in the heart of Crips. Turning down Edwina Drive, Ridah could not help but think about Lanka. She was too quiet, which made her paranoid. Ridah knew she was plotting against her, and she was going to be ready to lullaby Lanka and whoever was standing with her. Ridah was not sparing anyone.

This street grudge was something Lanka had sparked. Now, Ridah was ready to light her up!

Turning the engine off, as soon as Ridah hopped down out of her truck, she was greeted by a few cuzs immediately. The minute Ridah was up the steps, she scanned the crowd, looking for Smirky. Putting the pound cakes she bought with her on the table with the variety of the other food dishes, Ridah felt so out of place, like she was invading Kia's mother's private and last moment with her daughter. Ridah went to stand off to the side of a table.

Kia's mother appeared out of nowhere. Grabbing Ridah's hand, she pulled her into her arms for a motherly hug. Ridah almost broke down in Kia's mother's strong and warm embrace. She almost forgot what it felt like to receive such a strong, let alone motherly, hug.

"Thank you for coming by," Kia's mother said in a tired tone as she pulled back.

"Thanks for allowing me to come." Asking if she was doing all right did not seem like the right question to ask someone who had just buried their child. Instead, Ridah told her that she was praying for her.

"Oh, child, you was all Kia talked about. She got a picture of y'all at the park sitting on her dresser," Betty stated. "Baby, my doors will always be open to you." Betty hugged her affectionately.

Hearing that Kia thought highly of her caused Ridah to become so overwhelmed and, at the same time, made her feel lower than she already felt. "Thank you so much, Miss Betty."

Seeing Kia's mother in pain made it much easier wanting to get back at Lanka. Let her mother feel what Kia's mother was feeling. Ridah did not care if she was an imposter, but she was going to act like God when the time came to destroy Lanka. He would have to forgive her later.

As Ridah made her way out, Betty called after her, "Baby." She turned back to face her, and Kia's younger sibling stood beside her. "This is Kia's brother, Kell."

Ridah grinned. "Hey. I heard a lot about you." Kia always talked about how her little brother got on her nerves, but she loved him so much. "I hate we have to meet under these circumstances."

Kell lowered his eyes. With a distant smile, he sadly said, "Me too."

"Kell, honey, go make sure the table is stocked." When Kell was out of earshot, Betty turned to Ridah. "Baby girl, I'm not going to preach to you. But please let Kia's death be a wake-up call for you. Don't make your mother feel the same pain," she said with a hand across her chest and tears spilling down her cheeks.

Ridah was very thankful for the short sermon. Unable to look Kia's mother in the eyes, Ridah said, "Yes, ma'am." Ridah knew she would never understand what she pledged. Walking away was not an option for Ridah. Death was the only way out, and she was not trying to die anytime soon.

Betty hugged Ridah tightly. She tried her best to hold back the tears that threatened to fall, but tears fell anyway. After the two parted, Ridah went to sit on the sofa. She could not help but think of Kia while looking at the framed picture of her and Kell sitting on the end table. Ridah bet Kia's mother never thought she would lose her daughter to gun violence. Ridah shook her head sadly, deep in her thoughts. She did not think Kia's life would be snatched so soon.

K.J. and Smirky seemed to have appeared out of thin air. K.J. swaggered his way to where Ridah was sitting and sat down. Just as she looked up, she noticed the same two women she had words with on the church ground earlier were looking in her direction. Ridah tried her best to ignore them as K.J. looked unbothered.

Ridah's mind quickly shifted to K.J. She knew it was wrong to feel what she was feeling when it came to him, but she could not help it. Sometimes, you could not help who you were attracted to. K.J. happened to be with the woman who was once Ridah's mentor. To make matters worse, he and Lanka shared a child. Ridah hated the situation, but she was going to enjoy sexing K.J. She knew that would hurt Lanka more than anything. When the time was right, Ridah was going to end Lanka's chapter.

Napoleon Bonaparte said, "You must be slow in deliberation and swift in execution." With all that said, I'ma have my foot in that ho's neck.

Ridah was in deep thought when K.J. tapped her on the shoulder. "Yeah." Ridah was tired. It was not the kind of tired where she needed sleep. Ridah felt drained and robbed. She only had herself to blame because this was the lifestyle she chose.

"Where your mind at?"

K.J.'s question irked Ridah. She wanted to scream, "On killing your baby's mother," but instead, Ridah smiled sadly as she shook her head, like it was not apparent enough that she was emotionally drained.

Ridah was really battling round for round within. She was starting to feel like the other part of herself was getting the best of her. Ridah felt like throwing her hands up and surrendering to the streets. She could almost hear it now, whispering and rejoicing over her soul. Chills ran through Ridah's body at the mere thought. Deep in her heart, she knew that just because she was born into the gang didn't mean she had to step up and join in. Her twin was the proof of that. Watching her pops made Ridah want to be a gangsta.

Ridah had done so much wrong that she felt like a failure. Her mother, Tina, sent Ridah to a group home, saying that it was her way of saving Ridah. She did not have a clue that was when Ridah went full speed after meeting Smirky and Bagz. Ridah really started raising hell in the streets with thoughts of her mother's voice in her head, telling her that she could not do anything right to save her life. There had been times when Ridah wanted to show her that she could be like Prissy, but then again, that was not what she wanted. Ridah was going to be herself and pray she changed her life before the streets came to collect her soul. If Ridah did not change before then, it was what it was.

CHAPTER TWELVE

We attack not only to hurt someone, to defeat him, but perhaps also simply to become conscious of our own strength.

—Friedrich Nietzsche, 1844–1900

"Kia is the only female beside you who make a nigga stumble. You know how solid I am and how I stand on my shit." Closing his eyes, Smirky sighed. "I'ma miss Kia's wild ass, man! I swear whoever killed her gonna have a fucked-up day when I catch them."

Ridah could not shake visions of Kia's twisted-up body bleeding out on the concrete. She wished that she could trust Smirky with the one secret that kept her up most late nights, but Ridah knew she could not, and because of that, she held Kia's secret close to her heart.

Ridah pulled Smirky's arm to follow her to get something to eat. K.J. was already filling up a second plate. Ridah shook her head at his greediness. She made Smirky's plate with fried chicken, collard greens, mac and cheese, cornbread, and a few other things. After passing the plate to Smirky, she started to fix hers. Looking up, Ridah caught the sour look K.J. gave her. She held in the smirk that was slowly appearing on her face. She knew that look anywhere. K.J. was jealous.

"You didn't make my plate," he had the nerve to say.

Ridah cocked her head up at him. "A closed mouth don't get fed," she sassed.

"One, I didn't see his mouth open. And two, I thought you were fucking with a nigga. I shouldn't have to ask."

Ridah was amused by this statement. "Right," she sang, sitting down seconds after stuffing her mouth with mac and cheese. Closing her eyes, Ridah savored the taste, making her miss her mother's cooking. Tina slayed soul food on her worst day.

"Damn, you actin' like somebody gonna take ya shit." Smirky chuckled.

"I know, right?" K.J. added, not believing how Ridah was eating, like she hadn't eaten in days. "Most females tryin'a act like they ain't hungry and be hungry as fuck." They shared a few chuckles.

"We all know I ain't like most of these hoes," Ridah stated after swallowing her food.

"If you say so." K.J. chuckled as he thought back to the day he was at Ridah's house.

Ridah gave K.J. a quick jab to his rib cage. Laughter filled the air. It broke some of the tension that had built up between the two of them. In that moment, nothing was wrong. Everything was good, until the second passed, putting each one of them in their own private thoughts.

Ridah got up again, heading toward the table, this time for dessert. Seeing the same females who were at Kia's funeral, Ridah silently begged God to help her. One of them wore a smirk that Ridah so badly wanted to knock off her face.

"Something funny?" Ridah's face turned stone cold.

"Excuse me?" The female was taken aback by Ridah's approach.

Ridah glanced around the room, making sure Kia's mother was not around to witness the confrontational moment. Once the coast was clear, Ridah gave her the nastiest look she could muster.

"Bitch, you heard clearly." Ridah stared into the woman's eyes, causing her to look away.

"Girl, ain't nobody worried about ya thirsty ass," the woman replied, smacking her lips.

Ridah frowned as she put the plate down on the edge of the table, glaring at the women evilly. Right when Ridah was about to attack, Kell came up without knowing he saved the woman. God was favoring all of them today.

Ridah glanced at Kell with a smile. "What's up, Kell?" she asked.

"My momma wanna give you something." Sensing the tension, Kell looked back and forth between Ridah and the other women. "Everything good?" he asked no one in particular.

Ridah gave a half smile before saying, "I think y'all should thank Kell and God too while you at it." Ridah never took her eyes off them.

"Thanks," they both replied, and then they hurried off.

"Kia said ya ass was hell. I just witnessed it." Kell chuckled, watching the women rush off.

Ridah mustered up an innocent smile, then told Kell to lead the way to his mother. Walking toward the back of the house, he stopped, pointing Ridah in the direction where his mother was. Ridah walked to the cracked door. Pushing it open, she found Betty sitting on the edge of a queen-sized bed. Betty patted the spot next to her, and Ridah sat down, not knowing what to expect. Betty held a small book in her hand. Her fingertips traced the design that was in the book.

"This was Kia's. I think she'd want you to have it," Betty said below a whisper.

Both of Ridah's hands went up to her mouth. She was overwhelmed by the gesture. "Oh, my God. Thank you so much, Ms. Betty," Ridah could not help but say. "I'll keep it close to my heart," she promised as she fell into

Betty's embrace. This was all Ridah had left of Kia, and she would protect it with her life.

"Come check on an ol' lady sometimes. I need to make sure you are taking care of yourself out there too," Betty stated.

"I can do that!" Ridah responded.

By the time Ridah made her way back to the front of the house, the crowd had thinned out. She hung around with Smirky and K.J., watching people making their exits with paper plates tightly in their hands.

"K.J., you coming over tonight?" Ridah straight-out asked. She did not have to beat around the bush with it.

"Yeah, I'ma swing by," K.J. replied.

Betty observed Ridah and K.J. from afar. She could tell by their body language that the two cared for each other greatly. Kia told her about Ridah and K.J.'s baby momma's dilemma. Shaking her head sadly, Betty could not help but think of the demons she was fighting daily.

Betty used to be so high that she never noticed Kia's empty bed most nights. She wished she could have been stern as a mother, but the drugs had her mind so far gone that all she wanted was to chase her next high. Betty made so many mistakes in her life. If only she could go back in time to correct her wrongs. Instead, Betty was here, stuck in the present, dealing with her actions. Her reality nightmare. With one child left, she was praying it wasn't too late to save him or love him with a clearer and sober mind.

Betty had been clean a full month now and was afraid her daughter's death would be the reason she relapsed. Betty wanted to stay clean. She needed to stay clean, not only for herself but for Kell. He needed her. She had let her children down so many times due to her drug usage. This would be the one time Betty had to step up and be strong for the one child she still had alive.

While Betty was in the kitchen, putting food up, Smirky came up beside her, asking if she needed any help. When she declined, he helped her anyway. Smirky wished he could ease Betty's pain, but Kia was her daughter, and he knew the only thing he could do was be there for Betty in her time of need.

Smirky was going to miss Kia. She grew on him without him realizing how much he enjoyed Kia's company until she was taken away. Smirky had lost too many homies in the streets to count, but losing Kia, his newfound love, messed him up mentally.

Betty brought Smirky out of his thoughts. "Kia used to talk about you a lot. I guess she thought I was too high to hear her. But I was actually cleaning myself up. Smirky, it was so hard. I'm so scared I'm gonna get high again because, at this moment, I wanna get high so bad to numb this pain. I'm scared of failing, Smirky. I need help." Betty sobbed loudly.

Smirky exhaled as he held Betty tightly. He had never been good with words, so he had none to speak. They stood in the same position until Betty calmed down.

Pulling back from him, she sniffed. "Don't be a stranger, Smirky. Come see an ol' lady sometimes." She walked off, leaving him drowning in a pool of his own thoughts.

Smirky knew he already had two strikes against him. The white men wouldn't show any clemency toward his color. It was not the gangs these days that people had to watch out for. It was the police, the ones who were doing all the killings, ripping Black men and women's lives away like Black lives did not matter. They painted a picture of gangs and drug dealers being a menace to society when the truth was that the police were the real gang, orchestrating and killing behind badges. They were the real menace to our society.

***

When Ridah got home, she sat down on the sofa, holding Kia's journal tightly. Her eyes burned with tears. Inhaling, Ridah slowly opened the book. Tracing Kia's words with her fingertips, Ridah felt like she was invading her most intimate thoughts. She wanted to know Kia's deepest thoughts, and Betty blessed her with the book that would give Ridah the chance to get to know Kia with her no longer existing in this world.

Reading the first words caused tears to spill silently down Ridah's cheeks as her heart began to ache. She was not ready to know Kia's hidden pain. Closing the journal, Ridah went to her room to strip out of her clothes and get in the shower, hoping the water would wash away the gritty feeling of her skin. Ridah wanted to scrub her soul until it was clean.

After showering, Ridah got in bed with a racing mind. She tossed and turned. Glancing at the book on the marble nightstand, she felt unworthy of having a part of Kia. Kia had been riding hard with Ridah. It never mattered what time it was. If she called Kia and said, "Let's ride," Kia never questioned it. She was coming with force. Ridah would miss her hitta dearly. When Lanka decided to end Kia's existence, she wrote her own ending. Ridah had no other choice but to see Lanka through her demise.

No one could have told Ridah this was going to happen with her having a thing for K.J., betraying Lanka, and meeting someone who was like her in so many ways. This had to be how Judas felt after his great betrayal. The thought itself made Ridah weep silently. She went back to the old days, to a session she had when they first met.

That men may appreciate wisdom and discipline, may understand words of intelligence.

—Proverbs 1:2.

"*Do you read the Bible, Ridah?*" *Lanka asked everyone who walked through her door the same question. Students tended to look confused when this question was asked, but this was something Lanka lived by and applied in her everyday life.*

"*Huh?*" *Ridah was totally caught off guard by her question. Lanka repeated her question. Ridah then asked, "What do me reading the Bible gotta do with me being down?" She did not fully grasp what Lanka was getting at.*

Lanka leaned up and placed her elbows on her legs. She was about to lay some heavy knowledge not only on Ridah but on the other youngsters in the room as well. "The fear of the Lord is the beginning of knowledge. I enforce this to everybody who comes through that door." Lanka pointed at the closed door.

Ridah frowned. Not comprehending what Lanka was saying, she smacked her lips. "Are we having Bible study or are you giving me history?" Ridah snapped only for lack of understanding.

Lanka overlooked Ridah's comment and said, "A fool despises wisdom and instructions. You don't strike me as a fool, Ridah. Go home and read the Book of Proverbs. Don't come back until you are finished!" When Ridah did not budge, Lanka stood and pointed at the front door.

On the way home, Ridah's mind was full of confusion. Blu Foxx never told her this part of the game. She tried to recall a time when she had seen him reading the Bible. She couldn't. What Ridah did not understand was that if her pops did not read the Bible, why did Lanka want her to read it? How did the Bible fall into her daily life in banging? She would eventually discover when the time came.

"Whatever!" Ridah thought out loud as she continued to walk home. She was so deep in her thoughts that she did not notice three rivals heading her way.

"What's up?" one of them posed with a mischievous smirk.

Ridah jumped at the sound of the unexpected voice. Her reaction caused the trio to laugh out loud. She felt it in her gut that something grimy was about to take place. With that thought in front of her mind, she began to prepare herself mentally.

"What y'all want?" Ridah suddenly stopped, turning to face them, clearly frustrated.

"Oh, it's like dat?" one female asked, leaning down to grab an abandoned beer bottle off the side of the road.

The trio was looking for trouble, and with Ridah being solo, it made her an easy target. Not focusing on the female who did most of the talking, Ridah kept her eyes on the other two females who were slowly surrounding her. In the blink of an eye, the one talking swung, catching Ridah completely off guard. It did not take long for the other two to jump in. Ridah may have been getting beaten, but she put up one helluva fight against the three.

An older man stepped out on his front porch, threatening to call the police if the girls did not stop fighting. The trio took off running but not before Ridah sliced one of them in the face with a piece of broken glass. Then she hurried home. When Ridah made it home, reading the Bible was the last thing on her troubled mind. Instead, she went straight to sleep.

The next day, Ridah was up early in the morning, reading Proverbs. She finished the thirty-one chapters in no time. She read the Book of Proverbs for a week straight to engrave it in her heart.

Lanka was pleased with Ridah's progress yet didn't show it. "Now, you're ready to move on to the next level." Lanka gave her a smile.

CHAPTER THIRTEEN

Beef is when I see you, guaranteed to be in I.C.U.

—Biggie

Street fact: It's never ya enemies you have to watch. It's the closest ones!

Ridah jumped up out of her sleep with urgency. Her eyes automatically roamed the darkness, stopping on the door. She stared at it oddly, going back and forth in her mind about the unknown. Ridah decided to get out of bed. After she peeked out the door, Ridah then crept into the living room. A little gasp escaped her lips after discovering her front door was ajar.

"What the fuck?" she thought out loud. Ridah knew she was not that distorted to have left her front door open. Something was not right.

Before Ridah could close the door, a fist caught her on the side of her temple, blinding her instantly. Tears burned her eyes from the sharp blow she received. Although the impact did not knock her down, Ridah lost her balance but recovered quickly to protect herself against the big, masked man.

With one of her hands wrapped around his wrist, Ridah poked him in the eye, then applied pressure, causing him to release her quickly. He slapped her to the floor, then snatched her up like a rag doll. Throwing her over his shoulder, he carried her outside to the trunk of a car, which was already open.

Ridah started to buck and put up a fight. She knew once her kidnapper had her in the trunk, her chances of surviving were slim to none. He threw her in the trunk, slamming it shut. Darkness surrounded Ridah as she started hyperventilating. She knocked and beat on the trunk until her hands were aching and swollen.

It was at that hour that Ridah feared the unknown. Thoughts of Lanka being behind her kidnapping sent her into a frenzied rage. Filled with aggravation, Ridah felt like her body was on fire as she raged on the inside. She was done playing around with Lanka. If she made it out of this situation, Lanka would die by her hands, and if Ridah had to die in the process, she did not care. Macon was not big enough for the both of them. Somebody had to go, and Ridah did not plan on leaving. She was comfortable.

When the car finally stopped, Ridah felt around in the dark for anything to use as a weapon to protect herself. Luckily, she found a wrench. Gripping it tightly, Ridah's heart pounded as she waited anxiously for the trunk to open.

Ridah thought she was tripping when she heard a familiar Jamaican voice. Her body stiffened. She closed her eyes tight with the thought that this could not be happening. The voice belonged to Demya, one of Lanka's most trusted and dangerous followers. She was the one Lanka called when she wanted a quiet clean-up. Ridah leaned closer to the crack of the trunk, getting herself ready to strike her prey first.

"Me want fifteen tousand. She don poked me mon eye out," Demya said into the speakerphone.

"Keep an eye on that sneaky bitch!" Ridah heard someone say.

"You musta forget who you talk dat to, gal?" Demya laughed.

"All right. Just remembered she been to a couple of ya trainings."

Demya continued to laugh, shaking her head at Lanka's foolishness. She had yet to meet one who could go blow for blow with her. Not even Lanka stood a chance against her. The thought tickled her almost to death without realizing how close to that statement she was.

Ridah had the element of surprise on her side. Whoever opened the trunk, she would go hard in attack mode. Minutes went by and still the trunk was not opened. Ridah began to relax her tensed body until she heard the loud click noise, causing her to grip the weapon tighter. She welcomed the night air that rushed into the trunk. Too caught up in a heated conversation, Demya was not paying any attention, and because of her slip-up, Demya was now being preyed upon.

Ridah pounced on her, and a quick blow to the head caused Demya to stumble and grab the top of her forehead where she was struck. She was too shocked to scream for the driver to help. This was a fight for survival, and Ridah could not afford a mishap. With that in mind, Ridah sent another blow to Demya's head that caused her to drop like a sack of potatoes. Ridah got into the squatting position and leaped out of the trunk.

Landing lightly, Ridah stayed low and crept slowly up on the passenger side door. Her kidnapper was too occupied doctoring his damaged eye to realize danger was lurking closely. Ridah noticed the gun lying on his crotch. God was definitely on her side tonight, and she took a minute to thank Him. Ridah snatched the gun so quickly, and he sat, stunned. With no hesitation, she squeezed the trigger, sending his thoughts out the driver's side window into the night.

Demya was still on the ground, trying to make the fog from her head disappear, when Ridah grabbed her by her curly mane. She mustered up as much strength as she could, kicking Ridah in the face, opening up a small gash right above her eyebrow. The sickening sound filled the night air as Ridah's blood rained down her face. Ridah fell to her knees, and Demya did not waste a minute. She took her legs and locked them around Ridah's arm and applied pressure. Ridah grunted while holding a death grip on Demya's hair with her other hand. She tightened her grip until Demya was forced into full submission.

"Let me hair go!" Demya yelled, breathing heavily.

"Fuck nawl! Let me go first," Ridah growled, out of breath, ignoring the pain Demya was inflicting on her arm.

"This ain't supposed to be no fucking street brawl!" an angry voice shouted in the night air.

When Ridah heard Lanka's voice, her body stiffened for the second time within a day. When Demya loosened her grip, Ridah had to act fast. She didn't plan on dying tonight. She flipped around within seconds, now having Demya in a headlock. Lanka's eyes revealed how impressed she was with Ridah's survival skills. After all, Lanka was one of the ones who helped put the training drills together to strengthen her team.

She smiled as she applauded Ridah. "Well done, soldier."

"I got your soldier, you coward-ass bitch!" Ridah snapped.

Placing a hand over her chest as if Ridah's comment truly offended her, Lanka grinned. "I may be a lot of things, but a coward"—Lanka shook her head, disagreeing with Ridah—"ain't one of them!" she said in a confident matter.

"Bitch, you killed Kia and went into hiding. That's some coward shit!" Ridah spat. It was hard to keep her anger in check. Lanka knew that was one of Ridah's biggest flaws, so she decided to play on it.

"Bitch, I'll never be like you. You disloyal as fuck! Fucking on ya nigga best man, having babies and shit!"

Balling her fist up, Lanka brought it to her mouth. Shock covered her face. No one had ever spoken her secret out loud because the heavy punishment behind it was death, and no one wanted to lose their life behind something that wasn't their business in the first place. The thought of K.J.'s pillow talking with Ridah was like someone had stabbed her in the heart as she pictured K.J. betraying her.

"That ain't all he told me. But fuck all that. Story time is over!" Ridah pushed Demya toward Lanka.

In one swift motion, Ridah grabbed the gun off the ground, squeezing the trigger. Ridah sent shots at her targets, missing by an inch. Lanka pulled a disappearing act as if she were magical. Demya attempted to get in the car, where her dead partner's body remained slumped over in the driver's seat, but she was not fortunate enough to make a getaway.

"Aye, I wouldn't do that if I was you!" Ridah said to Demya, whose eyes widened with what Ridah believed to be terror.

"Fight without that gun, girl!" Demya challenged. It was all she could think of doing since she could not make a run for the forest behind Lanka.

Grinning, Ridah dropped the gun. "Let's go!" She rushed Demya.

Ridah slammed Demya's head against the concrete, and a sickening sound filled the night. Demya grabbed at Ridah's leg in an attempt to pull her to the ground. Without thinking, Ridah kicked Demya so hard she thought she broke her toe. Demya's body went still.

Ridah grabbed her phone, quickly dialing Smirky's number. Leaning on the side of the car, she breathed heavily while she kept her eyes alert. For all Ridah knew, Lanka could still be in the woods, waiting for the chance to attack. Ridah wouldn't be taking any chances of Lanka sneaking back up on her.

When Smirky answered in a sleepy voice, Ridah was relieved. She was so overwhelmed and could not seem to catch her breath. She started talking so fast that Smirky could not understand a single word that came out of Ridah's mouth, but the urgency in her voice was what made him alert.

"Calm down. I can't understand shit you saying!" Smirky was now fully awake.

"She had me kidnapped!" she said, instantly regretting it. The last thing she wanted was for Smirky to know Lanka was behind Kia's murder and him telling K.J. She and Smirky may have been close and all, but Ridah knew his loyalty to his cousin came first. That was something she just had to accept and respect.

"Who you talking about?" Smirky frowned at his phone.

"Demya," she found herself revealing.

As if he had not heard her correctly, he repeated, "Demya?" Something dawned on him. "As in Lanka's people Demya?"

If this was true, then it was not looking too good on Ridah's behalf. He could not help but wonder why Lanka would send Demya after Ridah. Dealing with K.J. would not make Lanka bring Demya out. This was deeper than his cousin. Demya was only brought out when it was time for a deep cleaning. So, this had to be a street grudge.

"Where you at now?" Smirky asked, jumping out of the bed to throw on some clothes.

Ridah gave him the location from the GPS. Still leaning on the car, she bit down on her bottom lip in deep thought. Ridah hated that she had to call him. She did not want Smirky to know about Lanka's involvement. When Ridah saw Demya stirring and trying to sit up on her side, she pushed herself out of the car and made her way toward Demya.

Demya put a hand up in surrender. "Wait, me tell ya what ya wanna know!" Demya stilled herself with thoughts of ways to appear less harmful.

"Smirky on his way. What I need for you to do is keep Lanka's name out of this!"

"Oh, I see. You want me quiet so you get her, ah?" Demya shook her head while smiling wickedly. "You sneaky bitch you! I tell you everything. Smirky kill me, yes?" she asked. If Smirky killed her, he would do it quickly. Ridah, on the other hand, would probably torture her.

"You smarter than she. But you gotta know I tell you none of she planned for you."

"Bitch, shut ya no-speaking-English ass up!" Ridah needed to think. She already knew Demya would not reveal Lanka's plan. Demya was hard to break, so Ridah already knew that was a no-go. "Lie down!" Ridah suddenly demanded.

Demya shook noticeably, not because she was scared but from straining her body. She sensed the reaper inching toward her. "I tell you!"

Ridah could not help but laugh. "Damn, you really gonna try dat method on me? Defense up. Convince them you don't know. Do whatever it takes." Ridah kicked Demya in her midsection. "And when they get closer, go in for the kill. Because nine outta ten, you gonna die." Ridah recited one of their lessons in training. Smiling through her pain, Demya rested on her back as she struggled to breathe.

Headlights grabbed both women's attention. Both were relieved to see Smirky's navy blue Chevy coming to a stop. Demya was ready to get it over with. Smirky was hot-tempered, so he would put a bullet in her quicker if she pushed him. Ridah was questionable. Demya knew Ridah would love to see her suffer before she crossed over to death.

"If you make him take his time killing me, I'll spill everything," Demya threatened with a clever grin.

"Bitch, shut the fuck up!" Ridah moved in to strike Demya again.

Smirky jumped out of his car, taking long, quick strides toward Ridah. As soon as she was in reaching distance, Smirky snatched Demya up by her hair. She let out a low grunt as her eyes found Ridah's.

"I'ma only ask you once," Smirky warned. He had no patience for nonsense. "Why you after Ridah?" He knew it was pointless to even ask such a question.

Smirky knew how Demya and Lanka moved out in the streets. The move she was making on Ridah only meant she knew something. Lanka sent Demya to silence Ridah before whatever it was that she knew was leaked. Lanka had to know Ridah would not fold for anyone. She would not speak to her enemy. Smirky was so confused by this sudden movement. He felt like he had been thrown into a chess game with a gun to his head to keep him off his game.

Demya looked up at Smirky, then dropped her eyes. Gripping her hair tighter caused her to gasp in a way that almost sounded like she was turned on. "I can't tell you dat!" Demya displayed a small smile. "But she can!" She nodded her head at Ridah, who gave her a death stare for making the statement.

"Stop tryin'a play games, bitch!" Ridah snapped, hoping Smirky would kill her before she revealed everything she did not want him, or anyone else, to know.

"Am I playing, Ridah?" Demya eyed her, silently challenging her.

"Fuck all dat! It's judgment day, bitch. Get on your knees and plead ya case," Smirky stated with his gun in the air.

Demya smiled, falling to her knees. Though she had always been prepared mentally for death, it was not easy to face emotionally, due to her leaving behind her son. The tears that filled Demya's eyes were not for herself but for him. Thoughts of him missing her made facing death hard. It made her vulnerable, and anyone who knew Demya Tuff knew she hated to appear weak, even if it was only for a second. Demya looked toward the sky and said a prayer of protection over her son's life. After primping her curly mane, she raised a hand in the air like she was in school. Smirky nodded his head for her to speak.

Demya requested an open casket for her son. Smirky gave his word to honor her wishes. "Guilty by association," Demya stated with her head held high.

"Yes, you are, Demya. Yes, you are!" Smirky smirked as he let two bullets kiss her upper chest. Blood began to seep out of Demya's body into the concrete of the street.

Ridah grabbed Smirky's gun unexpectedly before he could resist. Pointing it toward Demya's slumped body, she released two bullets tearing into Demya's face. Stepping back, Ridah admired her work.

Smirky was beyond stunned by Ridah's sudden action. "I gave her my word, Ridah!" Smirky yelled after recovering from the unexpected twist of Demya's fate.

"I didn't! Fuck dat bitch and her son!" Ridah snapped. She did not feel bad for Demya. If the shoe were on the other foot, Demya would have eliminated Ridah with no mercy, let alone a thought.

"Ya ass cold as fuck, cuz!" was all Smirky could say. Cutting curious eyes at her, he could not help but ask, "What's up for you and Lanka?"

"It's complicated, Smirky." Ridah shifted uncomfortably, hoping he would settle for her response. This beef was deeper and different from the kind Ridah was used to. She genuinely had a love for Lanka, yet Kia's death could not be ignored.

As Smirky pulled up in the parking spot, Scott ran up to the car, banging on the window in a desperate but alerting way. His sudden movement caused Smirky to aim his gun. Luckily, Ridah's reflexes were quick enough to knock his aim off as a bullet ripped through the night.

"Nigga, that's Scott!" Ridah's voice shook out of fear. She could not fathom the thought of Scott getting caught up in her mess. He was the only friend Ridah had.

"Scott's ass abouta get smoked the fuck up! He betta start announcin' his self!" Smirky stated, already on the edge. Smirky sighed, relieved the bullet missed Scott by inches.

With Demya's execution, it was only a matter of time before bullets started hailing their way. Smirky knew the moment he pulled the trigger that he had sealed his and Ridah's fate. For his impulsiveness, the consequences were death. Smirky's loyalty to Ridah would not allow him to walk away without ending Demya's existence. If he did not end her, she would have continued aiming for Ridah until her heart no longer beat.

The one person who could stop this death storm was Lanka. Smirky had to get in touch with Lanka before the streets started ad-libbing and adding fire to the situation. Smirky wanted to be the one who gave Lanka facts, and he hoped she would accept them. He knew she would not send fire his way, due to her dealings with his first cousin, but Smirky wanted to keep Ridah out of the line of fire, too.

"Fuck! Are you fucking serious, man?" Scott shouted. Bewildered, he ran his hands through his auburn hair.

"Oh, my God! I almost got fucking shot!" Scott continued to freak out.

Another time and day, Ridah would have been cracking up had Scott freaked out without a bullet whizzing past him. But on this day and time, shit was deep in the streets. With the heat blasting on high, the beef was now sizzling. Ridah knew Lanka was coming. When, was the million-dollar question.

Ridah jumped out of the car before Scott gave himself a heart attack. She grabbed him by his shoulders, attempting to calm him.

"You all right, baby boy. It is okay. He didn't know who it was." Scott's face was as white as a ghost. Ridah felt bad for her friend. "What's going on?"

"I saw a man in ya house. He looks really dangerous." Scott's eyes filled with tears. He did not want any harm coming to the one true friend he had.

Ridah sighed as she took a glance back at Smirky, who was still sitting in the driver's seat. He got out, eyes sweeping the dark area carefully before following behind them. When Ridah opened the door to her apartment, she froze, speechless. Her furniture was flipped over, pictures knocked down. It looked like a tornado hit. It took everything in her not to break down.

Smirky took one look around and knew he had to holla at Lanka. Pulling out his phone, he started texting her. "Aye, Scott, help her pack some shit right quick," Smirky said as he continued texting Lanka.

Smirky had to find somewhere Ridah could go lie low until he got to the bottom of Ridah and Lanka's issue. After no response from Lanka, Smirky sighed loudly. Grabbing his bottom lip, he pulled at it while in deep thought. Smirky did not want to call K.J. and alert him. He had to figure this out on his own.

Once Smirky was out of sight, Scott turned to his longtime friend. "Ridah, you in trouble, huh?" he asked innocently.

Scott was getting bullied every single day until Ridah defended him one day in the hallway. From that day forward, Scott's bullies almost broke their necks to stay out of his path. Every time he had asked Ridah what happened that day, she'd change the subject. He heard people whispering around in school about Ridah being a dangerous gang member.

"Scott, go home," Ridah sighed. She did not want to put him in any danger by being around her. Kia had already lost her life. She would be damned if she lost Scott to the streets. Ridah could not allow the streets to take a soul that was too sweet and worthy for the streets.

"No." Scott paused. His light gray eyes penetrated Ridah's. "I'm not leaving you out here."

Closing her eyes tight out of frustration, Ridah clenched her teeth. "Boy, ya ass ain't no fucking gangsta. This shit ain't no play. You can lose ya life, and I can't live with dat on my conscience."

"I'm not giving you no choice." He smacked his lips. Scott may not have been a thug or ever shot a gun before, but he was riding to the end with his friend.

In the bedroom, Ridah and Scott were packing some of her stuff when a front room window unexpectedly exploded, causing the two of them to jump. Ridah's reflexes were automatic. She pushed Scott down to the floor and told him to stay down. Ridah took a second thanking God silently after grabbing one of the hidden guns Smirky installed in different parts of her apartment. She could have kissed him right about now. She crawled out of the room where Smirky stood with his tool locked, loaded, and aimed toward the window.

"Where's Scott?" Smirky asked without taking his eyes off the window.

"Right here," Scott answered, causing Ridah to jump at the closeness of his voice. She did not even hear Scott behind her, which meant she was really slipping. Ridah gave him a look that made him feel like a child about to get scolded. "What?" he said innocently.

"I told you to stay still, Scott. I don't know what's going on," Ridah said in a loud whisper.

"I'm scared," Scott unashamedly admitted. "I know you'll protect me if I'm with you." Ridah sighed as she pushed him behind her.

Making their way out of the apartment, Ridah pressed her body against the wall while Smirky pushed the door of the building open. Seeing his damaged car made him step back in quickly. Smirky knew it was possible that someone could be lurking out there in the darkness. He would not chance them making a run for the pathway trail, which led down a steep hill.

As much as Smirky hated to admit it, the three of them were now sitting ducks. If they made an exit, there was no doubt in Smirky's mind the three would be gunned down by whomever waited in the darkness for them.

Passing Ridah his phone, Smirky said, "Text K.J." Turning to Scott, he said, "Go upstairs. Don't come down until I come get you." Smirky had an afterthought. He turned back to Scott. "I really need you to listen to me."

"But what if you don't come back?" Scott whined, scared out of his mind.

"Scott, I'm not leaving you," Ridah assured her friend. "Here, take this." Ridah handed him a .22. After quickly showing him how to use it, Ridah sent him upstairs.

When Scott was safely up the steps, Smirky and Ridah exited the building. No sooner than their feet hit the threshold, gunshots echoed and lit up the night, forcing them back in the building for cover.

"Fuck!" Smirky roared as a bullet pierced his left hand. He rushed toward the steps with Ridah backing him, making sure no one entered the building.

Scott turned to look behind him after hearing footsteps. He was glad to see it was Smirky and Ridah. An elderly man opened his door after hearing the commotion outside in the hall.

He opened the door and found them squatting in the corner of his door. The man shook his head. "I called the police," he warned. "Y'all young bucks always in some shit," he uttered.

Turning back to face the older man, Scott said, "Just let us in please, man."

"Y'all can't come in here. My wife sick. Now get the hell away from my door." The man stood his ground and attempted to close the door on them.

Scott put his foot in the opening of the door to stop him from closing the door in their faces. The man took his shotgun from his right hand to show them that he meant business. Smirky took his chances and rushed him, sending the man falling backward and the shotgun sliding across the floor. Smirky tussled with the man for a couple of minutes, not to hurt him but to get him under control.

Ridah quickly bent down to retrieve the shotgun. Thankfully, there was a small window at the top of the building. Taking the butt of the shotgun, Ridah knocked the glass out of the windowsill, then peeked out of it for any signs of movement. Two dark figures were moving so swiftly that Ridah almost missed them. Sliding down on the floor, she sighed. One look at Ridah and Scott knew whatever it was that Ridah had seen wasn't good for any of them. He wished that he had taken her advice and gone home when he had the chance to do so.

Ridah made sure Scott was prepared to shoot if anyone came up the staircase. Scott was scared to death. He had never used a gun but was determined to prove that he could be hard when needed. Scott closed his eyes, praying whoever was coming up would not come. *Wishful thinking,* he thought after opening his eyes to find the top of someone's head approaching. When the man got closer, Scott pulled the trigger, but nothing happened. Glancing down quickly, he discovered the safety was still on. Clicking it off, he pulled the trigger again.

Scott continued letting bullets spit disrespectfully through the air. Caught up in the moment, he ran down the stairs, shooting wildly. Scott suddenly came to a halt as he locked eyes with the man he saw earlier. He had a scar on the right side of his ear that traveled up to his nose. The man looked on in amusement at the inexperienced Scott, but he underestimated him after Scott pulled the trigger, sending him to his demise.

"Ridah. Smirky. We cle—" Scott's sentence was cut off by a bullet lodged in his throat. Trying to breathe caused blood to squirt from his throat.

Never in a million years did Scott, the white boy who always wanted to fit in, think he'd die such a cruel death. He relaxed a little when one of Ridah's homies entered the building, but his face tensed as Capone raised the gun. It was do or die, and with that in mind, Scott used the little strength he had to pull the trigger. Sending a deathly kiss straight into Capone's stomach caused him to double over and exit the building quickly in fear of being exposed.

Ridah barely heard Scott when he called them due to her ears still ringing from the gunshots. Smirky and Ridah rushed to make an exit out of the older couple's home. Passing a body on the step, Smirky came to a complete halt as he eyed Scott, who was lying in a small pool of blood.

He kneeled next to him. "Fuck!" Smirky said with frustration in his voice. Interlocking his fingers, Smirky placed them on his forehead. "This ain't supposed to happen to you, li'l homie."

It pained him to know Ridah was about to witness this sight. Smirky grabbed Scott's hand and told him to fight and hold on. The shaken Scott looked into Smirky's eyes and nodded. Scott attempted to put on a brave face, although he was terrified of dying. Hot tears stung his light gray eyes before rolling down the side of his face. In that moment, he wished he were back at home with his mother and sister, who always fussed at him about hanging out in this very area. Now here he lay, struggling to breathe. Scott felt like he was drowning in his own blood.

Knowing how Ridah felt about Scott, Smirky hated that he had to be the one witnessing him being caught in a war that had nothing to do with him. That was how it always seemed to go. "The good die young" was a big fact. Smirky was staring at Scott as proof. Ridah rushed to them. Bursting into tears, she fell to her knees and stroked Scott's pale and pasty face. The fear of not knowing whether he would make it petrified her.

"It's gonna be all right, baby boy," Ridah attempted to assure him. Scott shook his head, disagreeing. He felt death coming for him, and there was not a thing anyone could do to stop it.

"Ridah, I know you don't wanna hear this, but we gotta go. The police will be here soon." Smirky spoke in a low tone.

Ridah's head jerked in Smirky's direction, eyeing him like he'd lost his mind. "Did you leave Kia?" Ridah asked, filled with raw emotions. Looking down at Scott again, her voice trembled. "He's a good kid. He didn't deserve this."

Dropping his head, Smirky felt bad for even thinking Ridah would leave her friend. He was trying to save them a trip to the county jail. Smirky did not have the heart to tell Ridah that Scott was about to cross over, and the two of them would still be there to face whatever trouble awaited them.

"Let's get him up." Ridah got off the floor. She could not sit there and watch another person she was close to die. She had to do something.

Smirky helped Ridah pull Scott up. After both of Scott's arms were secured around his and Ridah's necks, the three of them struggled down the steps. Scott's feet were dragging while thick blood dripped down his chin to his T-shirt.

Smirky's mind drifted back to Kia's sudden death. He understood why Ridah could not leave Scott out there like that. He felt beyond bad for even speaking that out loud. Once they made it to Ridah's truck, she began cussing after discovering the tires were sliced. She felt like this was a death trap.

The nosy neighbors stayed well hidden behind the blinds and curtains of their homes, fearing the consequences of assisting the group, for it could cost them their lives. So, the peers stood back, watching the young white boy struggle for his life, and they watched in silence.

A heavyset woman stepped down off her front porch and rapidly walked in their direction. "Y'all come with me." She continued walking to her parked Honda. Scott's feet were dragging while his blood painted the concrete.

After everyone was secured in the car, the woman went speeding through the streets, deep in her own thoughts. The ride to the hospital was the longest ride ever. Ridah attempted to wipe the blood from the side of Scott's mouth.

"I'm so sorry, Scott. I'm sorry you got caught up in this shit," Ridah uttered repeatedly. He attempted to speak but began choking on the thick blood that came out of his mouth. When the blood began to spray out of his mouth, he went into a coughing fit. Smirky helped Ridah turn him over on his side.

Ridah remembered Scott used to beg her to tell him one of her crazy, wild stories about her life. He always thought her life was something like a movie. In his final moments, she decided to grant his wish and tell the last story he would ever hear from her in this lifetime. She began telling Scott what it was like when her pops was alive. She even told him why her mother moved them to Macon. Scott smiled painfully as his grip on Ridah's hand loosened. Closing her eyes, Ridah bowed her head and lightly squeezed Scott's hand, knowing he was gone forever.

"He didn't deserve this." Ridah's voice cracked as she broke down in the back seat of the Honda.

CHAPTER FOURTEEN

Laughter can conceal a heavy heart, but when the laughter ends, the grief remains.

—Proverbs 14:13

Ridah's troubles weighed heavily on her tonight. It was one of those nights where she felt like life was too much, and the gunshots echoing throughout her mind were too long, exploding pieces of her stained and troubled soul. Gripping the same .22 Scott had the night he got killed, tears blinded her sight, promising to fall at any given moment. Ridah was tired of carrying the crosses of her sins.

Ridah thought that because she moved to Anthony Arm apartments, things would become better. However, the dark cloud seemed to continuously gloom over her head. There were nights when Ridah jumped up out of her sleep in cold sweats from having nightmares of her own death. It was hard to find peace within herself, and though she was not big on angels, Ridah often felt like someone was watching over her.

Placing the gun to her head, Ridah closed her eyes. She inhaled deeply, then exhaled as her tears began to spill over. An unexpected noise from the back room caused Ridah to jump. Her body stiffened as she held her breath, listening intently, but silence filled the air. Drawing her finger around the trigger, Ridah squeezed her eyes tightly as she prepared herself for the outcome once the trigger was pulled.

Click.

Squeezing it again, Ridah got the same results. Frustration but relief caused her to drop the gun on the floor.

An unexpected knock on the front door snatched Ridah's attention. Getting out of the chair, Ridah wiped her face to get rid of any sign of disarray. Looking out of the peephole, she saw K.J. on the other side. Ridah's lips trembled as she put on a smile and opened the door. "Hey."

K.J. automatically saw straight through Ridah's charge. She appeared so vulnerable. A part of K.J. wanted to protect her from whatever had her in distress, but at the same time, he knew that he could not save Ridah from her demons. K.J. was running from some of his own. Life sure had a way of messing up a lot of people mentally, emotionally, and physically.

He admired how Ridah stood tall in the trials that had come her way. Since being around her, K.J. could not recall a time when he had ever heard her complain. If she did, he had not heard her utter one. Ridah had tried to go out the cowardly way only seconds ago.

K.J. entered the door and made his way to the sofa. Lanka's obsession with him communicating with Ridah only made him want to be around her more. At first, it was a game to hurt Lanka. Now, K.J. could not bear the thought of not being a part of Ridah's life. If he had to be honest with himself, K.J. had developed feelings over the few months they had spent time together. Shaking his thoughts away, K.J. put Lanka in the back of his mind so he could focus on Ridah.

"Ya ass gotta get up outta dat funk."

Ridah cut her eyes in his direction with a scrunched-up face. "I feel stuck," she admitted for the first time. "Scott was my friend."

"Man, you taking what I'm saying outta context." K.J. stood up, trying not to walk back out the door. He was already dealing with a lot, and the drama with Lanka made it worse. "Yeah, it's fucked up, real fucked up how the ones we love die." Shaking his head, he acknowledged the brutal truth. "But life goes on, baby girl. It ain't stopping for no one."

Ridah bowed her head as tears streamed down her face, dropping on her hand. "I'm just tired. I've taken a lot of losses." Ridah had finally reached her boiling point. Her emotions were starting to spill. No matter how hard she tried to contain it, it came with force, cracking her wide open for K.J. to see the broken young girl she had hidden for so many years.

"I have too." Lifting her head with his hand, he added, "We gonna lose more homies, maybe not good like Scott but it's gonna be so many more. The streets don't have a soul or love nobody."

Ridah never thought about the downside of the life when she first chose it. All she ever focused on was becoming a gangsta like her pops. She used to study him, and when he was not around, she would mimic his moves. Ridah had never witnessed Blu Foxx appearing to be the slightest torn over losing one of his homies to the street life. She could not help but wonder how anyone could remain mentally intact while dealing with something so vicious as the streets.

Ridah attempting to end her life would have been a disgrace and a blow to her pops's legacy. She wanted to change her life and live a better one than the one she was living right now, but Ridah had made such a mess of her life that she did not know how to go about cleaning it. She had already seen the signs of what could happen if someone continued to live by the double-edged sword. Surely, it would lead them to death. Ridah did not want it to be too late for her. She would prove to society that she was not going to be another statistic.

She looked K.J. in his eyes with a newfound confidence. "Thank you. Now, let's blaze one." Ridah held up a box of cigars and the best Kush in town. She enjoyed the smoke sessions with K.J. Some of their deepest conversations came out when they were high.

"I had other plans." A hint of desire was in his voice. K.J. had convinced Lanka that he would never betray her by sleeping with Ridah. Now, he was ready to move forward and take it up a notch. There had been so many nights when K.J. and Lanka would be having sex and his mind would turn to Ridah.

"And what would that be?" Ridah gave him a half grin as she leaned back against the La-Z-Boy chair with an amused look plastered on her face. Ridah had been daydreaming about this day.

K.J. circled her like she was his prey. He suddenly went in for the kill. Grabbing both of her feet, in seconds, he had them in the air before she knew it. K.J. snatched her lower body down, causing her to hang off the end of the chair. A soft moan escaped Ridah's lips. Instantly, her panties were wet. She had been wanting him for so long. This moment felt like a dream, and she was not trying to wake up anytime soon. Ridah wanted to sleep for however long as K.J. was in her dreams, too.

"Get up," K.J. demanded in a low but sexy voice.

Ridah was in a trance. She would do whatever he said as long as he stuffed her with his prize. K.J. picked her up and carried her to the cabinet, which was slightly taller than him. He looked up at Ridah with a cocky grin.

"What?" she said with a girlish grin. Ridah had to admit that he looked good. Ridah made a mental note to thank Lanka for sharing her man.

"This is what I need for you to do," K.J. started.

"What?" Ridah questioned, cocking her head in an amused way.

"Put action behind dat name. Ride this face," K.J. challenged her.

Sucking her teeth, she rolled her eyes. "Nigga, I'm abouta give you the ride of ya life." Ridah gripped the back of his head and ground her hot, wet pussy in K.J.'s face, releasing a deep moan.

K.J. grabbed her legs, putting them on his shoulders. He lifted Ridah off the cabinet while still sucking and licking on her clit. Ridah held on tight as K.J. carried her to the back bedroom, laying her down on the bed. Ridah arched her back and locked K.J.'s head between her toned chocolate legs.

"Damn, you tryin'a kill a nigga," K.J. said as he pulled back to catch his breath. "I got something for ya slick ass." He quickly unbuckled his belt.

"I'm waiting," Ridah said while rubbing her swollen clit and biting her bottom lip.

K.J. took one of her legs and put it in the air before crossing it on his left shoulder. "I been thinking about fucking the shit outta you," he almost growled.

Cocking her head to the side, she said, "What you waitin' for?" Ridah released a soft moan after sticking her finger in her slippery tunnel. Bringing her coated finger to her mouth, Ridah sucked the juices off while staring K.J. into his eyes.

So caught in the moment, K.J. quickly stuffed her with all ten inches. Ridah moaned loudly as he grabbed her throat with his free hand, giving it a light squeeze. She placed her hand on top of his to apply more pressure.

Arching her back, Ridah licked her lips as K.J. dug his hand deep in her hips as he pulled her pelvis to him. When he could not take any more, K.J. lifted her up.

Ridah wrapped her legs tightly around him as he gripped her butt and pumped away. The way K.J. was sexing her let her know she was not the only one who had been waiting for this moment. He put Ridah in so many positions that her body was hurting in a good way. Now, she knew from experience what made Lanka act so crazy. K.J. was a passionate lover. He knew how to make a person feel loved. His sex skills should be banned.

Ridah sat up in bed, watching K.J. get dressed. She moaned softly as images of their sex scenes flashed through her mind. Catching chills at the mere thought, Ridah felt like a fiend, fiening for him and his thick and juicy penis.

"You going to that party everybody's hyped about?" K.J. pulled Ridah out of her lustful thoughts.

Ridah recalled Smirky talking about it, but she had not decided whether she would attend. "I don't know yet." She did not feel up to being around anyone.

K.J. cut his eyes her way, not believing she'd pass up a party, especially one he was attending. "Come on, ya ass can't keep being shut up in this apartment."

"All right," she said quickly. "We betta not be jumping in no swamps and shit," she added, laughing before accepting the blunt K.J. retrieved from the nightstand.

"Take dat shit to the head," he said. "I'm abouta get up outta here. I'ma holla at ya later." He turned to exit her room.

"All right." Ridah fell back into the bed, releasing a sigh.

Lighting the blunt, she took a couple of pulls before sitting up again. Ridah had to get in touch with Smirky. As long as Lanka was out there, she could not relax.

Ridah had a blunt in one hand and the Swiffer in the other as she cleaned the kitchen floor. Thanks to K.J.'s visit, she was on cloud nine. Just when she was about to give up, K.J. came through and came up off that wood. "Just amazing," Ridah said aloud, shaking her head filled with lustful thoughts. Ridah's mind raced with thoughts as she loaded clothes into the washing machine.

Someone beating on the door like they were the police snatched her out of her thoughts. Ridah retrieved her .380 from behind the La-Z-Boy recliner she was sitting in earlier and made her way to the front door.

"Shanna, open the door. I know you see me," her twin yelled from the other side.

Ridah laughed as she opened the door. Her twin stormed in with a frown that deepened further after seeing what was in her sister's hand.

"Why you got dat?" she quizzed. For the life of her, she could not understand why Ridah idolized their trouble-some pops. She couldn't bear the thought. Tina always told her that pretty girls took flight when it was time to fight, and they were too cute to be fighting. She took heed, but Ridah was not hearing it at all. She was thugging eternally through her heart.

"Never know who on the other side of the door. But anyway." Ridah waved her hand. "What's up?" Ridah was curious to know.

"I can't bless you with my presence?" her twin asked as she went into the kitchen to get a glass of the apple juice that Ridah made sure she kept for her.

"Yeah. Whatever, Prissy." Ridah called her by the nickname their mother gave her. "How's Mom?" She sat down at the kitchen table.

Prissy took another sip of apple juice before replying. "Worrying as usual. Momma scared your ass gonna end up like Pops."

Prissy decided to leave the real reason for her visit out for now. It was that someone had been following their mother for a while. This had caused Tina to become cautious of her surroundings. Because Tina wanted Prissy to also be aware of her surroundings, she had no choice but to reveal her suspicions. The people who murdered Blu Foxx years ago had somehow discovered her location. It was only a matter of time before the people who murdered Blu Foxx caught their targets and carried out the botched order from years ago.

Prissy wanted to reveal what their mother confided in her, but the pact the two made kept her lips sealed. Besides, Ridah had Blu Foxx's traits. Both of them were hotheaded. Tina was not chancing Ridah acting out of impulsiveness and messing up her plans. Tina wanted Blu Foxx's killers to continue thinking she was not aware of their presence.

Ridah rolled her eyes toward the ceiling. What irritated her the most was that their mother always wanted to remain quiet and act like nothing was wrong and everything was fine. She swept everything under a rug, but Ridah? She could not bear the thought of ignoring the past. There was the legacy Blu Foxx left behind, unfortunately to no boys but girls, and Ridah vowed to make him proud.

Deep in Ridah's soul, she had dark moments where she did not want to be helped. She did not care if banging could be the death of her. In her mind, we all had to die for something. Why not leave the world banging? It was the death of her pops. Tina made sure Ridah did not forget she was just like her pops. So, why not leave the world like him? When she felt like this, Ridah was not trying to hear anything pertaining to her changing and all that "get on the right path before it's too late" stuff.

It was too late for her when she caught her first body, or maybe it was when she hid her pops's gun when the police were chasing him one night when she was with him. Ridah hid with his gun as he ran off into the darkness. She could not just sit back nonchalantly like her mother, especially with their mother's past, the one she tried to run from for so long for fear of it exposing light on her dark past for everyone to see.

Ridah smacked her lips as she rolled her eyes again with a mug. "Here we go again with this shit. So, she sent you over here to save me?" Ridah shook her head while looking at her sister. "Momma done hyped ya ass up to get cussed out. I don't wanna hear no come to Jesus talk. He ain't stopping them bullets from flying out here in these streets," Ridah snapped. The one thing Ridah hated the most about her mother was that Tina acted like she had been a saint all her life. "Stop wasting ya time, twin."

Prissy knew how stubborn Ridah could be, but she was not giving up on her sister like Tina had. She believed if she could get Ridah to hear her out, maybe she would not be so hard on their mother. "Why you always gotta make Momma feel guilty about the decision she made when she was younger? She only want the best for us, Ridah, damn!"

"Nawl, she acting like she ain't never did shit, then always judging and looking down on me. I'ma make my own decisions, and right now, I ain't tryin'a change. I'm good with being a gangsta-ass bitch dat will ride on any muthafucka dat step wrong," Ridah vented.

Prissy knew there was no sense in continuing to go back and forth with Ridah. She was in her own way right now. It was pointless. Walking to the sink, Prissy said, "Momma wanna hear your voice."

"Sis, I ain't tryin'a hear all dat shit Momma be on. 'Shanna, come to church, baby,'" Ridah mocked their mother. "Hell, next thing you know, people at the church are gonna be calling me a church gangsta. Then what she gonna do?"

The twins both laughed and slapped hands. Though Ridah was only joking, it would most likely happen. Ridah and Prissy may have been identical, but the twins were nothing alike. Prissy was a thinker, who listened intently before responding or even reacting to things she heard or saw, like their mother.

Someone knocking on the door brought them both out of their private thoughts. On the way to the front door, Ridah picked the gun up. Prissy shook her head but knew it was a necessity, especially if the black Honda followed her to Ridah's house. She sat back quietly, conflicted with her thoughts of loving and hating her pops introducing them to this type of lifestyle. Prissy was relieved when Ridah lowered the weapon. She exhaled without realizing she was holding her breath.

Ridah opened the door, greeting her longtime friend, Darius, with a one-arm hug. "I ain't seen ya ass in a while, nigga." Taking a step back, Ridah took in Darius's swag.

Darius was a peanut butter brown–skinned stud with a low fade who happened to be crushing on Ridah. Even if Ridah were into women, she and Darius could never be an item. Darius was affiliated with the Southside Bloods. Due to the pledges made to their sets, Ridah and Darius knew their loyalty to one another was limited. However, the two of them had a mutual understanding and vowed to always respect each other, no matter what happened.

"You gonna let a nigga in or what?" Darius asked with a coy grin that Ridah secretly loved.

"Oh. Damn. Come on in." Ridah stepped back to let her in. Every time Darius was in Ridah's presence, the thought of crossing over or simply straddling the fence would float around in her mind. Ridah had acted on her thoughts a few times, drunk of course, but never sober.

Darius eyed the gun in Ridah's hand and could not help but wonder what kind of problems she had that had her on high alert. "What's up with dat though?" Darius nodded toward the gun.

"Better safe than sorry, right?" Ridah replied, cutting her eyes at Prissy. "Why you looking crazy?" She could not help but laugh at her sister's discomfort.

Prissy's heartbeat increased as she watched the interaction between the two. Back in New York, she had witnessed the outcome of two rivals being seen together, and foul play was suspected. That was just how it went down in New York. If one was not one of them, then they were enemies. And if there were enemies, bullets were hailing heavily. Prissy was glad to be away from the violent state.

Prissy stood up. "I'm about to go. Make sure you call Momma." Prissy got to the front door, and then she turned to say, "Y'all be safe. I love ya, sis."

"Love you too," Ridah replied.

"You do the same," Darius said.

When the door closed, Darius pulled the blunt from behind her ear. Lighting it, she inhaled deeply into her lungs, then released a thick cloud of smoke. Darius sat down in the recliner, joining Ridah, who had already popped the first season of the *Saints & Sinners* series in the DVD player. Although Ridah had been wanting to watch the series from the beginning, she could not stop her thoughts from drifting back to one of her sessions with Lanka while she and Darius smoked the Kush in silence.

A fool is quick-tempered, but a wise person stays calm
when insulted.

—Proverbs 12:1

"I'm tryin'a get you past seeing color. This isn't about colors." Lanka eyed the heated youngster. She and Ridah had been going back and forth for an hour now.

"What the fuck it's about then?" Ridah asked. "'Cause last time I checked, if you go in any hood with the opposite color of what they reppin', you gonna be dodging bullets." Ridah really didn't understand where Lanka was going about colors.

Lanka could see the confusion written all over Ridah's face. "Do you know why our color is blue?"

Ridah remained quiet as she went back to her and her pops's many conversations. She did not recall him ever speaking on why blue was the color for Crips. Looking up at Lanka, curiosity filled Ridah's eyes. Although Ridah still had some growing to do, Lanka knew it was possible for Ridah to be one of the few who would help keep peace and bring unity to all colors. Lanka smiled as she placed her pointer finger on her full lips.

"Baby girl, you have so much to learn. We were Crips before we had a color," Lanka revealed.

"How do you know?" Ridah hated how Lanka thought she knew everything, and Smirky would have to find someone else to teach and help mold her.

"Because I read, Shanna. Dat's how." Lanka picked up on Ridah's energy and smirked. "I want you to go home and read Matthew 26:14-16."

"My name is Ridah." She sized Lanka up. She hated it when Lanka called her that, like they were on a personal level. "And why I gotta read Matthew?" Ridah folded her arms across her chest and sighed loudly.

"Da betrayal. Judas Iscariot betrayed the Son of God for thirty pieces of silver. Your very own cross you for

less. Even though Judas was remorseful, many won't be."

"I'm out. These some fake-ass gangs down here anyway," Ridah spat, *kicking the chair over as she walked out the door. She did not understand why Lanka was so adamant about her reading the Bible.*

CHAPTER FIFTEEN

*Do not think that I came to bring peace on the earth: I
did not come to bring peace but a sword.*

—Matthew 10:34

By the time Ridah finished dressing, she realized she
was thirty minutes late. After her house was secured,
she hopped in the truck, heading to her destination.
Ridah made a quick stop at the Chevelle station to get
some gas and a pack of cigars. After noticing a few
dudes leaning against the corner of the building, looking suspicious, Ridah pulled out a .38 Special, making
sure it was fully loaded. Satisfied, she tucked her baby
comfortably behind her back.

When she exited the truck, one of the dudes immediately started making cat calls, which Ridah ignored.
Noticing a gun print in the small of her back caused a guy
to state, "Damn, baby, it's like dat, baby?" He didn't wait
for a response. "If I was ya nigga, ya fine ass wouldn't
have to be out in these streets with no tool. Shit ain't
ladylike."

Ridah stopped to address the guy, who was obviously
talking too much for her liking. "What I need a man
for when I got two of the hardest bitches with me?" she
snapped before entering the store. "These lames niggas
do the most." Ridah spoke to herself without realizing
one of the dudes was walking behind her.

"Aye, bitch, what cha said now?" He hated when a female tried to act hard. It was not appealing at all to him. "If the shoe fits, wear it." Standing at a rack of chips at the coolers, Ridah put her hand on her bitch after peeking him putting his hands on his tool. "What's the problem?" Ridah asked, almost in a tired tone.

"Y'all bitches wasn't built for the streets," he snapped.

"Nigga, this lifestyle chose me. So, if you wanna shoot me in here for the way I live my life, then take ya best shot," Ridah voiced with no emotions. Taking her hand off her tool, she turned her back to the dude to grab a grape soda.

After Ridah paid for her items and gas, she headed out of the store to fill up her gas tank. Putting the cap back on, she was not in the truck good before gunshots rang through the quiet and cool night air. Not knowing which direction they were coming from, Ridah ducked down in her seat, praying she did not get hit by a stray bullet.

When the gunshots stopped, Ridah lifted her head and saw the same guy she left in the store running out the double glass doors with money flying everywhere. The Arab came out behind him with a crazed look in his eyes. Docking the shotgun, he squeezed the trigger, causing his target's body to grow wings a split second before he landed face-first to the ground. It rained money, and Ridah became stuck in a daze as bloody bills landed on her windshield.

Ridah made it to the party with another stain on her soul. She hated being in the Hillcrest area. It always felt like a trap to her. Ridah prayed nothing else popped off tonight but knew when liquor got in systems, intoxication mixed with egos and someone was going to start acting stupid. When the driver of a silver Pontiac honked the horn, Ridah exited her truck, then made her way to the car. A thick cloud of smoke coated the night air when Smirky opened the back door. Ridah grinned.

Hopping in the back seat, she hurriedly joined the smoke session.

Licking his dry lips, Smirky asked through low eyes, "What took ya so long, cuz?"

"I ran into a li'l problem," Ridah replied, not feeling like going through the motions of telling them about the incident at the store.

"Shid, let's hit this party, cuz!" K.J. suggested, slapping his hands together, then rubbing them.

"I'm with dat!" Ridah replied, running her fingers through her short bob.

Ten minutes later, the three were exiting the car. K.J. led the pack to the front door. A heavyset, short dark-skinned female blocked them from entering the house. She frowned deeply while sizing them up. "Y'all ain't coming up in here!" She rolled her neck and said it too nasty for Ridah's liking.

"What, bitch?" Ridah stepped up in full beast mode, ready to attack. She did not come there looking for any trouble, but she was not going to back down from any either. No one was going to disrespect her or their crew, definitely not some nothing-ass female.

The woman grabbed a wooden baseball bat that sat beside the door. Most of the people were in the backyard partying and enjoying liquor, drugs, and the grilled food. That did not stop the woman from swinging the bat at Ridah. Taking a blow to the side of her head, immediately blood started squirting from the wound. Seconds passed before Ridah reacted. She snatched the bat and began attacking the woman with her own weapon. People started crowding around, pulling out their phones to record and post the drama.

K.J., Smirky, and Capone held down the porch as the women continued to fight. When K.J. felt like Ridah had gotten enough steam off, he grabbed her. Still heated,

Ridah snatched away from him and went for the woman again. Smirky quickly pushed the woman back in the house to keep them separated. Ridah dropped the bat and wiped the blood from the gash on her forehead, breathing heavily.

The woman licked the blood off her lip. "Like I said, y'all ain't coming up in here!" she said in a trembling voice. She was not worried because she had her people there with her.

When Ridah spotted Chase, she was taken aback at how his eyes were filled with coldness toward her. Toni stood by him with a smirk, almost daring Ridah to get stupid. She clenched her teeth and gripped the .38 Special, returning Chase's deadly glare. Before this moment, Ridah did not realize things between her and him had reached this point. Jumping at the unexpected gunshots, everything became a blur. Smirky grabbed Ridah's wrist, leading them toward Capone's car.

Three dudes in all black and dark brown Dickies blocked them from the car. "I thought y'all came to party, dawg," one dude said as he took a drag of his Newport. He also made sure his chrome tool was visible.

K.J. had a wicked smile as he approached. "I'm always down to party, my dawg!" He displayed his tool as well, letting him know that neither he nor his crew were backing down from anyone.

K.J. did not care how many of them there were. They could all go out in a blaze of honor. Ridah's heart rate increased as she began to feel sick. This situation was like déjà vu. When Smirky pulled his tool out, she knew he was about to get it cracking. Ridah shut her eyes tight as she waited for sparks to fly. She could almost feel the burning lead entering her body.

"Nigga, move the fuck outta the way before I put a slug in yo' ass!" Smirky warned the dude who was leaning against Capone's car with no worries.

Chase walked up behind Smirky, who quickly spun around, pointing his tool at Chase, whose eyes loudly begged Smirky to pop off. The tension grew thicker within seconds. Without thinking, Ridah jumped between Chase and Smirky. A frown of confusion covered Smirky's face, but he was able to stay on point.

"What the fuck?" Smirky shouted in her face, making sure Chase didn't try to take advantage of the opportunity.

Although Chase had been real shady toward Ridah, he was once a friend, and because her love for him was real, she did not want to see him hurt. Ridah could not allow this situation to go down if she could help it. It was in this very moment that everything Lanka taught her made perfect sense. It did not matter what set a person claimed. When it came down to it, everyone wanted the same thing. Money. Power. Respect. The sad part was the price that was paid was in blood. Ridah thought about the position she had now put herself in. She turned around, facing Smirky, and his .44 now pointed at her.

"Let's just go," Ridah tried reasoning with a hotheaded Smirky.

"Fuck nawl!" Smirky's deadly eyes burned a hole in Chase's. He continued, "These niggas wanna gangsta party! Ain't dat right?" Smirky's top lip twitched as he stood tall with a cocky smirk on his face.

"Indeed." Looking at Ridah, who stood between them, Chase shook his head, disgusted.

"But I don't think she do!" He chuckled at Ridah's stupidity. Chase would have never gone against his own kind for her.

Before Ridah could react to Chase's remark, K.J. pushed her out of the way, causing her to stumble back. Smirky and Chase were now face-to-face. Neither one was backing down. Chase took a step forward; Smirky wasted no time raising his tool.

Chase's eyes filled with amusement. "Better make sure I die, nigga!" He never took his eyes off Smirky's. Chase's point was made. If he died today, he wasn't showing any fear or begging for his life like so many others had. If he was going out, it would be like the few classic legends who became a lot of the hood role models.

Smirky knew exactly what Chase was vowing. He would never allow another nigga to get the up on him. He had not run into anyone who did not care about his ego.

"Make ya final peace with God, my nigga!" Smirky wrapped his finger around the trigger.

Before Smirky squeezed off a shot, Ridah quickly squatted down to grab the bat. Blinded by rage, she swung the bat so hard at Chase that she missed. Catching the end of the bat, Chase snatched it and raised it in the air to strike her. Capone let off a shot at Chase, piercing a nickel-sized hole in his head, causing his body to hit the ground with a loud thud. Toni stood in the background, motionless, watching Chase's body go into a seize before going still.

It was like the Fourth of July as the night filled with light and gunpowder. The crowd was frenzied and started running for cover. Smirky and the rest of his crew took off running toward the truck while Capone stayed back off to the side, watching everything from the angle where he stood.

K.J. turned down Log Cabin Drive with two police cruisers right on his tail. When the lights flashed, he swore out loud. With the dirty guns in the car, he knew things had turned for the worse. K.J.'s worst fear was getting taken out by some undercover, racist cop. A car with three armed Black people in a dark area was all they needed. The officers were known for their famous line, "He had a gun," and as sad as it was, it would most likely be believable.

Looking at Smirky in the rearview mirror, the two spoke without uttering a single word. With Smirky being on parole for manslaughter, he could not afford to get caught up. Surrendering was never an option. K.J. knew his cousin had something up his sleeve.

Once he had the guns secured, Smirky threw the back door open, jumped out of the car, and took off running toward the dark woods. One of the officers took off after him while shooting wildly into the night. K.J. knew Smirky was going to make it. He knew those woods like the back of his hands.

The other two officers approached the car slowly with their guns drawn. "Get out the car with your hands up! On the ground now!" one policeman said in a raspy voice. He was silently begging for one of them to look like they were about to make a move. He wanted a reason to kill their Black asses.

At that moment, Ridah knew there was no getting out of this one. Glancing over at K.J., his facial expression was unreadable. Ridah sat on the ground with her hands up. A pimple-faced officer turned his gun on her and yelled for her to lie on the ground.

"I'm pregnant!" Ridah blurted. She did not want K.J. to find out this way. But the fear of the officer doing something stupid forced her to reveal her secret.

"Was you thinking about your got damn child when you killed that man? Huh? Yeah, I ain't think so. Now, lay your Black-ass face down on the ground before I blow your shit off," he warned as he dug his gun deep in the side of her face, praying she gave him a reason to fulfill his threat.

Fearing he'd shoot her, Ridah quickly did as she was told. "I ain't did shit!" Ridah replied with her face on the filthy concrete.

"Leave her the fuck alone!" K.J. shouted. Now that he knew Ridah could possibly be pregnant, he really had to save her.

"What the hell is this? A fucking nigger fairy tale?" The officer let out an obnoxious laugh. "I'll kill you, worthless-ass nigger, and ain't a damn thing gonna get done about it." Before he could make good on his promise, another police cruiser pulled up.

K.J. was relieved, seeing the Black officer, along with his white partner, jumping out of the cruiser. Taking quick strides to the other officer, he held his hand up. "Excuse me, Officer, we will take it from here." He could tell the officer was disappointed as he lowered his weapon and stormed off. He would not be killing any Blacks tonight.

When Ridah glanced over at him, K.J. turned his head away from her. He was livid. The fact that Ridah knew she was pregnant and was still in the streets wilding made him feel some type of way. She could have killed her child. After they both were cuffed, they were escorted to Bibb County jail.

CHAPTER SIXTEEN

K.J. had been living to learn the lessons life taught, which could be confusing, kind of like completing a puzzle without the picture. Sometimes, those pieces weren't what they appeared to be. Word on the streets was that someone in K.J.'s crew had been working with the other side for a few years. Although it was crazy to K.J., he knew most of them, if not all, couldn't be trusted.

There were times when something went down, and Capone would disappear for a few days and pop back up with no explanation. The thought of Capone being disloyal never crossed K.J.'s mind. Capone rode the hardest in the streets, which meant Capone had to lie low. Who would've ever thought old gangster Capone was one of the biggest rats on the west side of Macon?

K.J. built his street credit from the ground up. In all his years on the concrete, he could not think of anyone that had crossed him without karma catching them midstride. If K.J. didn't learn anything else, the lifestyle that he lived had taught him that people would bang with you day in, day out, while bragging about how gangster they were, but when things got hectic, the same people folded like beach chairs. Those were the ones spilling their guts before the detective could get in the interrogation room good enough to offer a cigarette.

*A life lesson: Never underestimate nobody! I don't give
a fuck how genuine they appear. Everybody is capable
of deceiving the next.*

—K.J.

K.J. pulled into the driveway of Smirky's mother's
small brick house. Hot as it was, the fiends were up and
down the scorching street like the heat did not faze them
at all. One of them approached K.J. as he exited his car.

"Baby boy, let me wash your car for some change. Look
out for me now!" a sweaty-faced man said with roaming,
bucked eyes.

"I always look out for y'all ass! Who's gonna look out
for me when I'm in need?" K.J. questioned as the smoker
fanned the gnats out of his face.

"Boy, who you gonna need? Nobody." He answered his
own question, hoping K.J. would give him some money
to feed the monkey on his back.

"Never know, man. Never know," K.J. replied as he
handed him a $20 bill. The smoker quickly thanked him
as he hurried off with a rough-looking woman K.J. had
never seen in the area before. Shaking his head, K.J.
watched them disappear down the alley. "Nigga didn't
even wash my car!" K.J. mumbled to himself.

Observing the scene, Smirky said, "Nigga, let me find
out you jocking Delosa's stinky ass!" He chuckled while
standing next to K.J.

Taking the blunt out of Smirky's hand, K.J. threw a
fake right then a sharp uppercut to Smirky's side. "Nigga,
you got me fucked up!"

Smirky groaned as he grabbed his side. "Damn, nigga,
dat shit hurt!" He frowned at K.J.

"Shut your dramatic ass up!" K.J. laughed at his cousin. As kids, they used to wrestle, and Smirky always complained about K.J. hitting him too hard. It made K.J. hit him harder, only to toughen Smirky up.

"Nigga, your momma!"

"Auntie! Smirky out here talking about ya sister!" K.J. said aloud, cutting his eyes at Smirky, who tried to snatch the blunt out of his hand.

"Snitch ass!" The two laughed until K.J. started choking after inhaling the Kush.

"Damn!" K.J. said as he looked at the blunt as he went into an uncontrollable coughing fit.

Smirky burst out laughing. "Nigga, yo' ass can't even handle this shit!" Smirky took the blunt from K.J. and stepped off the porch. "Come on, let's take a walk. I ain't tryin'a hear Ladybug's mouth if she smells this shit!"

"Nigga, it's too damn hot to be walking!" K.J. cocked his blue fitted cap to the left, dreading being out in the heat.

"Man, you better bring yo' ass on!"

K.J. jumped toward his cousin like he was about to attack him. Smirky threw his hands up in defense. When K.J. fell in step with him, they began to stroll down the street. Smirky asked, "How's Ridah holding up?"

Smirky had not heard from Ridah since the night of that incident at the party. She had been on Smirky's mind lately, especially after K.J. revealed that she was pregnant. Smirky was in his feelings for two reasons. Ridah didn't attempt to tell him anything, but she told K.J. The second was that Ridah had slept with his first cousin.

K.J knew that with Ridah being pregnant, Lanka would swear it was his. And he was not trying to catch any heat from that situation. He knew that Smirky and Ridah were close, and he could always get Smirky to do his dirty work. What he did not know was that there was a possibility that Ridah could be carrying Smirky's child.

Smirky had always had his cousin's back. This would be the first time Smirky went against K.J. He was so pissed, and Smirky planned to confront Ridah about the situation tonight.

No one knew of Smirky and Ridah's ongoing secret. In public, the two were homies. In private, they were lovers. Smirky never understood why Ridah wanted to keep them a secret. He wanted her so bad back then that he went with it. Their late-night arrangements made Smirky feel like he was not good enough. He loved Ridah so much, and he would do anything to make her happy.

The two made a pact years ago that neither of them would change up on each other, no matter what happened in their lives. As Ridah and Smirky got older, they started exploring other people. No matter how many females Smirky smashed, Ridah always remained his number one Cripette. He also valued their friendship too much to ever act on any of those feelings. Smirky would probably always be in love with Ridah.

"You know Ridah!" K.J. stated, wiping beads of sweat from his neck.

"Yeah, I do!" Smirky chuckled without K.J. having a clue just how close he was to the truth. Smirky could not stop his mind from traveling down memory lane.

Smirky was at a Halloween party that 2K4L (2Krank4life) Entertainment hosted by Bigg Murph. When he heard Ridah call his name, it was like music to his ears. Turning around, he almost choked on his Hennessy. There Ridah stood, dressed as an Egyptian. The jet-black short bob with the Chinese bangs fit her perfectly.

"What's wrong? Don't like my costume?" Ridah gave him a coy grin, knowing good and well Smirky was feeling her.

"Stop playing with me, girl, before I bend dat ass over for old time's sake!"

Smirky bit down on his bottom lip as thoughts of the last time he and his homie, lover, friend had sexed each other. He had been trying to get some more of Ridah for a month. But Ridah always brushed him off, saying he was the homie. There were times when Ridah was drunk and horny, and she begged him to thug her. Smirky made sure he delivered every time like it was the last time. Smirky never knew when the next time he was going to hit it would be, so he went all in. He was praying this was one of those times when Ridah would grant him access to do what he pleased to her body.

"Who's playing?" Ridah asked seductively, inches away from his face. "Remember the last time you had my li'l momma." She pointed to her private area, licking her glossy lips.

Before Smirky could respond, Ridah pushed him against the wall in the corner, causing Smirky's eyes to widen at Ridah's bold move. She had always made a move on him when no one else was watching. She stuck her tongue down his throat, and Smirky did not know if he should touch her or let Ridah have her way with him. Just as Smirky was starting to relax, Ridah pulled back and grinned.

"Them lips still soft." She giggled as she walked into the crowd, leaving him on hard. Smirky could have caught a charge that night.

K.J. called Smirky's name, snapping him out of his thoughts. Smirky looked at his cousin with a mischievous smile. "Why you got that goofy-ass grin on yo' face? What dat shit be about?" K.J. asked, flicking the roach to the ground as they made their way back to the house.

"You'll kill me if I tell you!" Smirky replied in between a joking and probably serious manner.

"Don't smoke no more of dat shit today, cuz!" K.J. said, glad to be back in so he could cool off. He stepped up on the porch to enter his aunt's house with Smirky trailing behind him.

"Whatever!" Smirky responded, cutting his eyes.

As soon as Smirky entered the house, he headed straight to his room while K.J. went into the hot kitchen, finding his aunt slaving over the stove. She took one look at him and shook her head in disapproval. Smirky had set him up. K.J. had forgotten how hard she tripped about the smell of weed.

"What's wrong, Auntie?" he asked, trying to act as if he did not know what had her in an uproar.

"Don't play with me, boy! You know good and damn well what's wrong! Coming up in my damn house smelling like dope!" Ladybug snapped, cutting her eyes at K.J.

Smirky entered the kitchen and butted in. "It ain't dope! It's loud!" He hated when his mother called Kush dope.

"Loud, Kush, Bush, whatever you wanna call it, it's still dope! When y'all asses start walking around here acting like these other muthafuckas, stealing and tryin'a sell shit, then what?" she asked, looking at them angrily.

Smirky rolled his eyes and walked back out of the kitchen. He was not trying to hear anything his mother had to say, especially while he was high. K.J. shook his head at his aunt. She was funny, or maybe it was the dope, as she said, kicking in full effect.

It took everything in K.J. not to laugh at Ladybug's theory. Ladybug and his mother, Pie, were too much to deal with at times. But K.J. loved the hell out of those two women. They were some old-school riders.

K.J. opened one of the many pots that was on the stove, and Ladybug hit him with a wooden spoon. "Boy, don't play with me. I'll still whoop your ass." Ladybug pointed her index finger at K.J.

"Dang, Ladybug." K.J. tried to shake the pain out of his hand. "What's wrong? You need some money?" he asked, knowing Ladybug would never turn down any money.

"Y'all need to move me up out this dump. That dope got these muthafuckers stealing and shit. They ass will steal dirt if somebody will buy it! Every time I get an air conditioner, they steal it!" Ladybug stressed as she continued to snap the peas into the yellow bowl.

"Where you wanna move to, Ladybug?" K.J. asked, giving her his full attention.

"Anywhere but in this dump!" she replied, then called Smirky's name. When he did not answer, she yelled, "Boy, get your narrow ass in here!"

Smirky entered the kitchen with irritation written all over his face. All he wanted to do was enjoy his high, but Ladybug was making it hard to enjoy anything. It seemed like she was always messing with him when he was high, like she got a kick out of blowing his high.

"What's up?"

Pointing her finger at Smirky, she warned, "Keep trying me, boy! Go get me a pack of cigarettes and play these numbers. Maybe I'll get lucky and win." She passed Smirky the piece of paper with the numbers on it.

Smirky frowned as he looked down at the paper, then back up at Ladybug. "I thought you stopped smoking."

"Boy, I ain't gotta answer to yo' ass! Now go do what I told you!" Ladybug shouted at Smirky.

Smirky rolled his eyes as he mumbled a few words under his breath. He was tired of her talking to him like he was still a child. "Come on, K.J.," he said, trying to put some distance between him and his mother as quickly as possible.

K.J. held his head down, so neither Ladybug nor Smirky would see the smirk on his face. K.J. followed closely behind him as he thought back to when they were young bucks.

K.J. and Smirky went to Riley Elementary School. One particular day, Smirky was walking ahead of K.J. and his friends when a younger boy threw a beer bottle that burst on Smirky's knee. K.J. attacked the boy and beat his face with a palm-sized rock. An older man had to pull K.J. off the bloody-faced boy and walk them home.

The man told K.J.'s mother only half of the story, how he attacked the other kid for no reason. No matter how much K.J. and Smirky told his mother the stranger was lying, she still beat them without mercy. K.J. could not understand how they were getting beaten because he took up for his cousin like they were always taught to do. Strangely, K.J. missed his childhood days when he was carefree and did not have the world on his shoulders and enemies trying to end his existence. He sighed then smiled to himself.

K.J. had always looked out for his younger cousin. The two of them looked out for each other. He knew if no one else had his back, Smirky did, and the cousins would ride 'til death for one another.

K.J. got in the passenger side, lighting up his Newport. He caught a glimpse of a familiar midnight blue Impala turning the corner. Not thinking anything of it, he inhaled the nicotine smoke while tucking the nine under his seat. Smirky had his head down, replying to a text. Looking up for a split second, he noticed an Impala with an AR-15 hanging halfway out of the back window.

"Duck!" Smirky shouted as the window shattered, causing glass to shower K.J.'s surprised and shocked face.

The Impala pulled off, leaving Smirky slumped over with a half-blown-off head. K.J. remained frozen, unable to take his eyes off of Smirky's body. Ladybug rushed out the front door in her green button-down housecoat. When she saw her son's car and window, she ran out to the car.

"Smirky! K.J.! Please, God, don't do this to me!" Ladybug screamed out in fear.

K.J. tried to speak, but when he opened his mouth, no words exited. He watched Ladybug open the driver's door, causing Smirky's body to fall over. Dropping to her knees, she screamed as pain ripped through her body.

Gunshots filled the quiet air again.

K.J.'s body jerked as bullets tore deep into his flesh. Ladybug's screams were cut short. It took K.J. a full second to realize what had happened. The Impala had made its way back to finish what was started. Reaching for his nine, which lay under his seat, K.J. gripped it tightly as blood dripped from his arm. Clenching his teeth, he pushed the door open and started shooting at the Impala.

Staggering across the yard as the pain spread throughout his body, K.J. fought to catch his breath. Every step he took was harder than the one before. Though his vision was blurry, K.J. could see a few people outside. No one came to his aid for fear of the killers coming back. Struggling to walk, the fiend K.J. had given money to earlier rushed to aid him. As the man stretched out his arms, K.J. collapsed, sending them both crashing to the ground.

"Hold on, baby boy. I got you!" he said as he and two others applied pressure on K.J.'s wounds. K.J. felt his body being lifted, and then the voices around him faded.

Ridah was awakened out of a deep sleep by the sound of her phone ringing. With her eyes still closed, Ridah reached to retrieve the phone while cursing whoever was calling her at three in the morning.

"Somebody better be dead!" Ridah spoke into the receiver, stretching her limbs and wiping cold out of her eyes.

"Ridah, come to the medical center!" was the only thing Anwar said.

"What happened?" Now fully awake, Ridah sat up. All kinds of scenarios went through Ridah's mind of who, what, when, where, and why. She started to panic. Going to the hospital meant death was brewing and grooming. Closing her eyes briefly, Ridah prayed. She could not bear the thought of losing someone else close to her.

Anwar refused to give Ridah any details over the phone. "Cuz, we'll talk when you get here. Just hurry up!" Anwar said, then ended the call.

Ridah felt like someone had cut off her air supply. She sat still for a minute, trying to get her breathing under control. Tears burned her eyes as she got out of bed. Ridah zipped her onesie up before slipping her feet into the fluffy house shoes. She rushed out of the front door, not caring whether it was locked. Ridah's only concern was to get to the medical center.

So many questions were invading Ridah's mind. She felt as if it were going to explode. When she reached the emergency room, Ridah scanned the crowded area. Her eyes fell on Lanka, who was leaning against the wall. Lanka's face was filled with grief. At that moment, Ridah felt like a ton of bricks had hit her. If Lanka was there, it could only mean that something had happened to K.J.

Ridah's eyes went to Anwar, who was pacing the floor, biting down on his bottom lip. Though no one knew of Ridah and Lanka's beef, she wished Anwar had given her the heads-up on Lanka being there. Ridah would have been unprepared if Lanka decided she wanted to settle the final score right where they stood. Ridah felt dumb for standing in front of her enemy in some fluffy house shoes.

Lanka cut her eyes in Ridah's direction, fighting the urge to put a bullet in her skull. Ridah must have felt the heat steaming off of Lanka. When she cut her eyes over her shoulder, she caught Lanka's cold glare. Another time, another place, Ridah would have been with whatever Lanka was with. But in the moment, she had to be there for her homie, lover, and friend if something had happened to him.

Ridah rushed over to Anwar. "What's going on?" She braced herself for the worst as she searched his eyes for a hint, but she found nothing.

"Smirky dead!" Anwar revealed while holding back his tears. He had never been big on emotions, but Smirky's death was breaking down his tough interior.

Ridah put both hands over her mouth, not believing what she was hearing. "Nooo! Anwar, please tell me you lying!" Ridah felt her heart crack. Smirky was one of the hardest she knew. No one was catching Smirky slipping! Ridah could not see it happening. "Nawl," Ridah said, shaking her head. "I don't believe that shit. I need to see a body." With blurry vision from her tears, Ridah attempted to go look for Smirky's body.

Anwar stepped in front of Ridah, dropping his head. No matter how hard he tried to hold back his own tears, they betrayed him. Whoever came up with the theory of gangstas didn't cry was a liar. Anwar was living proof. Holding his head up, he said, "That's not all. They killed his momma, and K.J. took a few hits, too."

Ridah suddenly became sick to her stomach. Bile rushed up to her throat and forced its way out of her mouth. Lanka suddenly stood next to Ridah with a suspicious face. Lanka touched Ridah's back, causing her body to go stiff. With fake concern and a half grin, Lanka gripped Ridah's shoulder tightly.

"You good?" she asked as if she cared. Ridah tried to pull away, but Lanka's grip became tighter. "Countdown!"

was all Lanka uttered before releasing her. "Hope you feel better soon!"

"Thanks!" Ridah glared at Lanka before she put some distance between them.

Ridah had underestimated Lanka. *Clever bitch!* she thought as her mind went into overdrive. Ridah glanced at Lanka as her thoughts continued to go wild. Lanka had to be tying up her loose ends. Lanka waited for the right opportunity to strike, so it would seem as if it was retaliation from the party incident.

Lanka appeared to be too deep in thought to notice Ridah dissecting her, or so Ridah thought. She could not prove it right now, but Ridah would bet her life that Smirky's blood was on Lanka's hands.

If Lanka was sending a message, she heard it loud and clear. Ridah knew how Lanka moved. With that in mind, she was not going to stop until their grudge ended with one of their demises in the streets. Though this was not the time, Ridah was ready to bang it out with her former mentor. It was now bigger than Kia's and Demya's deaths. Lanka would pay with her life for what she did to Smirky. No one was going to stop her. The next time the two were in the same space, it would be on-sight action.

Anwar went to stand beside Ridah, not knowing the tension between her and Lanka. Shaking his head caused chills to creep up Ridah's spine. "Shit ain't looking too good," he admitted.

"Can we see him?" Ridah asked but wanted to scream out her frustration. Instead, she hit the wall, drawing unwanted attention, including from Lanka, who was clearly irritated by Ridah's presence.

"Hell nawl," Anwar replied, walking Ridah to an empty chair to sit down. "Pull yourself together. Doing all that shit ain't gonna help! Cuz in there fighting for his life."

Ridah nodded her head as she faced the brutality of K.J.'s reality. Accepting Smirky's death was a hard pill to swallow. There were so many things she wanted to tell him, including her being pregnant with his child. Ridah would give anything to hit the reset button and go back in time. That was how it always was when something as tragic as that moment happened.

Hours passed without any update on K.J.'s condition. Ridah's thoughts were all over the place. Fresh tears began spilling down her face. Ridah began to panic after she realized Lanka had disappeared. She looked around frantically. Ridah could not afford to lose sight of Lanka. She would not put anything past Lanka, especially after her recent stunt.

Anwar pulled at one of his blue-dyed dreads as he sat down next to Ridah. Finally, a middle-aged male Indian doctor entered the waiting area. He clasped his hands in front of him as people started approaching him. In his profession, he had done this over a hundred times a day, if not more. The doctor searched the young faces that stood before him. Some of those faces were scared while others looked war ready. He knew whoever lay up in the back was someone of importance. The doctor also knew that he would most likely see plenty more young Black men laid up on a table, either fighting for their lives or dead.

"Who must I address concerning Mr. Plier's condition?" the doctor asked with roaming eyes.

Ridah stood among the group and stated, "We're his family, sir."

Lanka appeared out of thin air. "He's my fiancé," she exclaimed, then shot Ridah a deadly look.

"Okay. Well, the great news is Mr. Plier is out of the danger zone. However, we were not able to reach the bullet behind his heart. If we remove it, there's a sixty-seven percent chance he will die," the doctor explained carefully.

"When can we see him?" Lanka wanted to know. She needed to see K.J. before everyone else had the chance to.

"Yeah, when can we see him?" Anwar asked, still twisting at his dread.

"Tomorrow. He's heavily medicated," he quickly informed them.

Though it was a bittersweet moment, Ridah exhaled loudly while others clapped, relieved both cousins were not getting buried. Ridah's heart was torn to know Smirky was no longer among the living. She felt as if she had cried a million tears: J-loc, Kia, Scott, and now Smirky's death. If this was a wake-up call, Ridah was definitely paying attention. She had to get her life together before the streets came for her. And Ridah planned to do just that once she settled her final score. She had to get Lanka before she got to her.

After the crowd made a disappointing noise, some of them started hugging each other for comfort while others made their way out of the waiting area. It had been a long night for most of them. With K.J. being out of the danger zone, the crew was ready to wake up the whole neighborhood.

"Let's go, Ridah," Anwar said, taking long strides out of the waiting area. Following closely behind him, Ridah glanced over her shoulder to see Lanka still talking to the doctor.

Ridah began a battle in her mind of what was right and what she knew was wrong. Out of nowhere, her mother's voice filled the space in her troubled head. *"Exodus 23:2: 'You shall not follow a crowd to do evil nor shall you testify in a dispute so as to turn aside after many to prevent justice.'"* Shaking away her mother's words, Ridah tried to focus.

Fearing the unknown intensified the situation. No one had the first clue who was behind the shooting. Although there was not any proof, Ridah had an idea of who was behind the shooting. She hoped Lanka would slip up and expose herself. Ridah's loyalty would not allow her to turn the other cheek. She knew what needed to be done. She had to get revenge on behalf of her homies. Ridah owed that to Smirky for his faithful deeds to her over the years. Ridah was so deep into entertaining her thoughts that she bumped into a young woman.

"Watch where you going!" a light-skinned female voiced nonchalantly.

Already running off raw emotions, Ridah was in go mode. She blocked the girl's path, but before Ridah could fire off at the mouth, Anwar got between them. He had just lost his homeboy and was not in the mood for the petty mess these females were doing.

"Shit ain't that serious. Chill with all that extra shit!" he stated.

The female frowned as she sized him up. Without hesitation, she spat, "Nigga, you better get outta my face!"

"Bitch, I'm tryin'a help you!" Anwar replied, turning his head back to his crew. Before he could turn back around, Anwar felt the familiar coldness of metal kissing his neck. His expression said everything he did not utter. Anwar just got caught slipping. A big regret!

Lanka suddenly appeared, quickly pulling out a .44 from her light blue Polo pullover hoodie jacket. In one swift motion, she had the barrel kissing the young female's forehead, who did not look a day over 15 years old. Lanka was not fooled at all though. She and Demya had trained many youngsters, and the younger ones always felt they had something to prove. Most would pull the trigger quicker than the blink of an eye.

"Try me!" was all Lanka uttered, ready to unleash her anger. She stared at the girl deeply in her eyes, letting her know she would smoke her young behind out.

If pushed, Lanka would not hesitate to send the girl's thoughts flying through the air.

"Get that shit outta my face!" Gone was the hood chick from moments ago. Now, a young girl's voice trembled.

"Don't try to show out, li'l girl. Now my homie said the shit ain't dat serious. So g'on about yo' business," Lanka stated.

Two dudes walked up, and their frowns deepened.

"What's going on?" He didn't really wait for an explanation. He was already pulling his tool out, causing the light-skinned girl to grin proudly.

They were all caught off guard by the unexpected. Anwar took the awkward moment to snatch the gun out of the girl's hand and turn it on her.

"I told this bitch ain't nobody tryin'a be on no foul shit! She pulled out on me!"

As if they did not hear a single word Anwar said, one of them walked up on him with his gun down by his side. "Nigga, dat's my li'l sister!"

"I don't give a fuck who she is. She'll get her shit cleared the fuck out, pulling guns and shit on folks." Anwar's emotions were starting to seep out of him.

Ridah took the opportunity to chin check the young girl, who ate the blow she sent. The two of them began tussling. In the midst of them fighting, the sound of a gunshot ringing out into the early morning caused the two to separate from each other.

"Somebody get the police! These kids are gonna end up killing us!" a frightened woman yelled and quickly ran down the hall for fear of bullets entering the medical doors.

Both rivals began running in opposite directions. Neither crew was trying to get locked up. Ridah jumped in her truck, quickly reaching under the seat to retrieve the .38 snub nose. Laying it across her lap, her heart beat rapidly in her chest.

She drove aimlessly while deep in thought. "I can't keep living like this," Ridah exclaimed aloud with fresh tears in her eyes. Her tears came from pent-up, mixed emotions. Her beef with Lanka. Smirky being killed. Losing those dear to her and the self-battling from within of seeking change. Ridah's demons had forced her into a corner.

So many things had been going on in Ridah's life. It had become too much for one to bear alone. But even in her darkest moments, Ridah still held it together and pressed forward. Sometimes, she felt like she was just existing in the world. And now that Ridah had been indicted, she was not sure what the future held for her.

After driving around for hours, Ridah decided to turn it in for the night. Going to see K.J. the following morning put her at ease. Ridah could only pray that there was not any drama with Lanka.

Ridah pulled up to her apartment complex, turned off the engine, and sat there in her troublesome thoughts. Out of the corner of her eye, she could have sworn she saw movement. Maybe she was just edgy due to everything that had been going on. Ridah leaned over to retrieve the lip balm off the floor. When she sat back up, a barrel was pushed deep into the left side of her jaw. Squeezing her eyes tight, Ridah braced herself. She was not ready to meet the one person who had been chasing her for years: the grim reaper.

"Bang!" Lanka's voice mocked a gun as she smirked. "Yeah, bitch! Get out!" Lanka jerked the door open and snatched Ridah out of the driver's seat, causing the gun to fall out of her lap. "I've been waiting for this moment!"

Ridah snatched herself out of Lanka's reach. "If you gonna kill me, let's get this shit over with." Of course Ridah was not going to make it easy for Lanka, but she wanted her to believe she would.

Laughing, Lanka said, "Stall them! Pretty good but I ain't for dat shit. Remember I trained you!" Lanka giggled. "Good try though."

Ridah exposed a coy grin. Lanka may have trained her, but Ridah discovered her weakness, so she was depending on Lanka's emotions. "I know you ain't mad about dat nigga, K.J., telling me about li'l K.J. being his former friend's child." Ridah acted as if she were thinking while looking up into the sky. "What's his name?" She put a finger on her bottom lip as if she were thinking. "Oh, yeah, Fetticain. Dat's it!"

Lanka shoved Ridah back as if she had bitten her. "Bitch, you don't know what ya talking about!" Lanka vented. "K.J. would never tell a bitch our business!"

"Is dat what you really think?" Ridah began to walk up on Lanka, who suddenly had a face full of distress. Lanka was so off point that she never checked her for a gun. Lucky Ridah. The ball was in her court tonight.

"What do you think gonna happen when he finds out you was behind Smirky's death and him getting shot up?"

Lanka's eyes sparkled and widened. How could Ridah know of her dirty deed? She was extra careful and covered her tracks. Lanka now knew she couldn't let Ridah walk away. Dead people could not talk, and Lanka would do anything to keep her secrets from spilling.

"Who's gonna tell him?" Lanka raised her gun, leveling it at Ridah's head.

Ridah drew her gun and fired at Lanka. "Me, punk-ass bitch!"

"Ugh!" Lanka grabbed her shoulder as she fled in the night, yelling, "This ain't over, bitch!"

Ridah prayed that Lanka died from the gunshot wound. If she didn't, Ridah would have no other choice but to take the streets to Lanka's home. Lanka made the rules when she brought the drama to Ridah's house. Ridah refused to live her life looking over her shoulder every other minute. Lanka had the drop on Ridah and could have killed her on sight, but for some reason, she didn't. Maybe it was the years Lanka invested in her, since she was 13 years old, that made it hard to end Ridah's life.

On Ridah's end, she did not plan on sparing Lanka. Anything she felt for her before had been erased. To Ridah, her and Lanka's history meant nothing to her now. Lines that should have never been crossed were now crossed, and there was no turning back from that. If Lanka pulled the trigger on Smirky, Ridah could not chance hesitating to end Lanka's life.

CHAPTER SEVENTEEN

Ay, what I am today, I made myself
But I still ain't forgave myself
For runnin' to the grave getting closer to death

—T.I., "Still Ain't Forgave Myself"

It had been two months since the incident with K.J. and Smirky. The streets had been tight-lipped when it came to the topic of who was responsible for the hit. But that did not stop the blue team from being responsible for many of their rivals' deaths. The streets were soaked in blood, just like Smirky's and his mother's blood stained the concrete.

Ridah was having a hard time believing Smirky was gone. Smirky was one of the top three realest dudes known, and his presence would definitely be missed. Ridah took her pledge and loyalty seriously. Because of that reason alone, there wasn't a chance in hell Lanka would be walking around breathing while Smirky lay beneath the dirt. Lanka's life was on the countdown!

K.J.'s recovery was slow. He had to learn how to walk again. He also lost the use of his left hand, though the doctor said there was a chance the feeling could come back. K.J. said he felt like a cripple now, and despite the ugly scars that were left behind, he was thankful to have his life still intact.

Lanka stood by his side, playing her position, like she was not the cause of K.J. being inches away from death. Ridah knew Lanka's secret, and because she knew, Ridah could not sleep at night. The more she saw Lanka, the deeper Ridah's hatred for her became. She wanted to expose Lanka for what she truly was. When the time was right, Ridah would. Until then, she knew dealing with K.J. would cause Lanka more pain than anything else would right now. So, Ridah intended to do just that.

Lanka hated the fact that Ridah came to their house, checking up on K.J. Ridah got a kick out of getting under Lanka's skin. When K.J. told her Ridah was pregnant, Lanka wanted to blow a gasket. Although it wasn't possible that her child could be K.J.'s, Ridah still taunted Lanka by pretending it was his child. In reality, Ridah was no better than Lanka.

Ridah opened the bottom drawer to her dresser, which contained three plastic Ziploc bags of blue bandanas that belonged to three of the closest people she had lost. Ridah had Kia's and one of Smirky's many flags and her pops's, which was the most valuable one to Ridah. The others were from her younger days of fighting. Ridah could not help but shake her head sadly. She was unable to contain her tears, which fell freely as thoughts of her homies' lives lost to this gangbang tormented her brain.

Caressing Kia's flag brought out so many raw emotions. Ridah could not believe her Cripette was gone. The hardest thing Ridah had to do was look Kia in her eyes and tell her she would be all right. She needed Kia to survive. When she died that day, Ridah felt a stain on her soul, another burden, another cross to carry. Ridah pledged to her flag that everyone who had a hand in her hurt was going to feel her, even if she had to go on a suicide mission. They were going to feel Ridah's wrath.

Losing her homies did not hurt like the loss of the ones Ridah loved wholeheartedly. See, it was the oath that caused Ridah to ride for her set. But her friends, of whom she had very few, Ridah really took it to heart when they were killed. Her heart was still heavy about Scott's death. As much as Ridah tried to keep Scott away from that lifestyle, he still got caught up.

When Yo Gotti stated the good died young, he spoke nothing but the truth. Like so many others, Scott was the proof. What hurt Ridah the most was his mother would not allow her to pay her respects at his funeral. Ridah could not blame her. Scott's mother, who blamed Ridah for her son's absence, felt the same way.

A lot of people said they would trade places with the ones who lost their lives. But Ridah came to realize most people said that speaking from grief. Ridah could not speak for anyone else. She would ride to the very end for hers, but there was no one she would give her life up for.

As much as Ridah wished that she could change the past, she couldn't. All she could do was move forward. It was hard to leave the ones you loved the most in the past. Ridah would never know why the dark clouds moved right along with her. Sometimes, Ridah felt as if it only rained on her, and she could not reach her full potential.

When Ridah built up the nerve to say she was going to do better, the streets whispered her name through the night. She found herself in a trance of forgiving and falling back into its arms. Truth be told, Ridah was scared. She did not want to end up like most of her homies. Ridah wanted to live and make something of herself. Only then would she be able to help stop others from going through what she was going through. Ridah knew she could not fully live if she did not handle the street grudges against the ones who caused mayhem in her world.

Ridah's pops taught them that revenge was a promise, and the cost of violating her set was death! Revenge was the water that doused the fire on her inner pain. Ridah could hear her soul roaring loudly as the flames burned her mind and tried to settle the final score.

The sound of the phone ringing snatched Ridah out of her thoughts. She glanced at it, debating whether she should answer. It was one of those days where Ridah wanted to be left alone. Whoever was blowing up her phone was determined to reach her.

Sighing loudly, Ridah pressed the phone button. "Yeah."

"Forgot about a nigga already?" K.J. asked.

Ridah felt like every time she was going through dark hours in her life, K.J. always popped up. Her very own shining knight, shining his light into the darkness of Ridah's cold world. Because Ridah was good at masking her pain, she had no problem forcing her troubling thoughts to the back of her mind.

"Nawl. I'm not tryin'a deal with the extra shit that comes along with you." Lanka always found some kind of way to irritate Ridah by showing her that no matter what happened, K.J. wasn't going anywhere. That may have been true, but Ridah made sure Lanka knew she was there to stay as well.

K.J. picked up on the tension between Ridah and Lanka whenever the two were around each other. Ridah taunted Lanka so much, letting her know she was the one having K.J.'s first child! Lanka pulled a knife, threatening to cut Ridah's baby out of her. Ridah taunted Lanka so much, making it known that she was pregnant, whether she knew who her child's father was or not.

"I told you dat you don't have to worry about shit. Lanka knows I'ma help and be in the child's life. Dat's something you ain't never gotta worry about!" K.J. was not going to turn his back on Lanka either. Regardless of her deceitfulness, his heart would always belong to Lanka. But of course Ridah did not need to know any of that.

"Anyways." Ridah shook her head. She did not want to hear Lanka's name. "How are you holding up?" Ridah asked, trying her best to keep irritation out of her voice.

"Shid, still tryin'a process everything, man. My momma had to bury her only sister and a nephew," K.J. said, still in disbelief.

Ridah could hear the pain in his voice. Everything in her wanted to scream that Lanka was behind the hit, but she remained silent, loyal to Kia and ready to ride for Smirky. Besides, K.J. would probably not believe Lanka was capable of causing him this kind of pain. Regardless of what Ridah felt, she decided to take it to her grave.

"Tough times seem to last so long." Ridah wasn't expecting K.J. to reply. This was something she always wondered. If there was a God who truly sat high and watched low, why did He put people through this hell in life? Ridah did not understand the logic at all.

"What cha say?" he asked.

"Just thinking out loud," Ridah replied with a distressed sigh. She was so tired in the physical sense but too strong in the mental to give up. "When you coming through?" She wanted to see him but hated the thought of feeling needy. Ridah never experienced feelings like this. The growing fetus had her so emotional.

"I'll be there." K.J. hung up.

As soon as K.J. hit the door, he grabbed Ridah up and held her tight as if she would disappear. K.J.'s response let Ridah know that he needed her just as much as she needed him. Kicking the door closed, K.J. picked Ridah up and carried her to the bedroom. Placing her on the bed, he stood at the end, staring at Ridah intently as if he were peeking through a peephole of her soul, searching for something neither one of them were able to give fully.

K.J. pulled his shirt over his head. Ridah could not stop her eyes from falling on the hideous scar in the middle of his chest down his torso. She reached out to touch his scar. K.J. hesitated to step within her reach. Leaning forward, Ridah's fingertips traced the scar. Of all the times she and K.J. had sex, this moment was different. It was more intense. Ridah grabbed K.J.'s waist with urgency, pulling him on top of her.

"I love you, girl," K.J. said while staring in Ridah's eyes. He saw straight through her.

Ridah waited so long to hear those words from his mouth. Now that she had heard them, it seemed as though he was saying goodbye. The thought alone made Ridah's heart ache. She wanted this moment to last forever. Ridah hated herself for daydreaming of those hood fairy tales, knowing there would never be any happily ever after, especially while Lanka walked this earth.

One thing was for certain: the streets would continue after they were dead and gone. People were going to always find ways to taint a person's character. Not many would be able to tell what went down, but they would swear they knew what happened. Most of them would create their own story. The fact that Ridah slept with K.J. portrayed her to be another disloyal person. Although many would tell their version of what went down, no one would know the actual truth.

"I love you too," Ridah said. What she thought was going to take place didn't. Instead of them having sex, K.J. held Ridah close until they drifted off into sleep.

CHAPTER EIGHTEEN

A fool's mouth is destruction, and his lips are the share of his soul.

—Proverbs 18:7

Two Hours Later

"Court is now in session," the bailiff said with his hands behind his back. "All rise for the Honorable Judge Heimbruch."

Ridah and the others stood as the gray-headed judge entered the courtroom. Seconds passed before Judge Heimbruch told them they may all be seated.

"Have the jurors reached their verdict?" Judge Heimbruch asked. One of the jurors passed their verdict to the bailiff. There was no expression on the judge's face as she opened the folded paper.

Ridah felt it in her gut. This would not end well for her today. The sky was even dark at this hour, but Ridah would be damned if she allowed her peers to see her in the weakest hour. Her life was in the hands of twelve jurors who all failed to seek justice in not only her honor but in every young Black person's who entered the courtroom with a court-appointed lawyer.

"Nashanna Gier, correct?" Judge Heimbruch asked with a questionable look.

When Ridah gave a slight nod, her attorney gave her a side glance. Lowering her head, she said, "Ms. Gier, this is your life."

Ridah gave the attorney her full attention. She clasped her hands while cocking her head to meet her attorney's eyes.

"My life was in all of these folks' hands. You didn't kick up the smallest dust to defend me. If you don't have me back in court within two years, you see them boys back there?" Ridah paused as the attorney glanced over her shoulder. "They comin' for ya ass!" Ridah promised.

The attorney's face flushed red. Whether Ridah was bluffing or not, she was not going to risk her life nor her family's for a big scheme. "Ms. Gier, I'm going to do everything in my power to get you back in court," she vowed with a shaky voice.

Ridah then faced Judge Heimbruch. "Yes, I am."

"The jury finds you guilty of manslaughter, possession of a firearm during the commission of a crime, grand auto theft, and seven counts of aggravated assault." She looked up for a brief moment, and then she sighed. "Nashanna Gier, I sentence you to seventy-five years in a woman's facility."

Ridah removed her Prada eyeglasses as she made eye contact with the judge. "See you soon!" Ridah blew three kisses in each section's direction.

As Ridah was being removed from the courtroom, everyone was in an uproar, especially after watching the detectives escorting their star witness, Capone, out. Anwar sat back with a small smirk as thoughts of Capone being carried by his pallbearers crossed his mind.

Ridah held herself together pretty well, refusing to accept her fate, especially now that she would be giving birth to a child. Before she caught this case, people knew very little about her. Ridah was a private person. Now with this case, people only wondered if she was actually the killer on that fatal night.

It is the lips of the liar that conceal hostility, but he who spread accusations is a fool.

—Proverbs 10:18

K.J. leaned back in the wooden chair with an unreadable expression as he listened to all the rats testify against him. It amazed him how the ones who always hollered, "I'm real," the loudest would be the first to crumble like cookies within the first four minutes of an investigation.

K.J. would rather die before he helped the State put anyone away, including his enemy. He had never boasted about anything in his life, let alone spoken about anything that could lead to his downfall. Of all the things K.J. had gotten away with, this one time, he was actually innocent. He could not help but think that this was his karma though for all the stuff he had gotten away with. K.J. locked eyes with each witness who sold their soul for little to nothing. Knowing what to expect from people at all times was something that he had always engraved in his head.

Some people truly did love to feel important enough to get their five minutes of fame. As soon as the State got what they needed and wanted from them, the same witness they promised to protect would be tossed back in the streets with the vultures. K.J.'s one regret was Ridah getting caught up in the crossfire. Whatever the outcome would be, K.J. would make it his business to ride it out with Ridah and do everything to get her back in court.

K.J. allowed people to assume whatever they wanted about him. If he ever spoke in his defense, he would be his own star witness, leading the choir for the snitches. K.J. could never eliminate himself. K.J. was simply a street dude who happened to be street as well as book smart. K.J. had been busting his gun since the age of 13. The hood dudes gave him pointers, and the streets raised him. K.J. played the game raw, and in those streets, he went to war with anyone who was bold enough to bring heat his way. K.J. would go to war with the devil himself if he came wrong.

Living life had taught K.J. so many things. If a dude was a real gangster, he knew that he could not survive off the streets. He could get by but not survive. A lot of people thought that because they had been in the streets they had game. What people failed to realize was that the same game had been run since slavery. Women had been tricking men and men had been tricking women since God made the world. If you didn't believe it, read about it in the Bible. Genesis Chapter 3 verse 1-14.

K.J.'s intentions were not good with Ridah at the beginning, and he wanted her to get rid of the baby she carried. He wasn't comfortable with the idea of her being pregnant by someone else. And he didn't have the energy to go through the motions of explaining that Ridah's child wasn't his. K.J. still ended up feeling Ridah on a much deeper level. Ridah was the type of female a gangster wanted to have on his team. Not only had Ridah shown that she was one of the realest, but she also genuinely cared about people's well-being. K.J. loved that about her. She may not have reached his top four, but Ridah was closer than Lanka due to her sleeping with Fetticain. K.J. still could not believe the woman he gave his heart to did him like that.

Before K.J. got to know Lanka, she used to come around Duncan Block. There had always been something about her that pulled at K.J. Looking into her eyes told him a story of pain. While on the flip side, Ridah would chump dudes off every time one attempted to step her way. At one time, K.J. thought Ridah and Smirky had something going on.

When it came to Lanka, no matter how wrong K.J. did her, she always stayed down with him. Before K.J. and Lanka got together, he thought it was a man's job to smash females. With time, he learned that every female was not meant to be a smash and go. K.J. wanted to take his time to get to know some of them. Lanka happened to be one of those good girls K.J. ran across and exposed to that gangster. Although it was already in her, she now had someone like K.J. to bring it out of her. There were times that K.J. regretted introducing Lanka to this lifestyle. It was like the beast had awakened. Lanka took it to a whole other level.

"Keonte Plier," Judge Bankman said, bringing K.J. back to the present. "I find you guilty of felony murder and possession of a firearm. I sentence you to life plus five years."

Just like that, K.J.'s life was taken. The officers quickly escorted him out of the side door into the waiting white van. Once he entered the van, the first eyes he locked with were Ridah's. Seeing her smile made him all right in that very moment. Knowing that Ridah was going to prison pregnant kind of messed with K.J.'s mind, especially for something neither one of them had done. But K.J. knew Ridah would ride without folding an inch, and for that, he loved her.

There were other times when K.J. felt like Ridah was in competition with Lanka. Both women were unique in their own way and gave him something different. When it came to loyalty, Lanka would never win again, and Ridah would never have K.J.'s heart fully. K.J. secretly wished that he could mend.

"Hold it down," Ridah said while smiling at K.J.

"I'll always hold you down. Stay true," K.J. replied.

"'Til the death of me!" she said before the officer told them to quiet down. As the van led them on their journey, they sat back quietly in their own thoughts.

CHAPTER NINETEEN

*Bread of deceit is sweet to a man, but afterwards, his
mouth shall be filled with gravel.*

—Proverbs 20:17

Ridah entered the open dorm with her head held high.
Thanks to the news, everyone knew her business. Ridah
couldn't care less what anyone thought they knew. The
way she was feeling, any one of them could catch it, too.

Ridah made her way toward the back, empty bunk
in the corner by the restroom. She stopped dead in her
tracks after seeing the last person she expected to see.
Toni! Chase's chick! One thing was for sure: Chase was
not there to protect her now. The way Toni looked at
Ridah, one would have thought she had seen a ghost.

Ridah wanted to put her hands on Toni. She truly felt
that she was the main reason all of this happened. Ridah
could not help but think back to the day of the incident at
school. Toni did all that capping like she was really about
that life. Now, Ridah was accused of killing her boyfriend.
With that in mind, Ridah prepared herself and dropped
the State-issued stuff so that her hands could be free if
Toni decided to pop off.

"I ain't tryin'a fight!" she exclaimed. Toni fought to
control her emotions while looking at the one person she
hated the most.

Toni was not in a position to get at Ridah at this moment, but she vowed that when the opportunity came, she'd be the last one standing in the standoff. For now, she needed Ridah to think there were not any ill feelings toward her so she would let her guard down.

"I hear you!" Ridah replied with a smirk. She was not trusting Toni but would play her little game.

Toni wanted to knock the smirk off of Ridah's face while Ridah wished quietly that Toni was bold enough to try her again as she had done in the past. The reality for Ridah was that she was lucky Toni did not want to fight. Her fetus would be in harm's way.

The inmates sitting at the table playing cards stopped their game, dying for some entertainment. Everyone in the county jail heard Toni popping off loudly about what she was going to do when Ridah hit the county jail. When Toni did not pop off, many of them clowned Toni among themselves and refocused on their game.

Ridah quickly picked up on the setting. She had never been the type to get hyped off crowds. On her way to the back, Ridah glanced over her shoulder after hearing Toni call her name. Smiling, Toni asked if Ridah needed help putting her things away. Ridah nodded that she did as she continued to walk toward the bed with Toni following closely.

Ridah threw the flat pillow and thin wool blanket on the top bunk and made her way to the phone on the wall. She dreaded calling her mother and secretly hoped she would not answer the phone. Ridah let the line ring three times, and as she was hanging up, she heard her mother's voice. Ridah debated whether to act like she did not hear her mother and hang up. She already knew she had a few sermons coming her way, and right now, Ridah was not prepared to hear her mother preach.

Ridah observed Toni from afar. She could not put her finger on it, but she knew Toni was up to no good. All of a sudden, Toni wanted to be friendly after all the drama she started in school about Ridah sleeping with Chase. Now that Ridah was there for killing Toni's man, she was calm and humble. The more Ridah thought about it, the more she was convinced that something was definitely up with Toni. If she didn't do anything else, Ridah was going to find out if it was the last thing she did.

Toni may have thought she was slicker than Ridah, but if Toni wanted to play, Ridah was going to play the same game and act oblivious to what was going on. Ridah had her own personal reasons why she chose to deal with Toni.

Shaking her thoughts away, Ridah focused on her call. "Hello," Ridah said into the receiver.

"Hey, baby. K.J. paid for you to get a new attorney. But you know it doesn't mean nothing if you don't fall on your knees and pray. It ain't over 'til God says it's over! They may have won this battle, but they haven't won the war." Tina spoke with deep passion.

Ridah rolled her eyes, thinking, *here we go with this shit!* Although she felt where her mother was coming from, Ridah did not want to hear all of that right now. All she could think about was the seventy-five years for something she did not do. And Tina had the nerve to say prayer changed things. If that was the case, then why did God take away people we loved? Ridah had so many dead homies. She could probably start her own cemetery.

Ridah was sure most of her homies had praying mothers. Some may have even lived in the church. Scott's mother almost got evicted, giving up her whole check to pay tithes. But prayer was supposed to change things, let them tell it. That always sounded like a bunch of bull crap to Ridah.

"I feel you, Momma!" Ridah said in a bored tone. She was tired of hearing the same old thing.

"I don't want you to feel me, Nashanna. I want you to listen and understand what I'm saying. I told God if He got me through the stuff I was caught up in back in New York, I would change my life around. I moved us here to give y'all a chance at life without looking over our shoulders. I needed this fresh start. That's why we have to pray, baby. Cry out to the Lord. I can do all the praying in the world, but if you don't do your part, then it's not going to work. Read Psalm 29 and 35 every day."

Changing the subject, Ridah asked her mother something she'd been dying to ask her. "Who's lookin' for you?" When Tina did not respond, Ridah said, "Hello," to see if she was still on the phone.

"Yes, I'm here. We'll talk about that another time," Tina said in a nonchalant manner.

"Why can't we talk about it now?" Ridah pushed.

"I'm not talking about this shit over the phone!"

And there it was. Tina had finally broken through the stuff she was covering up. This was the real her she hid from everyone. Ridah used to love listening to her pops tell them stories about him and their mother when they were younger. He used to say Tina was meek and very timid. But when Blu Foxx told her to do something, she turned into a beast.

"Call me back later!" Tina rushed off the phone.

After Ridah hung up the phone, a woman came up beside her, causing her to grip the phone tightly.

"Still the same old Ridah, huh?" the woman stated with a pleased smile.

Ridah stared at the woman as a huge grin spread across her face. She threw her arms around the woman. "Roxy! Oh, my God! I ain't seen ya ass in years."

"Yeah, it's been a while since I saw them streets!" She pointed at a table full of food and snack cakes. "We got some stuff over there. You welcome to come chill with us whenever you through handling your business. But Toni ain't allowed."

Roxy was an old head from around the way. Roxy ran a gambling house and a ho house. She was well known for her famous fish and chicken plates on Rice Circle. Officers bought her plates and turned their heads on whatever went on in that area. When it came to parties, Roxy threw the biggest parties on the west side. If she was hosting your parties, you best believe she'd have her hoes there milking everyone who attended. To this very day, Roxy's parties were still talked about.

Roxy had a house off Lowe Street before she cut two of her hoes up for stealing money from her. Word on the streets was that Roxy had killed one of them for pressing charges and ended up with a murder charge after her former worker sided with the State. That was like three years ago. Ridah could tell even in this moment that Roxy was still plugged in thanks to her most loyal worker, Bam.

"I heard about you and K.J. That was some foul shit Capone pulled. You can't do people wrong and expect to live peacefully. Karma's a bitch, and when she comes, she hits hard."

"Yeah." Ridah did not care how cool Roxy was. Her and K.J.'s business was not up for discussion. Changing the topic, Ridah asked, "What's up with Toni?" She was curious to know the juice on her.

A frown formed between Roxy's brows at the mention of Toni's name. "Honey, dat ho made a lot of enemies." Looking Toni's way, she continued, "Bitch got desperate and started writing checks and shit." Roxy licked her chapped lips.

Shaking her head, Ridah stated, "Roxy, your ass ain't changed a bit." She could not help but laugh. "Listen, though, I can think of some ways to use her ass as a pawn."

"What can we use that trifling-ass ho for?" Roxy asked with a deep mug. "Bitch owes everybody, especially them hoes over there." Roxy nodded her head in the direction of some old heads.

"I tell you what. I'll clear her debts. She can work it off for me," Ridah replied as her mind started to turn.

"All right. I feel where you comin' from," Roxy finally said with a grin.

"Let me make a few more calls and I'ma come kick it with y'all. "

Ridah stood by the phone until the officer cleared them for count. Once the inmates were able to move around freely, Ridah walked over to Toni's bed, making light conversation. Toni was acting as if the two of them were the best of friends, but both women had their own reasons for dealing with one another.

Ridah went to Roxy's table with Toni close behind her. She could not believe how Roxy had hooked the jail food up. Although she did not eat much, Ridah had a good time and ate the Debbie snacks that were made into a chocolate cake. When it was time for lights-out, Ridah lay back in her iron bed with one question floating through her mind: was the party a welcome for her since they all knew she was coming to jail?

"Cure for the itch."

K.J. could not stop thinking about Ridah. He wondered how she was holding up. Then again, he knew Ridah was just that: a rider. After he handled all his important calls, K.J. did his routine workout, then freshened up and lay down. He tried to get comfortable but kept shifting his legs. K.J. could not help but put his hand deep in his pants to discreetly scratch his genital area. He cussed under his breath, thinking about the last female he was with. The biggest ho on Duncan Block was Amanda Davis. K.J. was intoxicated that night when she begged to suck his penis and bend her over. It was a life lesson he would always remember.

K.J. chuckled to himself, thinking of his current situation. He had never been offended by the word "crab," so it was very humorous to him that he was a Crip who had crabs. When K.J.'s itching became unbearable, he threw his legs off the edge of the bed and headed to the restroom.

There was an ashy Black dude standing up, butt naked, with his hands against the wall while another man was on his knees, pleasuring him.

"Nigga, do that shit somewhere else!" K.J. nearly yelled as he scratched his genitals in a frustrated way.

Both men jumped, quickly grabbing their jumpers. K.J. looked at them in a disgusted way as he made his way to the stall. Leaning against the back wall, K.J. sighed loudly while he tore into his skin. After K.J. scratched for what seemed like a lifetime, he went back to his bunk, hoping to go to medical the next day to cure his itch.

Lying back on his bunk, K.J. could not help but think of the old days when he and Lanka first met in middle school. The good golden days. K.J. never thought he would be lying here wishing for those days again.

Lanka and her friends were sitting on the bleachers, dick jocking, as K.J. and his homies called it. K.J. was doing laps around the gym as a result of being late for basketball practice.

"Y'all sorry asses need to be practicin' while y'all drooling and shit," K.J. said, breathing heavy. He never

*understood why girls always sat there giggling like
something was so funny.*

*Lanka stood with her hand on her narrow hip. "Ain't
nobody drooling over you with your ugly ass."*

*"What you call it then?" K.J. challenged. When Lanka
smacked her lips, he chuckled. "Dat's what I thought."*

*"Let's go, y'all!" Lanka jumped off the bleachers, fol-
lowed by her homegirls. "It ain't like y'all ass gonna win
anyway." Lanka took one of the basketballs on the court.
Bending her knees a little, she went for a three.*

*After the ball went through the hoop, she smirked at
K.J., then rolled her eyes.*

*"Girl, take ya skinny ass on!" He was highly offended
by her statement. K.J. shook his head, watching her
attempt to twist out of the gym.*

*Two weeks after that incident, K.J. was rushing to get
to his first period class. Lanka was walking down the
hallway, looking over her assignment for the final time.
K.J. bumped into Lanka, sending her books and papers
flying everywhere. The look she shot him would have
killed him on the spot if it could. K.J. sighed and quickly
bent down to retrieve the papers while Lanka picked
her books up. Lanka did not hide her attitude when she
snatched the papers out of K.J.'s hand. What she was
not expecting him to do was snatch them back and cause
a few pages to be ripped.*

*"See what you did, stupid!" Lanka shouted in the
empty hall.*

*K.J. frowned and looked at her like she was crazy.
"Why you so fuckin' mean? I coulda left dat shit on the
floor!" K.J. was sick of Lanka's smart mouth.*

*Lanka looked up at him with a smirk, but she did not
utter a word. Finally, she had his undivided attention.
And for the first time in her life, she did not know what
to say. When K.J. saw that Lanka had the same dumb*

look the other girls were giving him in school, he knew right then and there she had a thing for him too. But Lanka had to get in line and wait like the rest of them. He grinned at the thought.

"Oh, you mean to tell me you ain't got shit to say?" K.J. asked with a boyish grin.

Smacking her lips, Lanka rolled her eyes so hard that K.J. thought they would get stuck. "Shut up!" was all she said, holding back her smile.

"Come to the game and bring me some luck." He ignored her smartness.

"In ya dreams! Who y'all playin' anyway? Westside? If so, you might as well hang it up. Those boys play hella defense!" She spoke facts.

K.J. frowned. "Damn, you dick ridin' them niggas going against Ballard Hudson."

Lanka shot him a nasty look. "Boy, don't get ya lip busted!" she warned.

"I'd rather you kiss them. I can do without the violence shit." He stepped closer to her.

"Not in this lifetime!" No longer caring about making it to class, Lanka walked in the opposite direction from her classroom. When she did not hear K.J.'s footsteps behind her, she stopped. Glancing over her shoulder, she said, "Come on!"

K.J. looked at her, confounded. One minute, Lanka was cussing him out. Now, she was demanding he follow her. He smiled at the bad girl image Lanka put on. He'd bet his last dollar she had never skipped school a day in her life. He decided getting more days in ISS would be worth seeing what was up with little Ms. Lanka.

"Where we headed?" he questioned.

Instead of answering, Lanka led him through a pathway most of the students took to and from school. Once they were out of the public eyesight, she pulled a *blunt from her back pocket. She passed it to K.J., and he examined it before placing it behind his left ear. He reached in his sock to retrieve a cigar. Before Lanka could ask what he was doing, K.J. took the blunt from behind his ear and unraveled the paper to transfer the Kush into the cigar he gutted.*

"Why you do dat?" she asked with confusion in her voice. Lanka was in a trance watching him lick and roll a perfect blunt.

"Rule number two, neva smoke a blunt dat's already rolled." K.J. schooled her.

"And rule number one?" she asked in an innocent voice.

"Neva get high off ya own supply."

Lanka smacked her lips as she rolled her eyes at him. But later that night, she ended up at the game with a sore vagina and a silly grin on her face. Lanka and K.J. ended up being the hottest hood tale couple. He had been hooked since that day. Sweet memories!

K.J. missed his better half. When the two of them were around each other, he and Lanka always clashed. But at a time like this moment, he would give anything to get mushed by her mean behind. K.J. missed being a family. He missed his family with her.

Watching the officers do their turnover count, K.J.'s thoughts suddenly shifted, and his blood began to boil thinking back to the night of the party that brought him and Ridah to this situation in the first place. Capone had to be dealt with. Loc or not, he did not get a pass on snitching. So many emotions were going through K.J. at this moment that he felt he'd explode.

K.J. gained control of his emotions as he watched Dartez approach his personal area. He eyed him until he was six feet from his bed.

"What's good, cuz?" Dartez spoke.

"Can't call it," K.J. acknowledged. "I need to get a message and some cigarettes to Ridah."

"I got cha, cuz. Let me know when," Dartez said before licking his lips. "Aye though, remember what we rapped about a while back?"

K.J. sat up fully, giving Dartez his full attention. "Yeah. What about it?"

"I'm out this bitch in two weeks. You already know what time it is," Dartez said, looking K.J. dead in the eyes, letting him know how serious he was about getting some money.

K.J. nodded his head, not giving Dartez the response he was expecting. He did not become hopeful because of someone else's plans, though the determination in Dartez's eyes made K.J. dubious of him. At the end of the day, if he did not follow through on what he said, then it was no sweat off K.J.'s back.

"I'm happy for ya, cuz," K.J. said as he got the package ready for him to pass off to Ridah.

Dartez had always looked at K.J. as his role model. He wanted the respect that the living legend had. Who didn't? But if any of them were paying attention, they would have noticed that K.J. moved a certain way. He wasn't playing gangsta. He lived that life for real and wanted people to learn from his mishaps and be better than him. But most could not see past the OG status.

This was not one of those hood movies where everything was rehearsed. But in real life, once it was over, you could not go back and hit the reset button on life. Dartez still had a lot to learn. Sadly, he was going to have to make his own mistakes in order for him to get it.

Dartez was locked up for fraud, along with his baby momma. He was a true hustler who did almost everything to stack his money up the strong way. If it meant kicking in doors, laying people down, he did it with no remorse.

Dartez had a daughter and a family who depended on him. He could not let them down. Dartez figured if he could pull off the assignment K.J. gave him, his troubles would be over. And K.J. would put him down without any doubts about his abilities. Dartez would not have to be a petty crook anymore.

Ridah was sitting at the steel table that was chained to the floor, playing cards with Roxy. Toni was relaxing Ridah's nappy roots when Officer Adams called her name. Ridah pulled away from the table, curious to see what she wanted.

"Hurry back before you start burning," Toni said as if she really cared whether Ridah's scalp was damaged.

Ridah rolled her eyes and smacked her lips as she walked off. She knew Toni couldn't care less about her hair. When Ridah approached the officer, she gave her an unsure look before telling Ridah to follow her. Ridah knew right then it had something to do with K.J. She had been anxious ever since he sent word for Ridah to be on point when someone called for her. A skinny, tall light-skinned dude nearly scared Ridah to death when he stepped out from behind the wall. In his hand, he held a small box that was wrapped in a brown paper bag.

"He said trust nobody," he said before turning to the officer with a mischievous smile and slapping her ass. "Dat ass pokin'."

Ridah took that as her cue to leave. Besides, she needed to get the relaxer washed out of her head before it started sticking to her scalp. Walking down the hall, Ridah shook the box out of curiosity. There was no telling what K.J. had put in it. She hurried back to the open dorm, ready to tear the package open. Roxy and Toni were the first ones to break their necks trying to see what

Ridah was carrying. Ridah told them her attorney sent her the package to keep them out of her business.

The rest of the day went by slowly. Toni and Roxy were stuck to Ridah like a second skin. She didn't need them clocking her every move. Ridah tried waiting until lights out but knew everyone would be in her business then. So, she decided to wait for the right opportunity to make her move.

"Listen, y'all, I need to check out what my lawyer sent. I'ma get up with y'all in the morning," Ridah said truthfully so she could have a moment to herself.

She could tell Roxy and Toni were disappointed. They wanted to know what was in the box just as bad as Ridah did. After saying good night, Ridah climbed up on her bunk and sat Indian style as she ripped the box open. Opening the note, Ridah couldn't help but smile as she read K.J.'s words.

Ridah,
I'ma always keep it real with cha, no matter what. A lot of people crossing over, selling their souls and shit. But it's a lesson behind everything that has happened. I really hate you got caught up in this shit. It breaks my heart to think about you having a baby in here. Don't trust none of them bitches. I heard Toni's ass over there. Stay clear from dat ho. She is poisonous.
One love.

Ridah read K.J.'s letter again and folded it back up. When she finished counting out the money, Ridah tucked the money safely with the other contents he sent. Saying her prayers, Ridah drifted into a peaceful sleep.

CHAPTER TWENTY

At that time, many will fall away and will betray one another and hate one another.

—Matthew 24:10

Lanka sat quietly at the round table next to Fetticain while Big Al ranted and raved on the speakerphone. He was beyond livid after discovering that the highly trained Demya was murdered. Big Al and Demya's father were childhood friends until life stole their innocence. Now, he had to explain what happened to his daughter.

Demya's father was the man who ordered the blackout on Blu Foxx's family back in New York. However, Tina made a move none of them saw coming. The same night Blu Foxx was murdered, Tina took her kids and fled in the middle of the night after she received a phone call from the last person she wanted to hear from, Anita. As much as Tina blamed Anita for Blu Foxx's murder, she was thankful that she saved her and her daughters' lives and helped them move to Georgia.

Lanka hated to admit it, but she underestimated Ridah big time. Her latest stunt was a blow to Lanka's ego. Big Al gave them twenty-four hours to deal with the problem before he came from New York and dealt with it himself. Big Al secretly admired Ridah for lasting as long as she had, but it was time to carry out their botched job. The sooner they got rid of Blu Foxx's family, the sooner everyone could move without anyone putting pressure on him.

Fetticain stared at each person who was present in the eyes. He would have liked to believe that none of them would turn out to be treacherous, but in this line of business, he could not afford to take such a risk. You could not put anything past anyone. Fetticain clapped his hands together, which meant he wanted their undivided attention.

"If y'all ain't down with the shit Big Al talking about, I suggest you leave now," Fetticain warned as he flexed his jaw muscle. He waited for the weakest link to reveal itself.

A tall, slender mixed woman stood up. She looked Fetticain in his eyes before speaking. Fetticain had a way of communicating with his eyes at times. With that being said, she chose her words very carefully.

"Sir, with all due respect, I feel like I'm no longer needed. I'd like to decline my position." She spoke firmly.

While looking in her dull green eyes, Fetticain nodded his head, understanding. He placed one elbow on the marble table as he leaned forward.

"I respect ya thoughts, but I despise your weakness," he stated calmly as he slowly retrieved his gun from beneath the table.

One shot in the center of her head made the others jump, some gasping unexpectedly. The message was loud and clear. Lanka sat in his lap and kissed him as she played with his curly ponytail that she loved so much. Fetticain took his time looking each one of them in their eyes.

"Anybody else wanna leave?" When no one replied, he was gleeful with satisfaction. Grabbing Lanka's hips, he lifted her out of his lap to stand. He demanded, "Somebody clean this shit up!" Fetticain walked out the glass double doors with Lanka closely by his side.

Fetticain had met Lanka through K.J. years ago. They never talked in private. He saw Lanka rushing out of Logan's with a few of her coworkers, and Fetticain refused to pass up the opportunity to talk to her without K.J. around. Fetticain acted as if he did not notice her. He "accidentally" bumped into her, causing Lanka to stumble a little then go in defense mode. Fetticain threw both hands in the air.

"My bad!" Taking a step closer, he said, "Lanka, dat's you?" He acted like he didn't know who she was. The truth was that he would know Lanka and that walk of hers miles away in the pitch dark.

Lanka released a sigh. "Fetticain, I almost fucked your ass up! What you doing out this way?" Lanka looked around, almost suspecting a female close by with Fetticain.

He laughed with his hand still in the air. "I don't want no smoke. Nawl though. I thought I was about to grab something to grub on. But I see I'm a little too late."

Lanka shifted her weight to one leg. Looking around the parking lot again, she suddenly felt uncomfortable being out there at night with Fetticain. "Yeah, it's kinda late. We close at ten thirty."

Fetticain knew it was wrong to lust after Lanka due to his and K.J.'s history of them growing up together. But on the flip side, K.J. violated first when he slept with Demya. Fetticain felt that it was only right to repay him. In a way, Fetticain did not think Lanka would even chill with him due to her relationship with K.J. and her loyalty to him. What Fetticain did not know was that the well-known couple had problems already. He was stepping in at the right time.

"What cha in a rush to do?" Fetticain threw caution to the wind. He had made up his mind that he had to have

Lanka and would cross that bridge when the trouble came.

"It's New Year's Eve, boy. I'm tryin'a turn the fuck up! Wanna ride with me?" Lanka asked in a flirty way that made Fetticain's penis stand at attention.

Fetticain felt like she was staring into his soul. "Where we going?" he asked, returning the intense look she was giving him.

"Honestly, I don't care as long as I can turn up." She gave him a daring look as she pulled out her lip gloss to gloss her full lips.

Lanka allowed Fetticain to grab her small wrist and lead her to his black Charger. When he pulled up to a Red Roof Inn, Lanka gave him a devilish grin as she licked her glossy lips.

"So, we doing it like dat, huh?" She giggled. Lanka had been checking Fetticain out for a few years. So, she was with the trifling road he was on.

"Baby girl, stop fronting like you don't know what time it is. I know you been watching me watch you," Fetticain said, killing the engine.

"Oh, I never front. I was starting to wonder what was taking you so damn long to push up."

That was all Fetticain needed to hear before he pulled her in his muscular arms and kissed her like his life depended on it. Lanka let out a deep moan, and Fetticain picked her up and carried her to the room he had already rented.

Breaking their kiss, Lanka said, "If I didn't know any better, I'd think you had this whole thing planned." She pulled at his thick, curly ponytail.

Fetticain laughed. She didn't know how true her statement was. Instead of responding, he laid her on the bed, wrestling her black Dickies pants loose. When *he had complete access to her opening, he pushed her silk panties to the side and slid two fingers deep into her. Lanka arched her back as she rolled her hips slowly into his fingers.*

While his hand was busy, he used his other hand to undo his pants, which dropped to the floor. Fetticain took his ten-inch hard dick out of his briefs and teased Lanka's opening with the head of his mushroom-shaped penis. Lanka let out a loud moan, so Fetticain lowered his body on hers, kissing her. Lanka begged him to feed her his thick beef stick. Without further hesitation, Fetticain plugged himself deep inside her. They sexed hard, fast, slow, and until the New Year came in.

When morning came, so did reality. Lanka began to panic and cursed herself repeatedly for allowing Fetticain to enter her without using protection. Fetticain rolled her on top of him, sliding his penis inside her wet folds. Grabbing her hips, he made her sex him again until he exploded deep inside her. Shortly after, her whole body shook uncontrollably. Lanka jumped up off the bed and went to the bathroom and slammed the door. Fetticain lay back with a big smile plastered on his sweaty face. He silently prayed that Lanka would end up pregnant.

Fetticain smiled as he thought back to his and Lanka's first encounter. The outcome was that God had answered his prayer. He discovered Lanka was pregnant with his child, and he could not have been happier. Lanka begged Fetticain not to put their business out there, but his hate for K.J. ran too deep to listen.

Fetticain was Filipino and Black. People always told him that he looked like a dark version of Ryan from the reality show *Black Ink Chicago*. Women loved his curly jet-black hair, which he kept pulled back in a neat ponytail.

Fetticain could have had any woman he wanted, but he did not just want any woman. He wanted K.J.'s woman. He did not stop until he had Lanka. Beef sparked between Fetticain and K.J. after rumors emerged that he and Lanka were messing around. Lanka became afraid of things getting out of control and becoming deadly. She was left with no other choice but to tell her middle-school lover that the rumors he was hearing were true. She was carrying his former childhood friend's baby.

Lanka could never forget the look on K.J.'s face when he discovered her deceitfulness. K.J.'s look said everything he did not utter. Lanka was supposed to represent him and make men wish they had a woman as real as her. Instead, Lanka embarrassed him in the streets, and it took nearly a year for K.J. to come back around.

Fetticain became so comfortable with Lanka that he started pillow talking. Lanka took full advantage of the situation she put herself in. She began taking money out of Fetticain's offshore accounts and recording him bragging about murders he had ordered as well as had committed himself. When the time was right, Lanka was going to stand back and watch it all crumble. Fetticain was going to pay for all the destruction he had caused in her life.

Lanka killing Smirky and accidentally shooting K.J. made Fetticain feel like she was truly down for him. However, Lanka had her own reasons as to why she pulled the trigger on K.J., but Fetticain did not need to know that. She was tying up all her loose ends. When the time was right, Fetticain would get what was coming to him as well. While he was focused on getting revenge on K.J. and Ridah, Lanka was plotting on him and could not wait to see the look on Fetticain's face.

"Bae, I love you so much," Fetticain said, leaning in to kiss Lanka. "Where's my son?"

"He's asleep," Lanka replied with her arms around his neck. "Why don't we make another one?" She knew she could not have another child, thanks to Kyleena, but he did not need to know that.

CHAPTER TWENTY-ONE

Unexpected

Ridah stood at the phone, not believing what she was hearing on the other end. Someone had shot her twin. Ridah automatically felt that it was meant for her. She had not felt this helpless since their pops was murdered back in New York. Ridah's mind raced as thoughts of Lanka filled her mind, regretting not running up on Lanka.

"Nashanna, I don't know if that shot was meant for you or me. It could be your dad's past coming back to haunt me," Tina revealed. She was tired of keeping her troubles to herself. One thing Tina knew about her daughter was she was just like Blu Foxx. Bold. Impulsive. With that being said, Tina needed her daughter. Sadly, there was only so much Ridah could do behind bars.

Ridah began to worry about her mother's safety. For her to reveal something of her past, Ridah knew it was serious and that it bothered her. But she also knew this could be Lanka's doing since they had unsettled beef. It angered Ridah more than anything because Lanka waited until she was in jail to pull this stunt. Ridah was really entertaining the thought of telling K.J. everything. The only reason why she hesitated to tell him was for fear of him not believing a word she said.

"Momma, I'll call you back. Let me see what I can find out," Ridah said, still in deep thought.

"Okay, but please call me back," Tina stated in an uneasy voice.

"Aye, Momma."

"Yeah."

"Pops taught us to shoot first if anybody come your way. Better safe than sorry."

"I will."

Ridah hung up the phone and went downstairs to the main floor where the officers' booth was located. She needed to get a message to K.J. A storm was brewing, and Ridah could only hope it did not head her family's way. If so, she vowed to make it hail blood.

Ridah became paranoid when she noticed two females eyeing her. Because she did not know who was who, she wasn't taking any chances with anyone getting in touching distance.

"What's up?" Ridah asked in an aggressive tone.

One of the females took a step back while the other one stood her ground, watching Ridah in suspense, welcoming a challenge. Before any words could be exchanged, a guard approached them. Ridah never took her eyes off the female to acknowledge the guard's presence.

"Y'all get out of here!" the guard demanded. Once the females were gone, she focused on Ridah. "What's wrong?" She made the mistake of reaching out to Ridah in a comforting way.

Ridah stepped out of her reach. "Tell K.J. I need to holla at him." Ridah did not want to sound needy but could not help it. K.J. knew all the right words to say to put her back in focus. The guard nodded her head as she walked off.

Before climbing the steps, Ridah glanced in the direction the females were standing. She decided to approach them. The worst that could happen was them jumping on her. They quietly watched with caution-filled eyes as Ridah approached them.

"Is there a reason why y'all keep jockin' me?" Ridah asked as she stood back on one of her legs, crossing her arms.

The heavyset female cut her eyes over at the other female, who nodded her head as if to say, "Speak."

"Let's get something understood. Ain't nobody jocking ya ass!" she snapped before getting to why they were standing there in the first place. "K.J.'s baby momma in cahoots with the people dat's after ya momma."

Ridah dropped the attitude to get the information. She knew her mother's worst fear had come true. Whoever was responsible for her pops's murder had resurfaced to settle the final score. What she didn't see coming was Lanka being tied into all of this.

"Do you know who shot my sister?"

The heavyset female looked at the other female again as if to say, "Speak."

"K.J. baby momma."

"I'm sorry. You mean Fetticain baby momma," Ridah couldn't help but say.

"Funny. She's sayin' Smirky is yours," the female said matter-of-factly.

"What?" Ridah heard exactly what she said with widened eyes. How did these females know her business? Ridah realized right then and there that she was no better than Lanka. Lanka may have slept with the best friend, but Ridah slept with K.J.'s first cousin. Closing her eyes, Ridah wished like hell her child would turn out to be K.J.'s. Wishful thinking. Ridah gripped the rail, suddenly feeling dizzy from the thoughts alone.

As if reading Ridah's mind, she said, "Smirky used to tell Lanka everything. She's the one putting it out there in the streets."

Ridah lowered her eyes while in her thoughts. If Smirky were alive, she would kill him right now. She could not believe he would tell Lanka, of all people, their business. Ridah looked up at the ceiling and shook her head like she was shaking it at Smirky.

"You gotta be fuckin' kiddin' me." That was something she wasn't expecting to hear.

Ridah felt an instant headache due to the stress from all the drama unfolding around her. With her sister lying up in the hospital, along with Blu Foxx's killers coming for her family, and Lanka spreading rumors, Ridah felt like she was about to explode. Although she didn't know these females, she took heed to what they were telling her. Some things couldn't be made up, especially when it was too close to the truth.

"Who sent y'all?" She was dying to know.

"Darius. She's been in the background lookin' out for your momma."

If this was true, Ridah needed to call her mother back and convince her to leave the house while she still could. She couldn't believe Blu Foxx's enemies waited six long years to come to Georgia for them. Her mother, Tina, wasn't built like her, but Ridah knew someone who was. Although her mother would kill Ridah if she knew who she had planned on calling, she didn't have any other options. She had to protect her mother.

As night fell, Ridah's family weighed heavily on her mind. Her only hope was that her homies would ride with her up against these uptown gangstas. Sighing loudly, Ridah turned over to lie on her side, caressing her swollen stomach, and her mind shifted. Ridah was afraid to bring a baby into this cruel world.

Ridah couldn't help but wonder if there was a God in the ghetto, or should she say turf? That was what everyone was fighting over these days. Sirens woke you up in the middle of the night as thoughts of who was killed this time invaded many peoples' heads. It was sad when little children were caught up in the madness and died young. It was a shame, but reality was that when you came from where Ridah was from, it was hard to stay alive.

It was nothing to see fiends walking up and down the streets for a hit, and worse than that, some were selling their own children just to catch that high, which didn't last long. Walking over chalk lines, the smell of gun smoke was so thick it choked you. That was Ridah's world, yet when things hit close to home, she often wondered if she could walk away and let it all go without looking back. That was something Ridah still hadn't been able to decide.

Feeling a light tap on her shoulder caused Ridah to jump up. Frowning, she didn't even realize she had fallen to sleep. Ridah wiped the sweat from under her chin then noticed the guard had a small package in her hands.

"Sorry to hear about your sister. If she's anything like you, she's going to pull through." Passing Ridah the package, she added, "Well, I won't be here for a few weeks."

Ridah could not resist her response, which was filled with hurt. "Dat's the point. Prissy ain't nothing like me."

The guard didn't reply. She wanted to do something that would lift Ridah's spirits. She rushed off without a word, and Ridah frowned, confused by her sudden action. She shook her head and lay back down, attempting to get comfortable. As she was drifting off to sleep, she felt someone standing over her. Ridah opened her eyes to find the guard signaling her to follow her. The urgency in her eyes alerted Ridah to move quietly and quickly. There wasn't any time for questioning.

Ridah's feet lightly smacked the cold, waxed concrete floor. Turning the corner, she stopped short at the sight of K.J. She broke out running toward him and burst into tears as she fell in his arms. He allowed her to cry as he rocked and held her tightly. Neither one said a word. K.J. was her comforter, the one who protected her from the world. At least he tried to. Within thirty minutes, Ridah filled him in on everything that had been going on, including the females downstairs. He told her not to worry and to stay focused.

"We abouta be shipped off to prison soon, Ridah." He looked her in her big, round brown eyes and prayed she would see that he was sincere. "I'ma make sure the attorney get you back in court. I can't have you giving birth to that baby behind these walls. Not if I can help it."

K.J. blamed himself for Ridah's mishap. If he had not invited her to the party that night, she probably wouldn't have gone. Ridah was in this situation because of him. It was only right to do everything in his power to get Ridah off those charges. Although K.J. wasn't guilty of the crime he had been accused of, he'd do the time without a single complaint. He would never roll over on Capone or any other person who went against him.

K.J. talked to one of his many homies who kept his ear to the streets. Dartez knew everything that went on in the hood thanks to his li'l homie, who wanted to impress him in hopes of Dartez putting in a good word for him. What Dartez didn't know was where Capone was being held. If Dartez could pull off the perfect murder, K.J. would put him where he needed and wanted to be.

But his next task would be even more difficult. Finding Fetticain. The streets were talking loudly. Lanka was messing around with Fetticain again. If that was true, K.J. had plans for her, too. He could forgive a lot of things, but disloyalty was the one thing that was unforgivable.

K.J. looked down at Ridah and placed a kiss on her forehead. Pulling away caused Ridah to grip his arm tightly. "Please don't leave me," Ridah said in a desperate voice. K.J. pulled his arm from her and walked away as if she had not uttered a single word.

The guard placed a hand on Ridah's shoulder, trying to comfort her and get her to calm down. The last thing she needed was for another officer to catch her with this inmate. She could not explain her reasons for having a female inmate in the male wing after hours.

"We have to go, sweetie." The guard put a hand on Ridah's back and gently pushed her back in the direction they came from.

Out of frustration, Ridah jerked her body away from the guard and rushed down the hall. The guard cursed silently as she trailed behind Ridah. She understood Ridah's frustration, but she was taking risks by trying to help her. If Ridah was going to be a problem, she vowed not to help her again.

Chow call was at four thirty in the morning. Ridah was still awake. She had tossed and turned through the night. So much was going through Ridah's mind. She felt as if her head would explode from the pressure. After saying a prayer that her mother taught her and her sister, Ridah finally began to drift into a peaceful sleep.

"Ridah, wake up. The stories are about to come on," Roxy yelled in Ridah's ear.

Frowning, Ridah mumbled, "I'm tired." Then, she turned over and put the covers over her head.

Moments after Roxy walked off, Toni went to Ridah's bunk. Toni had the nerve to ease her sticky fingers in Ridah's food box and pull out oatmeal pies and a Twix. Toni shoved the items in her panties, then hurried off. Toni made eye contact with Roxy, who rolled her eyes and looked over at Ridah's bunk.

"Hell nawl," Roxy mumbled to herself.

Roxy did not like the idea of being around Toni, but she tolerated the move. Ridah may have let her guard down, but Roxy didn't trust Toni at all. She wouldn't dare allow someone like Toni to get close to her, especially after all that had gone down between them. If Ridah couldn't see what Toni was up to, then she deserved whatever Toni had for her. Roxy shook her head. Ridah was really slipping.

Ridah sighed as she sat up to get herself together. After gathering up her dirty clothes, Ridah called her helper, Toni. Ridah gave her $10 a week on GP so Toni could have the things she needed.

"Have you eaten yet?" Ridah asked as she was putting lotion on her face. Ridah wanted to call Toni out on what she saw her take but decided to keep it to herself.

"Nawl. You must be hungry," Toni said.

"Yeah. Ask Roxy if she's eating." Ridah left Toni at her food box purposely and told her to get whatever she needed. Toni didn't realize Ridah was setting her up. Ridah couldn't believe Toni would take from her because she was the one who had been helping her.

"All right." Toni hated the fact that Roxy was eating with them. She had to come up with a plan to turn Ridah against Roxy.

A lot of the same stuff that went on in the streets went on in jail. Ridah had listened to so many females bragging about niggas buying them this and that. Everybody had the same storyline. You could be all you wanted behind the walls until someone called you out and revealed what you were really living like out there.

On the streets, every female and nigga swore they were slick and had game. It was the same behind the wall. It was funny because everybody was trying to fool the next person by running a game when the truth was that, on the street, those same ones who were boasting didn't have a bar of soap to wash their behind with. You could tell the real from the fake just like you could tell the strong from the weak.

K.J. and Ridah's situation was different for some odd reason. Now that he was forced to sit still, he had gotten the proper chance to get to know Ridah on a more personal level. But that was what happened when you were deep in the streets. It didn't allow you the time to really get to know anyone. K.J. disliked the fact that she was pregnant, but because she didn't fold under pressure, he was going to make sure she was good, and their communication was sealed.

There were two parts K.J. elevated carefully. One part came from the soul while the other came from the heart. Getting someone's heart only meant that a person loved you in mind and thought. But when you got love from the soul, that person was every essence of you, and you were on another height, seeing things differently. Although K.J. wasn't there with Ridah yet, he was willing to attempt to give her the best of both sides of a gangsta and help her raise the child she was carrying.

Ridah and Lanka were alike in so many ways that it scared K.J. Sometimes, he asked himself if he was feeling Ridah because she reminded him of Lanka from back in the day or because of who she was. If it weren't for them being locked up, K.J. didn't think he would have ever had the proper time to get to know Ridah.

Despite everything Ridah had been through, she still stood strong, even when times were tough for her. She had survived tougher times. In K.J.'s eyes, Ridah was that down chick every gangsta dreamed of and wanted to have ride by his side. Ridah was slick and could be cold when she wanted and needed to be. But K.J. "overstood" and dug all of that. That was what added to the love K.J. had at heart for Ridah. He saw how she rode with someone she had only heard of but never knew on a personal level until now.

Lanka was the only one with whom K.J. had that "grow old with you" kind of love. The little slick move Lanka allowed to happen between her and Fetticain folded a lot of K.J.'s feelings and emotions up. He felt like his gangsta was tested, and in his eyes, that was what females did to lames and suckers. K.J. was neither. Lanka carrying another man's seed didn't hurt his feelings. Truth was that the situation messed with K.J.'s pride more than anything. Now, he was extending feelings to Ridah and felt like he was starting to slip, and that was the last thing he needed right now.

K.J. picked up the phone to make some calls to his homies on Poppy Avenue. When Dartez bonded out, it took him a minute, but K.J. was impressed with how quickly he found Capone. He really thought the State was going to protect him. There wasn't a doubt in K.J.'s mind that Dartez was going to push Capone's top back as soon as the opportunity presented itself. K.J. knew how badly Dartez wanted to be a part of his movement. Dartez had something to prove.

CHAPTER TWENTY-TWO

But the way of the wicked is like total darkness. They have no idea what they are stumbling over.

—Proverbs 4:19

When Ridah heard the officer call her name, she cursed. "This is the good part," she said as she jumped up from the TV.

"Want me to hold your seat?" Toni asked like she really cared if Ridah's seat was taken.

Roxy sucked her teeth. She was fed up with Toni's ass kissing.

"We all know if someone takes her seat, you'll give yours up." Roxy smirked as she watched Toni's face turn red as beets.

Roxy knew exactly what she was doing. She had been waiting for this day. Ridah always talked her out of beating Toni's ass, but today was the day. Ridah was not there to stop her this time. Toni thought she could pull wool over everyone's eyes but not Roxy. Roxy closed the distance between her and Toni, putting her finger in Toni's face. The time had come to handle Ms. Toni, and Ridah could not stop what was destined to happen.

"Li'l girl, fuck all dat barking. Bitch, bite." Roxy wasn't backing down. Period.

"Get cha hand outta my face," Toni warned as she prepared herself to swing if needed.

Toni may have fallen off since Chase's death, but she would fight anyone who got in her way. And Roxy was in her way! Toni wanted people to sleep on her, especially Ridah, because when the time came to settle the score, Toni was going to win. She was going to get at Ridah for taking the love of her life. Toni could not wait to see their shocked faces. She vowed no one would be walking away from the situation but her.

"Fuck your face, li'l girl. I'm abouta get in yo' ass," Roxy threatened, now face-to-face with Toni.

Toni took a step back when Roxy entered her personal space. She was not stupid. If she fought Roxy, she could risk building a relationship with Ridah and would have to come up with another plan. Weighing her options quickly, Toni realized getting payback was way more important to her than anything at this point.

Looking Roxy in her aged eyes, Toni said, smirking, "I got you another time, Roxy." She slapped Roxy's hand out of her face.

Before backing down, Roxy let Toni know that she was only sparing her because of Ridah. Roxy sat back down and continued watching TV as if nothing had happened. She was from the streets, so she should have known better than to turn her back on Toni. Roxy's biggest mistake.

Ridah went through the double doors into a cold, small room with a stainless-steel table and stool. The guard advised her that her attorney would be in shortly. All kinds of thoughts were flooding through Ridah's mind while her eyes roamed the small room. Tapping her nails against the steel table, she couldn't help but wonder if she would somehow get out of this situation she was currently in.

"Damn. Where's this lawyer?" Ridah thought out loud. Minutes later, a tall, heavyset middle-aged Black man entered the room. Pushing his wireframe glasses to the bridge of his nose, he introduced himself.

"Good afternoon, Ms. Gier. I'm Brent Sims." Extending his hand, he took a seat across from her.

"Nice to meet you, Mr. Sims," Ridah said as she looked him over. Clasping her hands together, she began firing questions at him.

Although Ridah was innocent of what she was being accused of, they still had to prove it. When Mr. Sims answered every question carefully, he in turn told Ridah what to expect when she went back to court. He also shared with her that she had been railroaded, which was mostly the result when having a court-appointed lawyer.

There were so many things that went on in her case that were not addressed, along with many loopholes and errors. Mr. Sims promised Ridah a lesser sentence if not acquittal. He went over his notes with Ridah again, making sure he did not leave anything out. When he had everything together, Mr. Sims informed Ridah that he would keep her posted and would come back soon.

Ridah walked back down the hall, overwhelmed with thoughts of a possible second chance at life. She hated the thought of giving birth to her baby behind bars. Honestly, Ridah could not say she would do right if granted a second chance at freedom.

The reality of being loyal to her set hindered her. Ridah took the oath, so it was a must that she follow through with everything her set required of her. Ridah battled within often. There was a part of her resisting the bad and seeking and wanting to do good. Deep down, Ridah knew she would not have made it this far if it were not for the prayers her mother had been sending up to God. She would not have made it through the worst if it were not for God and the prayers.

Ridah wiped her face with the back of her hand and attempted to appear normal. The last thing she wanted was for anyone to be in her business and to appear weak. Ridah forced a smile on her face as if nothing happened. When she entered the open dorm, she could feel the tension in the air. After first locking eyes with one of the inmates, Ridah's eyes quickly followed in the direction the woman nodded her head in.

"Better hurry. Roxy's gonna kill dat girl!" she stated in a raspy voice.

"Nobody didn't try to break it up?" Ridah asked while irritation covered her face. "If it ain't one thing, it's another," she mumbled. Ridah could not enjoy the good news she received because of their foolishness.

A disgusting smell hit Ridah's face as soon as she entered the filthy restroom. Roxy was covered with feces while she was holding the back of Toni's head down in the toilet. Ridah took a step forward, yelling for her to let Toni up, while Toni's arms swung weakly. Ridah feared Roxy would catch another case, a murder case. The only thing she could do was grab Roxy, which was not an easy task being that Roxy was five foot ten and 200 pounds compared to Ridah's five-foot-five, 117-pound frame. Ridah was not a match for Roxy's rage. Besides, Ridah did not want to put her growing baby in any more danger than she already had.

Ridah stepped out of the restroom area, back into the open dorm, and shouted she would give someone $20 if they got Roxy off of Toni. Ridah stepped to the side of the doorway as the women raced in for a lousy $20. Everyone watched as three women tried desperately to pull Roxy off Toni.

Roxy sent a nasty elbow to the closest one, causing her to crash to the floor with a sick thud. While everyone else laughed, another inmate stormed over to Roxy.

She jumped on Roxy's back like a cat and put her in the chokehold. Roxy quickly released Toni and began to claw at the arms of her attacker until Ridah told her to let Roxy go.

Ridah asked the same three women to help Toni as Roxy leaned against the gray tile wall, still breathing heavily with her eyes closed. Ridah's eyes roamed over Roxy's cotton shirt again and realized she had two stab wounds Toni had inflicted.

"Roxy," Ridah exhaled in a now panicked voice. "If we don't get to the guard, she may die," Ridah yelled in fear. The last thing she needed was another death near her. She was already in a messed-up predicament. This situation would surely taint her character to her peers. Maybe she was being paranoid, but Ridah was not taking any chances.

Roxy slid down the wall, tripping Ridah in the process, sending her down to the cold, nasty tile floor. As Roxy gasped for air, Ridah was forced back into her dark past.

Ridah, Smirky, Bagz, and Petey jumped out the window of their foster home at about two something in the morning. Petey had been scoping out an older white man's house for about a week now and was anxious to see what he and his gang could get their hands on. Dressed in all black, the foursome hit Pansy Avenue, pulling down their masks to conceal their identities all while creeping through the morning dew. Ridah was on the lookout as Smirky worked the alarm system.

Once Smirky broke the code, Bagz rushed into the dark house first with Petey backing the rear. A gunshot chipping a picture frame inches from Smirky's head made their bodies stiffen. Recovering quickly, Ridah gripped her .380, aimed into the darkness, and dislodged two shots, sending a figure rolling down the stairs. Smirky shoveled his Timberland boot deep in the crease of the man's neck and asked where the safe was but received no answer.

The man knew his intruders were going to kill him whether he gave them what they wanted or not. Petey was too amped up, thanks to the powder substance he fed his greedy nostrils. He kicked the man in the side of his head so hard that his neck cracked. The wounded man rocked side to side in excruciating pain. The crew was so caught up that they never noticed another figure standing by the rail with a rifle aiming their way.

"Leave my papa alone." shouted a frightened female voice, causing them to jump.

Petey frowned. "Aye, bitch, I got something for yo' li'l ass!" Before he could climb another step, he was cut off by a single bullet ripping through his throat.

Ridah squatted to aid Petey's wound while Smirky and Bagz focused on shooting at the girl, who took off running. It was an unforgettable sight to see. The more Petey gasped, the more blood gushed out of his throat. Ridah's eyes filled with tears. She held his head close to her stomach, rocking him against her.

Ridah would never forget the sound of death taking over Petey's body. The two knew what was about to happen, and it pained her that there wasn't anything she could do to prevent his death. Smirky wasted no time knocking the teenage girl unconscious once she gave him the combination to her grandfather's safe.

As quickly as they crept in, the three crept out, leaving empty-handed and without their homie. Smirky was so heated that the girl played him that he went and put three bullets into her face. Bagz had to pull Smirky from the girl's body before they all ended up in jail.

As Ridah thought back to the unfortunate night, her heart filled with regret and shame. Who would have expected the young girl to give false information about the safe code? Petey's death was in vain. From that day forward, the three all vowed to protect each other at any cost.

All the commotion brought Ridah back to the present. Officers were shouting for the inmates to move out of the way as they entered the restroom. Ridah stepped back against the wall with her eyes locked on Roxy's bloody body.

"Who did this?" a male guard asked while putting on his black leather gloves.

Ridah looked him square in his eyes and told him she entered the restroom only moments before they arrived. If he wanted to put pressure on her, she, in turn, would use her attorney visit as her alibi. The officer told Ridah and the others that he'd need statements from everyone who was in the restroom. Ridah didn't plan to cooperate. After Roxy's body was removed, everyone drifted into their own thoughts. Some went on as if nothing had happened at all.

CHAPTER TWENTY-THREE

Doing wrong is fun for a fool but living wisely brings pleasure to the sensible.

—Proverbs 10:23

While shooting dice with a local Crip named Big Iron, K.J. heard a guard call his name.

"Yeah!" he answered, eyes still on the crap game.

The badly shaped guard walked up on them and kicked the jail-made dice out of Big Iron's hand. He then bent over to snatch up the money, only to pocket it. K.J. stood up, and the others followed suit.

Leaning in close to K.J., the guard asked, "We got a problem, boy?"

"Fat boy, seems to me you the one with the problem." K.J. stared the bumpy-faced man in the eyes, which were filled with hate.

A few of the inmates chuckled. Some went as far as to make it known they didn't care for the guard. One decided to sneak the guard since he was on their wing by himself. The attack only made him angry as he grabbed his club to swing it with force. Someone caught it in mid-air and snatched it from him, turning his own weapon against him.

After minutes of kicking, punching, and beating with the club, not wanting them to overdo it, K.J.

put his hand in the air, signaling them to stop. The heavy-breathing and now sweat-covered men fell back, leaving the guard bloody and barely breathing. K.J. bent down to retrieve his money. He also took the guard's license to memorize his address, which would save a lot of them in the near future.

Everyone started wiping down anything that appeared like it could be a crime scene while K.J. and a few of his homies picked the unconscious guard up and took him to another wing where Bloods were housed.

Ridah jumped out of her sleep from guards yelling at one o'clock in the morning. Still half asleep, her mind wasn't registering what they were yelling. Her late response caused Ms. Watkins to pepper spray her. Ridah screamed and cursed while wiping her face. Watkins grabbed the back of Ridah's neck and sent her to the floor. The minute she hit the floor, Ridah knew something was wrong. Ridah felt a sharp pain as her blood spilled onto the infested floor.

Ridah's hand quickly covered her stomach. She repeatedly yelled, "My baby!"

Officer Watkins quickly replaced her snooty expression with a fearful look after noticing the yellow band on Ridah's wrist for the first time. She knew she had made a terrible mistake.

"I'm so sor—"

Before Officer Watkins could finish her apology, Ridah had connected with her jaw. There was so much blood on the floor that three officers had slipped and fallen in an attempt to separate Ridah from the officer. Another officer noticed the large amount of blood coming from Ridah, and he immediately got on his radio to call medical.

Ridah felt herself getting weak as she fought to breathe through the pepper spray. Two nurses came to aid Ridah to walk with them. She waved them off as she limped toward the doorway, collapsing before making it in the hallway. Everything around Ridah was muffled. She floated unwillingly as her pain began to fade.

Two weeks had passed since K.J. learned of the loss of Ridah's child. He was informed that the officer who was responsible was on leave until further notice, but that wasn't enough for him. She needed to feel the pain Ridah was experiencing. The county jail knew they had messed up big time, and K.J. was going to get the best lawyer money could buy to sue the hell out of them.

It was time to test those who claimed realism. K.J. was ready to set things in motion and see just how real his homies were. There was a known saying that said, "Only time will tell." Well, the time was right now.

After the operator informed him to proceed, Cigar spoke in a gangsta tone. "What crackin', cuz?"

"Shid, I can't call it, cuz." K.J. knew he had to choose his words carefully due to their call being monitored and recorded. "Man, y'all heard what happened to my li'l folks, right?"

"Oh, yeah. Shit fucked up. It was on the news and shit." Cigar was already thinking of a way to make the officer pay. It was funny how this officer just so happened to be the same officer that treated him like crap almost a year ago.

On the day Cigar was to make an appearance in court, he woke up, tied to the bedpost, with a big fan blowing loudly on him. He cursed himself for trusting his first baby's mother, Jill. She would rather see him in jail than with his other baby's mother, Peaches. She made sure that happened after making Cigar miss his court date when she filed child support.

Officer Watkins booked him that afternoon. She tried to clown Cigar in front of her coworkers without knowing who he was. After Cigar made bond, K.J. made Cigar give him his word not to bring any harm to the rookie officer. Cigar frowned at the thought of the hot-breath officer. He knew he should have deaded her back then. If he had, there wouldn't be a problem right now. Cigar couldn't wait to see the look on Watkins's face tonight when he pulled up on her. Cigar smiled as he thought, *it's finally time to pay the piper, bitch!*

"Send my love to shawty. Tell her everything gonna be all right."

"I will." K.J. sighed, hanging up the phone. K.J. felt the pressure of the world pushing down on his shoulders. Dark clouds seemed to only be in his world followed by a series of storms rushing his way.

Word on the street was that Dartez was jumping and pulling out on any- and everyone to feed his new drug addiction, meth. K.J. knew Dartez wasn't built like he claimed. Dartez capped too much to be anything other than what he claimed. K.J. only had a few niggas who pledged and stood on their shit without question, homies he could always count on.

Lying down, K.J. reread a letter from Ridah.

K.J.,
Thanks for everything. I love you. Nothing could ever change dat but us. Lately, I have been reading

my Bible, tryin'a find out who God really is, and if He is as they say He is, then He needs to give me some understanding because I have none. I just have been in my head a lot. But anyway, please stay out of trouble and holla at God sometimes.

Always yours,
Ridah

CHAPTER TWENTY-FOUR

A scoffer seeks wisdom and finds none, but knowledge is easy to one who has understanding.

—Proverbs 14:6

Ridah finished up reading Psalms 56. Closing the Bible, she sighed. She was searching for something but did not know what she was looking for. Ridah often felt like no one understood how hard it was to mask her daily inner struggles. It had become harder to battle her demons each moment that passed. Neither her homies nor her mother could help her.

This was something she had to face on her own. Sadly, it took being behind bars to realize this was not what she wanted people to view her as. There was more to Ridah than banging, and she wanted her peers to see that. She wanted to help save the youth, but how could she save anyone when she was disturbed within and could not save herself in her darkest moment? Ridah had a long road to evolving, and though she looked forward to making that step toward change, a small part of her felt that she wouldn't make it.

Toni was telling Ridah about her cousin, who was in prison, when four officers entered the open dorm with urgency. Everyone seemed to tense up waiting on whatever it was that was about to unfold. It was only a matter of time until someone spilled their guts about what happened in the restroom when Roxy was stabbed multiple times. Some were surprised it took as long as it did to rat Toni out.

When the guards approached Toni, she stood up slowly with her hands lifted in surrender. She may have been crazy, but she was not stupid enough to pull a move. The slightest sign of aggression in her body language could put her in a messed-up situation. That was the last thing she needed, so she bowed gracefully.

"All right, Ridah. Nice knowing ya," Toni stated oddly.

Ridah only nodded her head as she and others watched the guards escort Toni away. Later, the captain made his rounds to inform them that Roxy was out of the danger zone and must now wear a colostomy bag. Everyone started clapping and was relieved of the rumors of Roxy being dead.

Ridah sent Toni items to lockdown every week until she was shipped off to prison to begin serving her sentence. Some nights, Ridah tossed and turned as the number of years echoed in her head. No matter how hard Ridah acted, in the moment of truth, she feared what was beyond those prison gates.

K.J. leaned into the Plexiglas window. What he was staring at caused his blood to boil. If Lanka did not have the evidence, K.J. would not have believed it. There was nothing worse than the feeling of betrayal, especially by someone you loved. Lanka laid the pictures of Ridah and Smirky having sex on the table. K.J. wanted to kick his own behind for thinking Ridah was any different from the other women he had encountered, especially Lanka.

If no one else knew, Ridah knew how he felt when it came to betrayal. She knew what he went through with

Lanka and Fetticain, and for her to turn around and do the same thing, he felt disrespected. K.J. could not help but wonder if the child Ridah carried was Smirky's. All he could do for now was wonder.

"All these young hoes wanna be able to say they fucked you. Ridah ain't no different from the rest. She tryin'a come between us because she already knew what we went through," Lanka stressed.

It took everything in Lanka to keep a straight face. She was hurt to know that Ridah's actions bothered him so much but knew right then that K.J. loved Ridah. The thought ate her up like acid and made her want to speed up on her plans to end Ridah once and for all.

"We may go through shit, but at the end of the day, I'm in the storm with you. We always got through it together, and we always will." Lanka smiled, thinking, *checkmate, bitch!*

One thing Lanka knew about K.J. was that when someone crossed him, there was no coming back. He had not invested the time in Ridah to work through it as she and K.J. had. Lanka knew he was going to cut all ties with Ridah now. He knew the truth. In her mind, once Ridah was out of the way, he could focus on them being a family again.

After Lanka made her last chess moves, she would call it even. One thing she'd take to her grave was being involved with the shooting of him and Smirky. Fetticain was the one behind the wheel of the Impala that pulled the trigger on K.J. the day she killed Smirky. Lanka hated that she had to kill him, but she couldn't take the chance of Smirky calling her out on being behind Kia's murder and Ridah's kidnapping. Besides, he killed Demya, so either way, Smirky had to go.

K.J. looked at Lanka. He did not feel the same energy he used to from her, but he shook it off as he was tripping.

"So, you ridin' with me or what?" He knew that he was blessed to have Lanka. No matter what had happened between them, they would always have each other's back. No matter what.

Lanka frowned, not believing he would fix his mouth to even question her loyalty. "'Til the end of time, bae!"

"Dat's all I need to hear," he said, still deep in thought.

Lanka blew three kisses as she stood to leave. She had to hurry up and tie up her loose ends before her secrets started reaching the surface, exposing things she worked hard to keep hidden.

While Ridah was getting ready for the shower, her name was called for mail. She threw on the gray shorts and a towel around her neck to cover her breasts. Rushing out in the hall, then down the steps, Ridah could not contain her smile when she saw K.J.'s handwriting also along with Darius's. She knew if no one else kept it real, those two always would.

Before she could turn, the officer told her she had legal mail, which she had to sign for. She tore into the first one and began looking over the contents. There was a handwritten statement with Capone's name and signature. Capone had been a CI (cooperating informant) for almost a decade. Ridah walked back to the door, waiting for the officer to pop it. She leaned against the wall as she thought back to the first sign of Capone's griminess. How could she not see it back then? Capone had always been for himself.

CHAPTER TWENTY-FIVE

Faithful are the wounds of a friend, but the kisses of an enemy are deceitful.

—Proverbs 27:6

Fetticain leaned against the edge of the oak-wood desk as Toni sucked his penis like it was her favorite-flavored lollipop. Glancing down through low eyes at her, he inhaled the thick smoke. Visions of Lanka invaded his mind as he leaned his head back and pumped in and out of Toni's mouth with a vicious pace until she caught all his throat babies.

Toni moaned, looking up at Fetticain with lustful eyes. "Daddy, you like—" Toni was cut off by Fetticain shoving his enlarged dick down her throat, causing her to gag. He held up his index finger to his lips, silencing Toni. She stopped like an obedient child until further notice.

Fetticain hit the speaker button anxiously to see what was so important to interrupt his sex session. "Speak to me." He looked down at Toni, who was still on her knees, waiting for directions. When Fetticain pointed to his penis, Toni quickly grabbed it and greedily took him in her warm, wet mouth. Just as Fetticain's body began to relax, his body stiffened as his secretary informed him of his visitor. Fetticain pushed Toni's head, causing her to fall flat on her butt. He pointed at the door, and Toni took the hint and dismissed herself. Since Chase had been gone, he was now her sole provider, so she felt like she had to accept the abuse Fetticain dished out.

Once the office door was shut, he adjusted his pants and sat back into the soft cream leather chair. Fetticain knew just who his visitor was, so he grinned wickedly before telling his secretary to send the visitor in. Anita entered his office seconds later, speaking in silence by nodding her head. Her nervousness showed by her fidgeting, which Fetticain noticed with a tight smirk.

It was a struggle for Fetticain to hide his disgust, yet he did not attempt to do so. Although he was known for preying on the weak, Fetticain despised a weak-minded person. If someone would bend easily for him, he knew they would do it for the next, and Fetticain was not willing to put himself in a position for it to come back and bite him in the butt.

While Anita was sleeping around with Blu Foxx, she was also having an affair with Big Al, Fetticain's father, for years. When Fetticain first discovered their affair, there was not a day that went by that young Fetticain did not show his hate for Anita. Now as an adult, he felt it was right to cause destruction in her world as she caused within his family over the years. It was an honor for him to watch Anita destroy herself and the ones dear to her. Fetticain smiled sadly as he took his feet off his desk and offered her a seat. Fetticain was his father's most evil son. She hated that she ever had any dealings with Big Al and his dysfunctional family.

Anita wasted no time getting to the reason why she was there. "I've done what you asked of me. I also turned the guns in this morning with K.J.'s fingerprints." Anita tightened her lips and braced herself for Fetticain's wrath after her next sentence. "Tina has gone in hiding." She knew Fetticain was not going to take this news well, and honestly, she couldn't care less. Anita was ready to cut all ties from Big Al and Fetticain.

Fetticain slammed his fist down on the desk in frustration. "Fuck! Big Al ain't gonna wanna hear this shit!" He clenched his teeth tightly.

"Her daughter, Ridah, has come into a lawsuit. The attorney representing her is damn good. It's possible that she'll beat those charges," Anita said, holding back a smirk that was creeping up on her face.

Anita had witnessed firsthand Fetticain unraveling at the mention of Ridah's name. Even though he had never met Ridah, Anita knew she got under his skin, and his obsession would cost him greatly in the future. When it did, Anita would be right there to watch it all unfold.

Fetticain slammed his fist hard on the wooden desk again. If Lanka were in his presence right then, he would probably kill her. She had slipped, and her slip-up could cost him big time. Fetticain was not willing to gamble his life, not for Lanka or anyone else. Looking Anita in her aged eyes, he began to wonder what his father ever saw in her. One thing Fetticain despised was weakness, and not only was Anita weak, but she was also blinded by love, just like Toni.

Anita feared him discovering she had tipped Tina off. She had to correct her wrongs from all those years ago. She was so blinded back then that when Big Al reached out for her to track Tina's family down, she did not realize the danger she led to Tina's doorstep until it was too late. All Anita knew was Blu Foxx had broken her heart and run off with Tina. Thanks to her own digging around, Anita discovered that Big Al had something to do with Blu Foxx being killed years ago. With this news, she had to be extra careful and as calculating as Fetticain.

While Anita thought she was not a step ahead, Fetticain had a few tricks of his own. If Anita was not too far in her own head, she would have known that judgment day for her had arrived today. Fetticain slid the paperwork over to her. Anita's eyes began to fill with tears as she glanced down at the consent form she promised to sign.

Fetticain did not care if she was Lanka's aunt. He did not want her in his son's life. The agreement was that after she wrote the suicide note, she would take the million dollars he offered her and leave town. If she was ever seen around Macon again, it would cost her her life.

After she signed the paper, he smiled. "Anita, your slate has been wiped clean."

Standing up, Anita dabbed at her tears. She was relieved that Fetticain did not have the first clue about her tipping Tina off about Big Al. "I better go pack my things. Have a great day." Anita's only concern was getting as far away from Fetticain as possible.

Holding up his hand, Fetticain said, "There's no need to rush, Anita." He then walked around the oak-wood desk.

Fetticain put his arm over Anita's shoulder and began to walk her out of his office. Anita tightened her grip on the off-brand tote bag she carried, not sure of Fetticain's intentions.

"Don't you wanna see them before you leave?"

Anita did not like the tone of his voice. She knew she had to prepare herself for the worst. When Anita stopped, Fetticain gave her an innocent look, but Anita was not fooled. "Damn, you don't wanna see them." Fetticain shook his head sadly.

Anita knew she could not trust him. She never once stopped to think that she was just as bad as Fetticain. If Anita turned on her own family, she would be the worst kind to keep around. Even Judas could not live with his betrayal. Could she?

Fetticain knew Anita was too self-centered to inflict her own pain, so his plan was to do her a favor by orchestrating her death. Fetticain led her to a dark room, causing Anita to stop in her tracks, displaying a worried look. Fetticain gave her a reassuring smile as he pushed her in the room. With fearful, widened eyes, Anita saw three people dressed in smocks.

Turning around, Fetticain attempted to grab her. "Your soul is unclean," he growled.

"So is yours, or did you forget?" Anita raised a perfectly arched eyebrow while sticking the concealed Taser deep in Fetticain's side.

After he collapsed to the floor, Anita quickly rushed toward Fetticain's office to retrieve the papers she was forced to sign. Smiling wickedly, she dismissed herself quickly. Now a step ahead of Fetticain, her next plan was in motion. It would bring her closer to settling an old score, one she daydreamed about over the years.

CHAPTER TWENTY-SIX

*A man of violence entices his neighbor and leads him in
a way that is not good.*

—Proverbs 16:29

K.J. slammed the phone down, and he punched the
wall out of frustration. Lanka was supposed to bring his
son to see him weeks ago, but now, he could not get in
touch with her. He found it very odd that he could not
reach her so suddenly. Then, he started to fear the worst
thing could have happened and he hadn't heard about it
yet, especially with the beef going on between him and
Fetticain.

This situation had him on the edge. The unknown
was what had his thoughts running wild. Picking up the
phone again with a sigh, K.J. dialed up one of his homie's
numbers in hopes of him having something new for him.

Hearing Big Iron's voice, he exhaled without realizing
he was holding his breath.

"What's crackin', cuz?"

Getting straight to the point, K.J. said, "Man, y'all still
haven't seen Lanka or Anita ass?"

"Bruh, you ain't heard what went down?" Big Iron
asked, not believing no one had informed K.J. on the
latest.

K.J. started to feel knots in his stomach but braced himself for what Big Iron was about to reveal. "What happened?"

"Fetticain shiesty ass tried to kill Anita, somethin' about she knew too much or some shit. Dat nigga was sleeping on Anita ol' ass though." Big Iron chuckled. "Bitch Tased his ass and got the fuck on. Nobody know where she at, but cha son and Lanka still with dat nigga."

"Dat bitch foul as fuck, cuz!" K.J. said, struggling to control his anger. "Fuck!" he suddenly shouted. "At the end of the day though, dat's Fetticain's son!" K.J. revealed. People had been whispering about it for years anyway, so why not say it out loud?

Big Iron could hear the distress in K.J.'s voice, and for him to speak on that, he had to be at the end of the rope. "Damn, homie!" was all he managed to say. There were no comforting words after K.J.'s comment.

The streets had turned Big Iron's soul black at the age of 11. He breathed, ate, and shit violence. Some people were amazed at how he blazed it out with the police and took nine hits. Big Iron was still walking around a free man. It turned out that the police opened fire on the wrong kid, or so they thought. Big Iron's youth had them all fooled, and he used it to his advantage to play on their intelligence.

K.J. hung up the phone. What he had just heard put him in a foul mood. He knew that if nobody else rode with him, Big Iron would ride to hell and back by himself. That was just how nutty the kid was, which reminded K.J. of his cousin, Smirky. Although K.J. was in a funky mood, he climbed off his bunk and walked into the small TV room, hoping to catch *Shark Tank*. As K.J. got comfortable in the hard plastic chair, someone called his name. Leaning forward, K.J. gave the dude an irritated look.

"What's up?" K.J. asked. He wasn't in the mood, and he didn't want to take his problems out on anyone.

"Let me rap wit' cha for a second."

"I'm listening," K.J. said. It was hard for him to not be irritated. Lanka was out there playing house with his former best friend. This was the second time his first love had embarrassed him, and he vowed Lanka would not get another chance.

K.J. could get his locs to wake up the whole neighborhood and have them hitting the floor. He had only felt like this twice: when his aunt and cousin, Smirky, were killed. Not being in control made him feel powerless and weak, and there wasn't anything weak about K.J.

"I'm looking for some work," the guy said with a nervous look.

K.J. leaned forward with his hands clasped. He did not believe this dude. No, the dude did not know his current situation, but he sure read his facial expression, which K.J. did not try to hide.

"Nigga, do I look like I'm in the mood to hear you out?" K.J. asked with his veins popping against the skin of his neck.

"My bad, cuz." Dude put his left hand to his chest.

"Nigga, you can't even look me in my eyes. Get the fuck outta my face," K.J. expressed in a tone so deadly it caused his own hair on the back of his neck to stand.

Grabbing his cup, K.J. made his way back to his cell. He had too much on his mind. Lanka had played a big part in his current state of mind. If he had ever thought Lanka would display the betrayal that she had, K.J. would have left her in the hallway picking up her own books many years ago. Lanka had made it through K.J.'s tough interior. He had given her the good side of him and catered to her every need while Ridah hadn't gotten that far with him yet. She had the OG side of him, which was meant to always protect Ridah at all costs. That went for anyone K.J. rocked with.

K.J. could not help but think back to the day Lanka came to visit him, telling him about Ridah messing with his cousin. He listened, but something told him not to feed into what she said. He knew how vindictive Lanka could be. And when he realized the pictures she showed him were Photoshopped, he knew just how far Lanka would go to keep him away from Ridah. K.J. never let on that he was on to her game. He just continued to let her believe he was buying her story. He never questioned Ridah about who she was pregnant by because it was before him. He was going to help her because he had love for her. If Ridah did pull something like that, it would have hurt her more than it did him because they had had conversations about how he felt about people not keeping it real.

K.J. admired the fact that Ridah accepted him for who he was and never attempted to change him. Lanka, on the other hand, always had something to say about how he lived life like she wasn't living the same lifestyle as him at once. Back then, K.J. wasn't ready to evolve, but as time changed, so did he. Although he had a few run-ins in the streets, it was a struggle for him to break completely free due to the streets having his soul trapped.

K.J. was sitting in his cell when the officer called his name. Putting the papers, he held down, he sighed. *What can they possibly want now?* He secured his locker box, then exited the cell. When he entered the dayroom, the officer told him he had to go to the library for a drug test. K.J thought about the Kush he and his partner burned over the weekend. If those water pills he took did not help, he was done! But so was the guy who sold them to him!

As K.J. hit the walk, he nodded his head a few times to people he passed. There wasn't an officer at the gate to let him through, so K.J. put his back against the brick wall and kicked his left foot up. He was not in a rush to find out what the outcome would be. When one of his homies named Bone came up, they did their signature handshake, then leaned against the wall.

"What's good out there in them streets, cuz?" K.J. asked.

"Word on the block is Fetticain done went wild, cuz. Crazy though because I heard he had something to do with Smirky being killed," he said, shaking his thin dreads.

"Oh, word?" K.J. tugged at his chin hairs as his thoughts went wild.

"Dat's word, cuzzo," Bone replied, licking his lips.

Finally, an officer came to let him through the gate. K.J and Bone showed their passes before they were allowed through the gate.

"Where you headed?" K.J. asked.

"Shid, to piss in a cup."

"I'm heading that way too."

As they headed to the library, they were deep in their conversation.

K.J. put the letter down that Ridah wrote. He sighed, rubbing his hand across his low fade. He knew there was more to Ridah than what met the eye. It was he who had to bring it out of her. With all the talks they had, K.J. thought he knew Ridah, but there was so much he did not know. The person who wrote those words that stared back at him was not the same person he knew.

He had told her early on that she needed to write her life story. Ridah always sent him a rough draft of her work. She trusted his opinion. Ridah's work was like the ghetto gospel. Picking the paper back up, he continued to read.

Definition of Real
He who believes he is real has wrongfully mis-
taken the whole concept. To be real means you
must be perfect, like God. Who is like Him? Tell
me. I would like to know, and if that person does
exist, how do we know? Confounded that somehow
our minds twisted the image of a picture that was
presented. How could we have thought the perfect
person existed?

How do you define real? What is real to you?
Before you answer, think about all the things Jesus
went through in His final hours for you, for me, for
us. Would you, could you, watch your friend be
nailed to a cross without guilt or shame? Knowing
the part you played in this situation, yet in His
heart you remained?

Could you, would you, stand up against the
world and die in His place for our sins like Him?
Would you become the woman who washed His feet
with her hair, or would you just stare at me as you
try to figure out where I am coming from?

See, this is real. We misinterpreted the whole
meaning of being real. Cain and Abel brought that
to light. And if that weren't enough, look at how
Judas tried Jesus. Betrayal will forever be upon us
in some shape, form, or fashion. Not only is that
real, but it's reality to me. I would never stigmatize
my own character or question it, but I have got to
face my truth like the next. As humans, we tend
to make mistakes.

Ridah's intentions were never to cross the lines and sleep with her mentor's dude. She knew that sleeping with Lanka's first love made her appear to be on some slick backstabbing, but Ridah wasn't. Sometimes, stuff just happened, but it didn't mean she was fake or couldn't keep it real. Ridah had to keep it real, and in the time of death, she would die being a real human. She would never mistakenly hate on her partners, let alone lead them in the blind. Ridah had seen it happen, though, many times.

"Bruh, what cha reading dat got ya all tuned in like dat? I been calling ya name," K.J.'s roommate asked as he tried to get a peek at what K.J. was reading.

"My homegirl be sendin' me pieces of the book she pennin'," K.J. said, still in deep thought of Ridah's words.

"Word! What is it called?"

"*Diary of a Goonette!*" he replied like a proud father.

"I'm already diggin' dat bluez! Make sure you get me a copy soon as it hit!"

"No doubt," K.J. replied with a distant look.

K.J. went back in time to when they were on the streets. He would never forget the desire in Ridah's eyes as she mentioned how she had the beginning of her book. He used to beg her to give him a sneak peek, but she was not ready to let him in. Now here they both were, locked up, and he was sitting in his prison cell, reading Ridah's most intimate thoughts that she had only shared with him.

K.J. closed his eyes, trying to picture Ridah leaking the depth of her mind on paper. He could not help but smile when he thought of her, but for some reason, it was hard to picture her face. When he tried to remember her touch, K.J. frowned, trying to force the picture to appear. Glancing down at the pages, Ridah's words jumped out at him as if they were alive. It was as if she was speaking to him. K.J. became so caught up in the moment of the story of a true Ridah, the moment of her truth.

One of K.J.'s homies came into his cell out of breath, bringing K.J. back to the present. "Man, the Cert team just snatched the homie up. They tore his room up," he stated and left as quickly as he came.

"Shit." Bone jumped off the top bunk as he went into his locker to get any contraband that would build a case against him.

The cellmates knew from experience that when the Cert team came, they came with force and vengeance. Privacy did not exist, not in prison anyway. They went through everything and would even read your letters. K.J. jumped up quickly and went to the spot and put his cell phone up. As he was handling his business, he heard someone yell, "Cert alert," which meant the Cert team was coming into their dorm. K.J. knew why they were coming, and he cursed himself for dealing with the dude. *The price you must pay for being real, trying to help a nigga come up. It never fails!*

"Fuck! Dat nigga didn't waste no time," Bone said with his heart beating rapidly.

K.J. told Bone to calm down and try not to look suspicious, although that would be hard when their cell smelled like fresh cigarette smoke. Bone quickly sprayed some blunt spray, which took the smell down a notch. K.J. peeped out the small window, and there they were, coming up the stairs, heading their way.

"Aye, they comin', cuz!" K.J.'s heart beat hard in his chest. He sat at the desk, and Bone leaned against the wall as they hurried up and waited.

Cert Robbins was the first to enter the cell with a cocky grin. Bone cursed under his breath as he put the chess piece down.

"Y'all niggas already know the routine!" was all Robbins said.

K.J. looked up from the chess game they pretended to be playing, matching Robbin's grin with his own. "How many times are you going to keep coming for me and come up empty-handed?" K.J. was dirty as hell, but he was cocky with it, which was what Robbins hated about him. Robbins could never catch him red-handed.

In flashing speed, Robbins was in K.J.'s face. "Boy, I got ya ass by the balls." Looking up at Bone, he added, "Ya ass too, nigga!"

Bone laughed as he replied, "Like playin' with balls, huh?"

Robbins mashed Bone in the face, causing his head to hit the wall. Bone's face turned red as he shook with anger. Looking over at the other Cert member, he asked, "So, you not seeing dat shit, huh?" When he did not reply, Bone said, "Right! Then you won't see this!" Then, he fired off and punched Robbins so hard that his jaw cracked.

The Cert quickly put his mask on and sprayed Bone and K.J. after beating them. Once they were finished, they locked them in their cell with cuffs on. K.J. and Bone coughed uncontrollably while their eyes burned. Both thought they were going to die from not being able to breathe.

"I'ma kill dat nigga!" K.J. vowed as he continued to cough and tried to control his breathing while his face burned.

"Man, this shit fucked up!" Bone retorted, turning over on his side as blood began to drip from his nose on the waxed floor.

The two of them may have been messed up, but K.J. was glad Bone popped off when he did. If he did not, their room would be torn up at this very moment. They would probably be in lockdown right now pending investigation. K.J. looked over at Bone, whose face was red, and started laughing. Bone frowned, thinking K.J. had finally gone crazy. He did not see or find anything funny about their current situation.

When their room door was opened, both were glad to feel the cool air come in the small cell. A female officer working the dorm came to unlock their door after being informed that two inmates were locked in their room. She was not aware that they were still in the building when she cleared it after the Cert sprayed.

"They didn't tell me y'all were still in here!" She shook her head as she bent down to take the cuffs off. "The warden needs to know about this shit!" Officer Lana stated once she finished. She leaned against the rail to let the other inmates in the cell to help them. Shaking her head, she watched them go outside with the other inmates until the building aired out.

CHAPTER TWENTY-SEVEN

There is a path before each person that seems right, but it ends in death.

—Proverbs 14:2

Three Months Later

Ridah sat at the table with her attorney. With Capone dead, there was very little Ridah could be charged with since the statement Capone wrote wasn't signed by him. The DA had an unsigned statement in which Ridah's name was not mentioned.

There were so many loopholes in Ridah's case that her attorney guaranteed her that she would walk away a free woman. There were witnesses stating that Ridah never had a gun the night of the crime. There were even witnesses saying that Capone was the gunman. After two long hours of debating at the table, the judge had finally reached a verdict.

"Nashanna Gier," the judge stated, but it sounded like he was questioning her.

"Yes." Ridah looked in the eyes of the man who held her freedom in his hands.

"I'm giving you time served on possession of a firearm and dismissing all the other charges. If you come back before me again, you will have a bad day. Do I make myself clear?" he asked, looking over the rim of his glasses.

"Yes," Ridah responded. She didn't care about his last comment. She was too stuck on going home.

Ridah's supporters stood cheering, saying that she was getting released. Some wondered if the wheelchair would slow her down, or would she go back out there on the same shit, banging until she ended up dead like her pops and so many of her homies? The thought burned most of their minds.

Ridah's gang family stood, dressed in the truest blue. They were ready to show out as they welcomed their Cripette home. The love was felt in the air, and only two people were missing in their circle: K.J. and Smirky. *May Smirky rest in peace.* Thoughts of Scott brought tears to Ridah's eyes. She could almost hear his voice saying, "I knew you were gangsta, Ridah!" She pictured him saying that with that contagious smile of his.

Ridah wished K.J. could have shared this joy with her but knew it would not be long before freedom found him. Thanks to the settlement she received from suing the county jail, Ridah returned the favor and got K.J. the best attorney there was. His freedom was worth the pretty penny she gave up. The fact that he used all his money to get Ridah off overwhelmed her. Real people did real things.

Ridah had been blessed with a second chance at life. It took her going to prison to want more and seek more out of life. She would forever be gang affiliated, a Gangsta Crip to the day she died. However, the banging part was now a thing of the past. If she did not get it right this time, she knew it was over for her.

Ridah realized this was never about following in her pops's footsteps. She could have chosen a better path as her sister did. But Ridah allowed her pride to cloud her common sense. She was so busy trying to prove to her mother that she was not scared to live the life she fled from. Ridah wanted not only her mother to know but everyone else as well. She went hard in the streets, and she did what most females were scared to do, went places some dared not go, in fear of being killed. Ridah lived her life fearlessly.

At the end of the day, what did she gain? Ridah became caught up in a world that was even more confusing than who she thought she was. All she had now was her story, and the truth was that some would daydream of being that girl Ridah once was. Some would fear these things happening to them and take Ridah's story and learn from her mistakes. Sadly, most of them would choose the former, trying to be cool until it happened to them.

Back to the streets, not much had changed. Everybody was still doing their thang. Anwar was still doing it big, and some of the homies were banging harder, along with new faces, younger faces, lost faces. They all wanted and were searching for something. Ridah's homies wanted to throw her a welcome back party, but she wasn't up for all the company. Besides, Ridah knew there was going to be somebody acting up. With that in mind, she settled for staying in her house around a few of her homies who had been down with her.

Ridah was also not comfortable enough going to certain places in a wheelchair. Surrounded by laughter, just having a good time, Ridah missed every close person who could not be there with her. Anwar passed the blunt to Ridah. As she leaned in to get it, the phone rang.

"Hello," she spoke into the receiver. Ridah's eyes lit up when she heard K.J.'s voice. Hearing his voice excited her. "Hey!" she squealed into the receiver.

"Congratulations, baby girl!" he said.

Tears filled her eyes before she knew it. "Thank you. I wish you were here with me."

"I'll be there soon enough, baby girl!" K.J. started filling her in on things Anwar had already told her.

In the midst of K.J. talking, there was a knock on Ridah's door. Anwar opened the door, thinking it was one of the homies coming back from the store. Instead, gunshots greeted him. Anwar's body flew back to the floor. No one was prepared for the unexpected. There was no time to react.

K.J. was yelling Ridah's name, but what she saw next left her speechless. Toni entered the front door with a big Kool-Aid smile, causing Ridah to drop the phone to the floor. She already knew what time it was. They came to collect. Ridah hated that she could not defend herself.

Crossing her arms, Toni cocked her head to the side in a cocky way. "What's good, Ridah?" She got close up on Ridah. "Damn, Moe fucked ya ass up, huh?" Toni giggled. "I dreamed of this day." Toni finally had the upper hand, and it felt good.

"If you gonna kill me, come on and get the shit over with!" Ridah showed no sign of fear. She never thought she would have to prepare herself for death. But as she sat helplessly, Ridah was ready. She had no other choice but to be.

Toni hit Ridah in the mouth. When Ridah reached to her mouth, a bloody tooth fell in her hand. She spat at Toni, then laughed, staring Toni in the eyes. It was like Ridah was taunting her, daring her to pull the trigger. Toni quickly placed the gun to her forehead, but Ridah never broke eye contact with her.

Before Toni could wrap her finger around the trigger, Lanka came strolling in. "What's up, tough girl?" The smirk on Lanka's face disgusted Ridah.

"Fuck you!" Ridah shouted. Her life may have been on the countdown, but her mission statement was still to be fearful of no one!

Ridah refused to die being scared and fearing another human being. At that moment, Ridah hated that she would not have the chance to go head-to-head with Lanka, especially after her killing Kia and Smirky. God knew it had been a long time coming.

Suddenly, Fetticain appeared. He was finally able to meet the one woman who had caused him so much hell. Fetticain looked Ridah over before closing the distance between them.

"It woulda been nice, too," Fetticain said. Leaning close to Ridah's face, he whispered in her ear. "But you a waste, a dead fuck. You can't feel shit!" Fetticain chuckled as he reached in to grab between her legs.

Ridah grabbed his hand and pushed it back as she glared at him. "Don't think because I'm in a fucked-up situation that I'm a weak-ass bitch. I'm still hood!" She shook with anger. It killed her pride that she could not do anything but sit there defenselessly.

"Fetticain, you doin' too much!" Lanka snapped after seeing him grab between Ridah's legs. She focused back on Ridah. "Still wanna put up a fight, huh? When the truth is you already lost. Game over, bitch!"

Ridah jumped at the sound of the gunshot, waiting to feel the burning pain spreading through her. When it didn't come, Ridah opened her eyes to find Toni on the floor, choking on her own blood.

"Lanka, since I'm dead already, tell me why you killed Smirky and shot K.J.," Ridah said.

"Since you're gonna die, I guess it wouldn't hurt to tell you, huh?" Lanka said, shrugging her shoulders. "Did you really think I was gonna let Smirky live to tell K.J.? Smirky killed Demya. You couldn't have thought I was gonna let that shit spill in the streets!" She shook her head. "Hell nawl!"

"But you shot K.J. too!" Ridah accused.

Laughing, Lanka shook her head, disagreeing with Ridah. "Nawl, I didn't do that. My child's father did," she admitted, nodding her head in Fetticain's direction.

"I'm ready now!" Ridah said, knowing she would rest in peace. If she did not know anything else, she knew K.J. was going to not only get revenge for Smirky and his aunt but for her, too.

Lanka's eyes filled with tears as she looked at her once protégé with a tight smile. Turning the gun on Ridah, she said, "See you next lifetime, bitch!" Lanka emptied the clip into Ridah's face.

"Count time!" the floor officer shouted, causing Ridah to jump out of a deep sleep.

Stepping down off the ladder, Ridah stood by her bed. She attempted to shake the nightmare of her being killed out of her troubled head. She had been sitting in the county jail going on three months waiting to be transferred to prison. No, she didn't commit the crime, but she was about to be doing time all in the name of loyalty.